A Corpse's
Nightmare

BY PHILLIP DEPOY

A CORPSE'S
NIGHTMARE

PHILLIP DEPOY

ST. MARTIN'S MINOTAUR
NEW YORK

A CORPSE'S NIGHTMARE. Copyright © 2011 by Phillip DePoy. All rights reserved. Printed in the United States of America. For information, address St. Martin's Press, 175 Fifth Avenue, New York, N.Y. 10010.

www.minotaurbooks.com

Library of Congress Cataloging-in-Publication Data

DePoy, Phillip.
    A corpse's nightmare : a Fever Devilin novel / Phillip Depoy. — 1st ed.
        p. cm.
    ISBN 978-0-312-69946-8
    1. Devilin, Fever (Fictitious character)—Fiction.   2. Attempted murder—
Fiction.   3. Coma—Patients—Fiction   I. Title.
    PS3554.E624C67 2011
    813'.54—dc23

                                                            2011026226

First Edition: November 2011

10   9   8   7   6   5   4   3   2   1

This book is dedicated, as is most of this life, to my lovely wife and best friend, Lee Nowell, playwright, director, bon vivant, but, alas, a person absolutely unaware of Kronos. I spend a lot of my time waiting for her, often at the door, clutching my keys, stammering about just how late we actually are. And in those painful, difficult moments, my mind eventually wanders. And in some of those moments, I began to piece together the various aspects of this book. So thanks are due. And, incidentally, when she finally comes down the stairs, it's always worth the wait.

ACKNOWLEDGMENTS

Acknowledgment is made to my band days, decades ago, when I began exploring the history and nature of jazz. A college professor of mine tried to arrange a trip to New Orleans so that I could meet Wild Bill Davison with an eye toward writing his biography. I was more interested in Appalachian folk music at the time, and didn't go. I now see that all things conspire to come together, as they have in this book, in order to tell a story. I would also like to acknowledge a moment, long ago, with Yolanda King, daughter of Dr. Martin Luther King. Yolanda and I were in a play together in Atlanta in 1964, a year in which an interracial couple was a magnet for ire. I kissed Yolanda on stage—never mind that I was a fox and she was a turtle—and that kiss so enraged someone or other that a contingent of Klansmen materialized at the next show. Many were frightened. Yolanda thought it was funny. I just wanted to kiss her again. I believe in that moment, the seeds of this book took root.

A Corpse's
Nightmare

1.

The dead can dream; I'll tell you how I know.

Things had been quiet in Blue Mountain for so long that we had all come to mistake inertia for contentment. An entire autumn afternoon, for example, could be spent cataloging the images in cumulus clouds. They rushed over the mountain on their way to other, more important places, each with great mythic import. On October 9th I noted three minotaurs moving in the clouds. I made a list of their various postures. Doubtless a propensity for classical literature and a bottle of French pastis combined to color these perceptions. My time at the university had given me a love of mythology. My friend Dr. Winton Andrews had given me the pastis. Indolence had done the rest. I might have remained in that happy state of suspended animation for the rest of my life. I've heard or read that some people have that sort of luck. Alas, lazy autumn turned to bitter winter. On the 3rd of December, just before midnight, a total stranger came into my home and shot me as I slept in my bed. I died before the emergency medical team could find their way to my house.

But in that sleep of death, what dreams may come? To begin at the beginning, childhood is of absolutely no consequence if it's

2 | PHILLIP DePOY

handled properly. All normal childhoods are exactly the same as Tolstoy's happy families: just alike. Unfortunately, my early years were handled as strangely as anyone could possibly imagine.

For reasons I can only guess, my mother always instructed me that it was impolite to tell the truth. In any circumstance, she thought she should make up something better. It was never a harmful lie. In fact, it was generally a lie that was meant to improve a situation.

She would say, "What a splendid looking dress!" no matter what the thing looked like. Or: "These are the most delicious Brussels sprouts I've ever eaten." (Clearly the oxymoron of placing the words *delicious* and *Brussels sprouts* in the same sentence needs little comment.)

The worst lies were about me. "My son? He's a fine, normal, average boy. We didn't really name him Fever, it just sort of happened."

I knew I was neither normal nor average. My IQ tested at 186; I liked the poetry of Wallace Stevens and the music of French Middle Ages at age eight; I had my first sexual encounter with a girl when we were both nine—it was wonderful.

I also may have had an angelic experience when I was eleven.

So while mother's application of the word *fine* might have applied—I won't judge that—the words *normal* and *average* seemed out of the question.

To be specific, the IQ test was given three times to verify its results, the nine-year-old girl's name was Alisa; the angel had no actual form. My IQ has been a source of trouble for me ever since I was tested. I never knew what became of Alisa, her family moved away to New Orleans. The angel, on the other hand, visited me again—possibly.

I first met the angel in something of an unusual way. I had read that Einstein posited curved space by imagining he was riding the Universe on a beam of light. I wanted to try the same experiment. It seemed a most obvious occupation for a Sunday morning while my father was at church.

I remember quite clearly that I sat in a chair by the window in my room, staring out at the morning sun. I was dressed in my usual blue jeans and flannel shirt. The room was bare then, save for a bed, a desk, and a Currier and Ives picture of a sleigh being pulled over a bridge by two horses. Just as I was beginning to feel light-headed from shallow breathing and concentration, the images of ordinary reality faded and there it was: the angel.

I saw a face that was not a face and it said, very softly, "Do you recognize me?"

"No," I think I said. "Should I?"

"No *should*. Just *is*." I might have imagined that an angel would proffer that sort of language.

I tried to focus on the face, but it kept changing. "I don't understand," I said.

"We only have a moment together." It hovered like a mist outside the window. "Look through the things in the box behind the clock on the mantel."

"What things?"

It shimmered. "They're in the box behind the clock."

I dared not take my eyes away. "What am I looking for?"

Then the angel vanished.

Without hesitation, I flew down the blond wooden staircase that led from the upstairs bedrooms. In those days all the rooms downstairs were, in fact, one big room. Bronzed oak beams framed the entire place. The galley kitchen was small then, still to the right as you came in the front door. There was a stone hearth wood-burning fireplace to the left by the large picture window. The quilts on the walls always seemed like church windows to me.

I went straight to the clock on the mantel. Behind it I found a blue tin box. I didn't even think to question why I'd never noticed it before. It had a forest hunting scene embossed on its lid.

In that box, I found the ingredients of several lifetimes.

The tin was old, nineteenth century, and had, I believed, once held candies. I opened it as if it were some sort of present. It contained mostly papers and letters, some photos—poems and documents—things that would prove quite puzzling for, really, the rest of my life.

The most baffling object in the box was a photograph. Just as I picked it up to examine it more closely, my mother appeared behind me.

"What are you doing?" she demanded.

I jumped because she startled me. Whatever she lacked in verisimilitude, she more than made up for in stealth. She always had.

I spun around. She was wearing her print dress with the giant blue roses on it, and a black cardigan with a collar. Her feet were bare. Her hair was tightly coiled copper around her head. She was smoking a cigarette.

"I didn't hear you." I tried to hide the box, but it was no use.

She stood over me. "I said, 'What are you doing?'"

"I'm looking through the things in this box," I answered calmly, "as would seem to be obvious."

She stared down at me. "Don't you get smart with me, buster."

"I'm not getting smart with you, Mother," I sighed. "I already *am* smart. And please don't call me *buster*."

"How about if I call you *Smart Mouth*?"

"Call me whatever you want to. I can tell a puzzle when I see one."

"A puzzle?" she asked.

I held up the photo. It was an ancient sepia image of a young woman in a bar, smiling for the camera. On the back of the photo it simply said, "Lisa, 1923."

My mother looked away. "What is that?"

"Oh, I have a feeling you know what this is." I moved toward her. "It says '1923' on the back, but that's a picture of you if I ever saw one. You weren't born in 1923. Your mother wasn't even born in 1923."

"That's not me," she said weakly, using the same inflections she always employed when she was making things up.

"I don't see how it could be."

"What do you want?" she sniffed.

"An explanation would be good," I answered.

She let out a sigh that I would remember for the rest of my days. In it I could hear all her heartbroken, impossibly gargantuan disappointment—in me, in my father, in an entire world that had not given her the things she richly deserved: normalcy, comfortable economics, and an escape from Blue Mountain. But all she said was, "I'll get the letter."

She went up to her room, and came back out a few moments later carrying the letter as if it might explode. She handed it to me and turned her back. I thought she was being overly dramatic, as she was always wont to do.

It was a plain envelope. It was sealed. On the front were the words *For Fever* in keen script. Just touching the envelope somehow made my fingers feel strange.

I opened. I unfolded the paper inside. I read.

> *Dear Fever,*
> *If your mother has given you this letter, you must already suspect something. You're looking at some of the photographic evidence. Maybe you've had an angelic visitation. Don't be alarmed. Everybody has those. If you decide to pursue this matter, you're in for quite a ride. If you find out who the woman is in that photograph, your life will change. Doesn't matter. Everything you think you know in this life? None of it is real.*

It wasn't signed.

I looked up at my mother. "Who wrote this?"

She still had her back to me, but I thought she might be crying.

"Did my father write this letter," I demanded, "or my grand-father?"

"You don't know the person who wrote this letter," she mumbled, "yet."

I set the letter in the box with the other foreign objects. "Are you crying?"

She nodded.

I took a step closer to her. "Why?"

"It doesn't matter."

"Then why are you crying?"

Her voice got stronger. "Don't do it, Fever. Don't chase after answers to these things. Forget all about it. Just stay around Blue Mountain and maybe work with me and your dad in the show when the time comes for you to earn a living. You leave here and go out in the big world: you're just asking for trouble and heartache. You look for answers to this particular riddle, and you'll find out things about people—about the whole human condition, in fact—that you don't really want to know. You don't really want to know just how awful everything can be."

I blew out a little breath. "That's just the sort of thing you say that eggs me on."

She turned. "What?"

"Maybe you don't realize it," I explained, "but when you say something like that, it makes me want to do the opposite."

She stuck her neck to the side. "What are you telling me?"

"When you say 'no,' Mother," I explained exasperatedly, "it only makes me want to find out what 'yes' is like. You drive me crazy!"

"Don't pay any attention to this mess, I'm telling you!" Her voice grew shrill. "Why can't you just stay an ordinary human being?"

"God! You *have* to realize that when you refer to me as *an ordinary human being,* you are engaging in what's called 'wishful thinking.' I'm about as ordinary as wings on a turtle!"

"And?" She narrowed her eyelids. "You never heard of a turtle-dove?"

"God, God, God!" I looked away. "If you aren't the most exasperating person I'll ever meet, I don't want to go on living."

"I see." She wagged her head. "And you call me overly dramatic."

"Where do you think I get it?"

"Brother!" She tossed her hand. "You can't blame everything on me. Some things you're just born with."

"Do you *see* why you make me crazy?" I rolled my head trying to untie some of the knots in my neck. "Do you see what you're saying? Whether I learned it from you or I inherited it genetically, it still comes from *you*!"

"You blame me for everything," she said again, feigning weakness. "Well, fine, then! Go on! Chase the ghosts for all I care. Be a freak!"

And at that—and I recall this feeling quite clearly, even as an adult—my entire body and mind relaxed. With a miraculously bizarre sense of what I was soon to learn could be called déjà vu, I answered her challenge.

"Well," I announced, "it's good to know my true nature so early in life."

At that she gave up, ascended the stairs a bit like Gloria Swanson in *Sunset Boulevard*, went to her room and put on the Frank Sinatra record of "Angel Eyes." It was a deliberate dig at me. She thought I ought to be more religious, more normal, more outgoing—all qualities that she seemed to think Sinatra embodied and I hated. Sinatra was a good American; I was a bad boy.

I knew, even then, the heartbreaking aspect of my mother's desires and accusations, lies and foibles, disappointments and fears. They all stemmed from an attempt on her part, in the younger days, to escape Blue Mountain. She and my father had both been born in our little hamlet, but had once wandered away—in

1961—all the way to Atlanta. They always told me that they had taken a journey toward spirituality and a dynamic sense of purpose, something that everyone had then. Kennedy was in the White House, Civil Rights were on the move, young people were speaking their minds—the world was changing for the better and forever. By the spring of 1963, everything in America was moving in the perfect direction. The country was filled with beautiful young people. Their ideology was beautiful. Even the president and his wife were beautiful. Everything seemed to be headed into the light at the center of the greatest century in human history. That's how it felt.

Everything was opening up. Even the interior of the White House was revealed. Previous first ladies had been shy about the decor of their four-to-eight-year home, but Jackie Kennedy took everyone on a tour of the place—on live television! She showed everyone the young White House, where their president and his smart, beautiful wife lived.

In that year, 1963, my parents were crusaders. They helped to arrange a folk-singing extravaganza on the steps of the Atlanta Capitol building. They were already gearing up for Kennedy's re-election. They were Young Democrats. They had convinced no less than Peter, Paul and Mary, Pete Seeger, and Joan Baez to perform.

Every song was the hammer of freedom. Every word was the bell of justice. Every glance they shared was a song about love between brothers and my sisters, all over this-a land. The feeling in the air that spring was that all human beings could, with very little effort, change the world for better, forever, and very soon. They felt it was the most exhilarating sense of power and change ever known to humankind.

Then, autumn came.

The president—the young beautiful president, the president that would live forever, the president that gave everyone a feeling of freedom and forward-moving idealism—was assassinated on national television. The gun exploded, blood erupted; they saw the skull and brains fly everywhere. President Kennedy lay dead in a Lincoln Continental.

Also that year: Robert Frost died. Jean Cocteau died. Edith Piaf died. Pope John XXIII died. A hurricane in Eastern Pakistan killed twenty-two thousand people. The entire world had a shocked sense of loss. Suddenly all the events of life seemed greatly random and inexplicably cruel.

It was no coincidence, my parents believed, that the popular American drug culture got a significant boost after the Kennedy assassination. If the icon of hopes and dreams could be shot through the head right in front of you, it was understandable that you might want to search for alternate realities, other possibilities; any means of turning away from the things that you saw.

My parents' choice—their act of turning away—was to go back to the strange carnival life they had known only two years earlier with their odd traveling show. They went back to Blue Mountain and resumed their deeply unusual lives. My father was a world-class magician and my mother was his hypnotically beautiful assistant. Together they were mesmerizing onstage, largely because they seemed too ethereal—as if they weren't entirely of this earth. They picked right up where they had left off, almost as if their dream of a better world had never happened. The Ten Show, as it was called, turned out to be their calling. Once they came home, they never looked back.

These events explain how I came to be born in Blue Mountain, not a more metropolitan clime, the product of strange parents and lost hope.

Whenever they told me these stories—and most of them came from my mother in her cups—I always had the impulse to tell them that they had not been paying attention. I thought they should have realized that no one could alter reality. They couldn't, as they'd dreamed, ever eliminate war, hatred, racism, sexism, governments, systems of economics, foundations of education, and all strife—not just by loving. I tried to explain it to them, at age eleven. I gave them the salient facts: (a) color television had become the single most popular form of entertainment in the world. After 10,000 years of human folklore, oral traditions, stories passed from person to person with great reverence, suddenly came television. Human interaction was quickly being removed from the process. (b) It's not possible for the human mind to hang on to a beautiful vision indefinitely. That vision changes in a very short time. Everything changes. It's a key function of the human psyche: visions are meant to fade. (c) No one can alter reality. All you can alter is your own perceptions—and not even that very well.

Which brings us back to the angel. It was very clear to me when I saw the angel that God was in everything. For months after that experience I could see His Light emanate from trees and rocks and hills and plains and water and air and most of all from the glorious, loving, all-embracing countenance of every human being around me. We were all very obviously one in God, I thought: safe, blessed, and free. It was the most beautiful vision of life that anyone ever had.

But it passed.

2.

I awoke to see Lucinda's face, bathed in clear light. No Pre-Raphaelite model, no mysterious legend of the silver screen, no medieval Madonna could have been more beatific or bright or beautiful. She was holding my hand, dressed all in white, and smiling. The windows of the room were impossibly blinding and she said my name over and over again, as if it were her only prayer.

Then a sudden sharp noise tore that vision away—and I *actually* woke up. I was in a cold, dark hospital room. I did not, at that moment, remember being shot. I only wondered why I might be in the hospital. It was clear that I'd been awakened when a nurse, standing at the end of my bed, had dropped my chart.

I blinked. She gasped.

"Oh my God," she whispered. "Fever?"

I slowly recognized the woman. She was Stacey Chambers, a friend.

"Hi," I managed to say.

My voice did not sound familiar to me. It was grating and garbled. And when I'd said the words, I'd felt as if I might vomit.

"Don't try to talk, sugar," Stacey said excitedly. "You've got a small feeding tube in your throat."

A quick survey of my physical situation confirmed that I not only had a tube town my throat, but an intravenous needle in each arm and several electrical wires depending from my abdomen. Everything was attached to machines. My bed was the only one in the room. The blinds were drawn. There was no television, no lamp, and no food tray. Only one chair sat in the corner. It was a beige hospital chair, all metal and vinyl. It didn't look particularly used.

"You try to stay awake, now," Nurse Chambers said, fussing with one of the machines to which I was connected. "I'm calling Lucinda right this minute."

She reached out and snatched the receiver from the phone by the bed with such force that it clattered across the small bedside table.

"Hey, Reba," she said breathlessly into the phone, "it's Stacey. Get Lucinda right away. Dr. Devilin's awake!" She listened for a second, then shouted, "I know!"

I tried to speak again, but a feeling of desperate nausea overtook me. It must have been evident on my face.

"Hold on, hold on," Nurse Chambers said, hanging up the phone. She hopped around my bed for a moment and then leaned close to my face. I was suddenly aware of her perfume, her warmth. "I'm just going to get rid of this old feeding tube, Fever. Close your eyes and think of England, that's what Winnie says."

With a slow but steady revulsion, I relinquished the thin tube from my esophagus.

"What happened to me?" I croaked. "And who's Winnie?"

"Oh my God," she whispered, "your memory's gone."

I concentrated, realizing that my memory, though not gone, was sluggish. This woman, Nurse Chambers, had come to dinner at my house with my best friend Dr. Winton Andrews. Andrews was the Shakespeare scholar at the university from which I'd been—what would be the word? *Released?* At any rate, Andrews and I saw each other often. He liked having a free place to stay in the mountains when the weather got too hot in Atlanta. And the woman he had recently begun seeing, thanks to me, was this woman, Stacey. She worked under Lucinda Foxe, the head nurse at the hospital. Lucinda was my fiancée and had been for—what? Seven years?

"You're Stacey, I'm Fever, this is the county hospital, Lucinda is my fiancée, and I must be pretty sick." I looked around at all the other tubes and machines. "But I don't know what happened to me."

"You were shot," she said, taking my hand. "You were shot bad."

"Shot? When?"

"Um," she said, and then drew in a large breath.

"Go on," I urged her.

"You've been in a coma for three months. It's nearly March."

Hearing that, for some reason, produced certain images from dreams and odd memories: patterns of clouds, the voice of my mother, the face of an angel. I'd been dreaming of my mother, my childhood, old stories.

"Is Lucinda in the hospital?" I asked. "I was just now dreaming of her."

"It's four o'clock in the morning, sweetheart," Nurse Chambers cooed. "She's at home. But she'll be here directly. She knew you'd be all right."

"Three months." I said the words, but didn't believe them.

"You know," Nurse Chambers confided as she glided around my bed moving machines, turning knobs, checking one of the IV tubes, "Lucinda . . ." but her voice trailed off.

"What is it?" I could tell that she wanted to say something important, but thought better of it.

"I'll let her tell you. Come on, sit up." She cranked the bed somehow until my head was nearly even with hers.

"I'm starving," I realized.

"You've lost nearly twenty pounds." She took wrist and felt for the pulse. "But we had physical therapy in here every day to work the muscles, so you should be able to walk fairly soon."

"Walk?" I looked down at my legs. "Where was I shot?"

"Oh, you were shot in the chest," she answered quickly. "We had physical therapy come in so your muscles wouldn't atrophy while you were unconscious."

"Shot in the chest." I blinked. "Who shot me?"

She shrugged. "Nobody knows. Sheriff Needle's been working on it most every day since it happened, and Melissa Mathews, you know, his deputy? But there's just no evidence. None. Near as they can tell, sometime right around midnight on December third last year, somebody came into your house and shot you in your bed. You were asleep. They might have stolen things from your house, too. It was a little disorganized downstairs, they said, but nobody could tell if it was because you're messy or the killer was looking for something."

"The killer?" I was beginning to feel the stiffness in my body, my joints, my muscles. "This person killed someone?"

Nurse Chambers stopped moving. "Oh. Well. Let's just get Lucinda to tell you all that." She wouldn't look me in the eye.

I was concerned that Sheriff Skidmore Needle, my oldest friend in Blue Mountain, had puzzled over a crime for three months without result, especially since it was a crime that so directly concerned me. I decided to concentrate on the immediate. The larger picture was too disconcerting.

"All right." I was slowly adjusting to my surroundings. "Is there any chance I can get something to eat? Something solid?"

"Not a good idea yet," she answered, "but I was going to call down for some soup."

Just then I realized that several other people were standing at the door to my room. They were all hospital personnel, two of them very young. One appeared to be something of a candy striper, eyes and mouth both wide open, her pink chewing gum quite visible.

The other was a tall, thin, sullen looking twenty-ish boy, crew cut, eyes dull as a butter knife.

"Why are they staring at me?" I asked Nurse Chambers.

She turned around and saw everyone. "You'uns scat, please," she told them good-naturedly. They disbanded immediately.

"Soup," I reminded her.

"Albert," she called out, "you bring Dr. Devilin some soup broth quick as you can."

"Yes, ma'am," the crew cut answered from down the hall in an unusually Midwestern accent.

"Winnie," I realized, "is your abbreviation for Winton. You were talking about Andrews."

"And now you're awake for real." She patted my arm. "We've gotten kind of serious since you went into your coma, me and Dr. Andrews."

"He's not here, is he?" I asked.

"He will be soon as I call him," she confirmed. "He's come up from Atlanta every weekend since this happened to you. He kids around with you like you were awake. Tells you his old corny jokes. Talks about his students. Reads Shakespeare out loud."

"Really." I couldn't imagine Andrews reading to an unconscious body.

"And poetry, sometimes. He said this one about a hundred times: 'Of the two dreams, night and day, what lover, what dreamer, would choose the one obscured by sleep?'"

"Wallace Stevens." I smiled. "I dreamed about that. You understand that he was trying to convince me to wake up."

The phone rang then. She picked it up instantly.

"Yes?" she said, and then listened. "Okay."

She held out the phone for me.

I took it, knowing who was on the other end.

"Lucinda," I said, my voice still gravelly, "It would appear that I've missed a few dinners with you."

"God you have no idea how good it is to hear your voice," she said softly.

"I was just dreaming about you," I answered, "in a very flattering way. Then Nurse Chambers, here, woke me up."

"How did she do that?" Lucinda whispered.

"I think she dropped my chart on the floor," I answered, "and it was very rude. You were standing over me and whispering my name, dressed all in white. Like an angel."

"You sound like Louis Armstrong."

"And I feel like the wreck of the *Hesperus*," I agreed, "but apparently I'm much better than I was yesterday this time. Are you coming to see me or not?"

"I'm getting dressed while I'm talking with you," she said. Suddenly I could hear the rustle of her clothes.

"No need to fuss on my account," I told her. "Come as you are. You do still sleep with nothing on, don't you?"

"I'd have to say that I admire a man," she said, her voice a little stronger than it had been, "who can come out of a coma pitching woo."

"*Pitching woo?*" I smiled. "Did I go back in time while I was out? What kind of a phrase is that?"

"I'll be there in twenty minutes." She hung up the phone.

Nurse Chambers was beaming at me. "You two act like teenagers."

"If I promise never to talk that way ever again in your presence," I said, shifting uncomfortably in bed, "will you promise never to call Andrews 'Winnie' when I'm around?"

"I think we can work something out," she said, adjusting the pillow at the back of my head. "You know, we were all really worried about you."

"I feel strange," I confessed. "Last night I went to sleep in my bed, and tonight I woke up in the hospital three months later."

"You don't know the half of it," she whispered softly.

3.

Lucinda arrived just before five that morning. The moon was full and low. Its light was neatly cut into stripes by the blades of the window blinds. When Lucinda appeared in the doorway, she seemed to have floated there. She already had her coat off. She was wearing a blue sweater, black jeans, and some sort of boots.

In seconds she stood over me, holding my hand. I had known her long enough to read her face. She was hiding something. I thought it might be that she was trying to control her emotions under the circumstances. I squeezed her hand.

"Why don't you pull up that chair," I rasped, glancing at the only empty piece of furniture in the room, "and tell me all about it?"

"All about what?" She didn't move.

"All about what happened to me. As far as you know. I can tell you've got something on your mind. Don't make me drag it out of you. I'm too weak. I've been shot. And then I was in a coma."

She smiled. "I know. But you're awake now, God help us all."

"Well, then."

She hesitated, but let go of my hand, dragged the chair close to the bed and sat, obviously trying to collect her thoughts.

"The best way," I encouraged her, "is to just let it all come out at once. Don't think about it too much. I can see that you have a lot to say, but don't try to organize it into anything coherent. It'll take too long and I've got other things to do today."

"Oh, you do?" She shook her head.

"Well, there's broth coming, and later I'll be trying to sit up on my own. Then I'd like to convince Nurse Chambers to give me a sponge bath. It's a pretty full day."

"I see," she said. "Then I'll get right to the point. Somebody shot you."

"That much I know. There's more to the story."

"There is," she confirmed. "The man who shot you called 911 after he did it. If he hadn't, we wouldn't be having this conversation."

"He called . . . how do you know?" I tried to sit up. I failed.

"There's a tape recording of his voice. You can hear it as soon as you want to. Skidmore's listened to it about a thousand times. He didn't call to save you. He called to let someone know that you were dead."

"Why would he do a thing like that?"

"Sounded a little like he was bragging," she answered.

"What did he say?"

She opened her mouth to answer, then obviously thought better of it. "I'll let you listen to it."

"Okay," I said slowly. "What else?"

"The ambulance had a hard time getting to your place. There was a lot of snow." She folded her arms. "I don't know if you remember that. It had snowed for three days before this thing happened. I'd been working overtime and we hadn't seen each other for a few days before that. Anyway, they ran off the road, the ambulance. They didn't get to you for almost an hour. They called in to the hospital. I was waiting in the emergency room. I was nearly out of my mind."

"I'm so sorry," I told her softly.

"I got in my Jeep and plowed on up there. Don't quite know how I did it, but I got to your house maybe five minutes behind the EMTs. I came up to your bedroom. You were—they had already started packing up. Everything was very still. No one was talking. They—see, they . . ."

Her voice trailed off. She swallowed. A single tear appeared in the corner of one eye.

"What?" I asked very softly. It only took me a moment to realize what had happened.

"They had pronounced you dead," she whispered.

"I see." I sat back a little. "But I'm not dead. You did something, I'm guessing."

She nodded again.

"Tell me."

"There's a lot of new work—articles about trauma victims and freezing." She fumbled absently with her watch. "I made them haul you outside and bury you in the snow. We stood around until you turned blue, and then put you on a stretcher, packed the snow around you—in your body bag. And brought you here."

"So I wasn't really dead," I managed to say.

"No. You were dead all right. But the freezing did the trick. With a little bit of electricity and slow warming, blood transfusion, and a breathing apparatus, you were alive again. Barely. You had three surgeries right away and two more a month later. Plus, you lost the littlest toe on your left foot, a patch of your backside, and the tips of both elbows."

"Lost?"

"Frostbite. You were lucky it wasn't worse. See, some moron packed you in freezing snow."

"Thank God she did." I smiled. "I don't know what to say."

"I don't guess there's much to say about that." She sniffed. "It worked. Here you are."

"After three months in a coma."

"Well, you lost some of that extra weight you put on from my cooking," she said, sitting forward. "And I got to concentrate on my work for a change. So it all worked out."

"Lucinda?"

"Yes?"

I didn't hesitate over a single syllable. "Let's go ahead and get married."

Her whole face relaxed. She stood up laughing. "Oh for God's sake. I was worried there might be some brain damage to come out of this."

"Look, I'm serious," I began.

"You come out of a coma talking about what I wear to bed," she interrupted, moving around the bed, "and getting a sponge bath from Stacey, and then you want to get married. Lord, what's next?"

Before I could go on, convince her that I was in dead earnest, the Sheriff of Blue Mountain walked into my room. He only took a few steps before he stopped.

"Fever?" He just stood there. "They said you were—are you awake?"

"Skidmore," I answered. "Are you coming in?"

He looked at Lucinda. "How is he?"

"He just told me we should get married." She raised her eyebrows.

"Jesus," Skid said, shaking his head. "You said there might be brain damage."

"I know you both think you're funny," I announced loudly, squirming in bed, "but it looks to me as if things have may have gone to hell while I've been out. Skid can't find a murderer even though he's got a tape recording of the man. Lucinda doesn't seem to want to get married anymore. And Andrews has taken Nurse Chambers way too seriously. Are we sure this is still Blue Mountain?"

Nurse Chambers strolled into my room then, on cue. She was completely naked except for her nurse's cap. When she smiled, her teeth were entirely transparent. She leaned over my bed and whispered, "Are you sure this isn't some sort of nightmare?"

4.

I found myself standing in a crowded nightclub staring at a yellowed photograph of a crowded nightclub. In the center of the picture there was a woman. On the back of the photo it said, "Lisa, 1923."

I looked around. I could feel the club, the whole world still celebrating the end of war. I could feel the year 1923. The war to end all wars had been won, and times were very good. Most people had money. Everybody had fun. Jazz was king, Gin was queen, and everyone else was royalty of some sort, at least for a night or two, until they sobered up. But most young people were full-fledged jazz babies. Jazz babies drank and danced and copulated with the frenzy of wild hares. France, for example, was a nation of 65,000 illegitimate births. Germany had nearly three times that many. Somebody should have been comparing those census statistics. If people in France had known there were that many more bastards right next door, they might have been more prepared for what was about to happen. If they'd been paying attention, they would have known that a young man named Adolf Hitler had just announced a twenty-five-point program at the Hofbräuhaus in Munich.

Unfortunately, everybody was too busy being a jazz baby. They sang in the streets. They drank thick coffee in cafés. They guzzled wine.

But to be specific and infinitely more personal, there I was, an idle observer in a particular place that would come to mean a great deal to my family and me. It was a Paris hot spot called *Le Chat du Jazz*, The Jazz Cat. A woman named Lisa owned it, but it was popular because of a great new soprano saxophone player from Chicago, an expatriate named T-Bone Morton, the grandson of former slaves.

After hours, I observed, ghostlike, T-Bone and other assorted young people arguing far into the next morning. They talked about philosophy and religion and politics and wine and other things vital to human life.

T-Bone gave what was obviously his favorite speech. Everyone reacted as if they'd heard it or variations of it many times before.

"The truly virtuous turn into pure light when they die," he opined. "They move out of this reality altogether. The merely good, they spend a little time in heaven, and then they have to return to this earth or, I suppose, other earths like this. They are shed, as rain, back to the ground, where they become plants, are eaten, become eggs in a female or sperm in a male, and are reborn. The pleasant people are reborn as great teachers and sages; the unpleasant people are reborn as pigs or slugs or something else. This keeps up until we can mend the torn places in our spirits. Those torn places are direct results of our actions on this earth. So, in conclusion, if you don't want to be a slug in the next life, don't act like a slug in this one."

Minor applause ensued.

T-Bone added, "These are all thoughts, of course, which originated in Africa, the cradle of civilization."

The French woman named Lisa, the club owner, responded, "I'm all in favor of this pride you have in your African heritage. All in favor of it. But not everything started in Africa."

T-Bone leaned back. "Name anything that didn't."

She shrugged, as only the French can, and I fell in love with her just a little. "Why not five? Without even thinking I can tell you five things that did not come from Africa: Greek theater, the Sistine Chapel, Shakespeare's plays, Impressionist painting, and truly great wine."

T-Bone did not even take a breath. "All African, at least theoretically."

The table exploded. All manner of objection—good-natured, bad-tempered, ill-conceived, well-thought-out—flew around in the air.

"All right, then." T-Bone held up one hand. "I'll concede your wine. The French beat everybody at that."

It was clear that he knew what he was doing. He could wear anyone down on any other subject, even where Shakespeare was concerned, but he would never win an argument with Lisa about wine. Lisa Simard was a holy terror in general, and no one could argue with her in her own club. The problem was that she loved to argue, especially about her favorite subjects: the rights of women in France, the growing horror of fascism in Europe; the best wines in the world. But she had been known to produce a small knife in the heat of such discussions, so the debates were mostly one-sided. Her customers tended to agree with her just to keep the peace. In fact, no one ever caused trouble in her café.

Also, there were wilder rumors about Lisa: that she'd killed her own father in a drunken brawl; she'd fought as a man in the World War; she had once crushed a man's left testicle between her thumb and first finger. That particular story was told all over Paris. An inebriated rowdy, the story went, had hoisted a glass in honor of Adolf Hitler's twenty-five-point program recently announced at the Hofbräuhaus in Munich. Her response was to kick his chair, shove him to the ground, and crush a part of his private world before he could think of a second thing to say.

She stood up immediately and announced, "Just like squeezing a grape."

The man passed into unconsciousness.

No one ever caused trouble in Lisa's café.

As it happened, Lisa knew all about crushing grapes, and that was the reason no one argued with her about wine. She had been born into the Simard family of the Château Simard, purveyors of good, sometimes great, St. Emilion wines for hundreds of years. Her ancestors had spent generations learning every nuance of soil and sun, rain and dew. They knew every plant that was planted for miles around the grape vines, every sound the grapes heard, every emotion the grapes felt. Lisa could tell, most times, what a wine was like just by looking at a teaspoonful of it—before she even tasted it. When she actually tasted it, she was quite capable, she insisted, of telling the color of the vintner's pajamas.

She had left the delightful family business and come to Paris because, she would always explain, priorities in the city were arranged in their proper order: wine, food, love, art, music, coffee, philosophy, politics, national pride, family, architecture, gardens, work, and cemeteries. In that order.

And of course there was the jazz. She loved it. She'd hired T-Bone Morton after she'd heard him play a single chorus of the song "Dr. Jazz." People flocked to Le Chat du Jazz to see T-Bone, to hear his wild improvisations. Each solo would seem to everyone a frenzy of rage and fear and violence and sudden, soul-shattering redemption. Each solo was like that. T-Bone poured himself out until he was empty at every show. He took the listener on a journey, and the journey was always transcendent.

Sometimes, when the girls were flirting with T-Bone, they would ask about the emotion in the solos. "What makes you play like that?" they would ask.

Soft as silk, low as a sigh, T-Bone would answer. "The Universe has a lot to say. I'm trying to translate as fast as I can. See, the Universe is not just big, it's infinite. And when it tries to say something through a finite little human body, it's always difficult, you understand. So I struggle with it. That's what you hear."

Everyone in Paris loved T-Bone Morton.

Alas, as he and Lisa would soon discover, T-Bone was not universally loved. There was a certain man from Chicago named Chester, who figured in the story of Lisa and T-Bone quite prominently. Chester was a barely literate bundle of rage who worked in the stockyards of Chicago. He was fleshy and stooped, with only patches of hair on his pockmarked head. He always wore coveralls and a flannel shirt. He lived with his mother. They were both sick most of the time and poor all of the time. But they saved up all their money. They never spent a dime. They were planning for a trip to Paris. On instructions from his mother, Chester was going to kill T-Bone Morton.

That is why, at the beginning of 1923, red with anger and anguish, Chester quit his job in the stockyards and signed aboard an ocean liner as an assistant to the cook. His job was to chop things—salads, pork loins, root vegetables—for the people who lived above in the sunlit cabins and sea-sprayed deck.

For agonizing weeks Chester lived in the kitchen and rested in a dark steel bunk. He was seasick all of the time. He was hungry all of the time. He couldn't sleep, he couldn't read, he couldn't think.

The only clear idea in his mind was that he was going to kill a man named T-Bone Morton and maybe then, at last, his mother would be at peace. Kill that man: it was his evening prayer, it was his morning ablution, it was his food and drink.

Everyone avoided Chester. There was a palpable air of menace and disease around him like a stinking aura. One evening, while he was chopping mutton and repeating his only prayer in the kitchen, a busboy accidentally bumped into him.

"Sorry. Gee." The bus boy smiled shyly. "Excuse me, pal. Guess I still ain't got my sea legs."

"I'll give you sea legs," Chester said, and without blinking cleaved off the boy's left hand. The boy passed out. Then Chester used the cleaver to slice the boy's legs to hamburger.

He hauled the bleeding carcass into a janitor's closet. Then he collected salt water from the bilge and doused the boy in it. The boy woke up.

"Sea legs," Chester mumbled.

Then Chester locked the closet. The boy began to scream. Chester went back to work in the kitchen, covered in sheep's guts and human blood. It was several hours before someone heard the boy screaming and took him to his bunk.

That was Chester.

The ship's doctor was summoned. He didn't know what to do. By then the boy was out of his mind.

"I'll never be able to fix those legs, not with the stuff we've got onboard ship. His muscles and nerves are all cut up. He tried to scream some more, but he couldn't. He just kept whispering 'sea legs.' Now he's in a coma. Exactly what am I supposed to do?"

The captain decided to keep the busboy's condition a secret from the passengers on board. Why panic paying customers?

The boy never regained consciousness. He bled to death in his coma. He died before the ship reached shore. He was buried at sea. Under "Cause of Death" on the official document, the doctor wrote, "Unknown."

A week later, the ship pulled into the port of Marseilles. Chester had arrived in France. It took him several more weeks to get to Paris. He couldn't speak French. At that point, he could barely speak any human tongue. Parisians would cross the street to avoid him even before they got a good look at his face. Chester was a snarling nightmare, a human wreck, because he was comprised almost entirely of searing vengeance. He was hoping to avenge a horrible crime that had been perpetrated on his mother. His mother had instilled that rage in her boy from the day of his birth.

He wandered the crowded streets of Paris all night and day. He still couldn't sleep, he hated the food, and the people in France were morons. For nearly five weeks he wandered aimlessly asking everyone the same riddle: "Where is T-Bone Morton?"

Most people ignored him. Another drunken American. What could one do? They seemed to be simply everywhere these days. Ah, well. On to a late dinner.

Then, early one morning in May, Chester found the object of his quest: Le Chat du Jazz. There was a sign out front that read in big, bold letters even he could recognize: T-Bone Morton. The rest of the scribbling was in French, but Chester knew he had found his prey. It was three o'clock in the morning. The stars above him were obscured by the street lamps. He checked his inside coat pocket, smiled for the first time in several years, and stumbled into the club. It took a moment for his eyes to adjust as he searched the room for any sign of someone who might be T-Bone Morton.

At first no one noticed the demon at the door. Everyone in the club had been there since early evening, drinking, talking, taking a dinner break, drinking, dancing. There were still three couples left on the dance floor.

Then Chester saw a man on the bandstand. The man was playing music. That man had to be T-Bone Morton. T-Bone played music. Chester grew calm and steady. He took a few staggering steps toward the bar and said loudly, "T-Bone Morton?"

The bartender nodded, heavy-lidded. "*Oui*, T-Bone."

Chester nodded and moved slowly across the dance floor toward the bandstand. His eyes were locked on the devil's musician. His hand moved slowly toward the inside pocket of his coat. He found his pistol, raised it, and pointed it right at T-Bone's head.

T-Bone saw the gun at the last minute. He didn't stop playing. He knew that bullets were faster than musical notes, but he wanted to finish his solo.

Then, at the exact moment Chester squeezed the trigger, Lisa appeared out of nowhere. There was a flash of something shiny, and she stabbed the man in his gun arm. Then she cut his throat. Chester's bullet went into the ceiling of the club.

Chester dropped to the floor like a broken elevator. Lisa's hand moved at the speed of light, her knife was gone, back in its hiding place somewhere in her dress.

In the chaos that ensued, several of the Frenchmen in the club hovered over Chester as he tried to talk. He managed to whisper a single word comprised of two syllables.

"Mother."

Lisa heard him but she thought at the time that he was saying good-bye to his mother because he did not take another breath.

Lisa looked at T-Bone. "Did he hurt you? What happened? What did he do to you?"

"Nothing," he assured her. "I think I'm okay. Man. Here's your proof of God right here. That bullet should have killed me."

"This isn't proof of God," Lisa objected. "It's proof of *me*."

T-Bone smiled with an overflowing heart. "Well, it certainly proves the rumor that nobody causes trouble in your club."

"Exactement!" She nodded curtly.

"Yes, ma'am," T-Bone said.

Lisa looked down at the man bleeding on her floor. "Who was he?"

"This guy?" T-Bone stared. "I don't know him."

"You never saw him before?"

He shook his head. "Don't think so. Maybe in the war. I knew a lot of guys in the war."

"Maybe in the war." She nodded. "Let's look at his wallet. See who he was."

His name was Chester Echo. He was from Chicago, where T-Bone had lived before coming to fight in the war. There were seven American dollars and fifty francs in the wallet, but there was no clue whatsoever as to why he would want to kill T-Bone.

"That's it." Lisa made a decision. "This man was out of his mind."

No one disagreed. The police were summoned. They pronounced the dead man dead. They asked everyone what had happened.

Lisa told a very simple lie. Two men, the dead one and someone else, had been sitting and drinking, arguing about a woman all night. Finally, in the wee hours, one of the men rose up and stabbed the other, then ran away from the club.

The police were satisfied. It was an *affaire de coeur*. What could one do? Ah, well. On to an early breakfast. That was that.

Lisa closed the club just around sunrise. T-Bone helped her. They didn't talk, but T-Bone went home with Lisa for the first time. They were both filled with life, holding hands. Everything on the walk to Lisa's flat was wonderful. The sky was glorious, the buildings were heavenly, and a certain bridge was filled with rapture. They were young and alive and in love. It was Paris in the twenties.

After they made love, T-Bone lay awake listening to the ticking of the clock on Lisa's mantel. He was too happy to sleep. In the late morning light, he could see several dozen blackbirds on the clotheslines strung in between the buildings outside of the window. He nudged Lisa.

"Look," he said.

"What?" She wasn't asleep either.

"Those birds. Out there on the clotheslines?"

"I see them." She sat up to see. "What about them?"

"Imagine that the clotheslines make a music staff." He stared at them. "Doesn't that look like sheet music? Aren't the blackbirds musical notes?"

"Ah." She cocked her head and looked again. "Yes they are. Well?"

"Well what?" he asked.

"What's the melody that they are making?"

"Oh." He squinted. "That's a good idea."

Softly, he began to whistle the melody made by the birds on the wires. It was unexpectedly melodic. In fact, as it went on, it was mesmerizingly complex, looping, repeating, strange, filled with mystery, and altogether remarkable.

"There," he said when he was done.

"Beautiful." She closed her eyes.

"See," he said, "that's a melody that God assembled just for us, just for you and me in this moment. No one else in the world has ever heard that."

Lisa took in a breath because she knew at that moment that she was in love with T-Bone. "You should use that melody."

"I don't know." He shook his head. "I don't like to steal from other composers."

"Idiot," she whispered, folding herself into his arms. "Who do you think composes everything anyway? Who do you think gives you all your fantastic solos when you play? You don't think He's giving you that melody now?"

"I knew it," T-Bone said, holding her tighter. "You do believe in God. The way you argue about the subject, I really didn't know until this moment."

"I'm Catholic," she told him, as if that were the perfect explanation. "You'd better write down that song before you forget it."

"Good point." T-Bone took another look at the birds and nodded slowly. "I'd better write this down."

He threw his legs over the side of the bed to get a pencil and a piece of paper. Just as he did, the birds flew away. He was already beginning to forget how the melody went.

"Gone," he said softly.

"Well, there you have it," she said, getting up to make coffee.

"What?" he asked, standing naked in front of the window and staring out at the empty clotheslines.

"*That* is proof of God." She reached for a cigarette. "Not somebody shooting somebody in a nightclub."

"What are you talking about?"

"Last night," she reasoned, striking a match, "you said that the bullet missing you was proof of God."

"Yes," he prompted.

"But this is much better proof."

"How?"

"Well." She lit her cigarette. "You and I both know there was a melody in the room a moment ago. You whistled it; I heard it. It's gone now, but it did exist. And in some way it still *does* exist because it's out in the air, *because* you whistled it. It exists but no one on earth knows it now. And if that is the case, where does it exist?"

"I don't know." T-Bone turned to face her. "In our memories?"

"No. You don't remember it anymore. Neither do I. But it does exist."

"Where then?" He sat back down on the bed.

She handed him her cigarette and said, "In the mind of God."

That was Lisa.

She was the woman in the photograph that I found in my tin box. She was the woman who looked exactly like my mother. She was the reason that a stranger came into my house and killed me.

5.

I felt Lucinda touch my face and heard her say, "Fever?"

I opened my eyes. She was looking at me very anxiously.

I turned slightly and could see that I was once more in a hospital room—or *still* in a hospital room. That would be the more accurate phrase, I thought. Skidmore was standing on the other side of the bed opposite from Lucinda. Deputy Melissa Mathews was beside him. She, alone, was smiling; smiling very sweetly at me.

I was happy to see Melissa there. She brightened the room. Her chestnut hair always seemed just-washed, her eyes were shy but her posture was bold, and her lips were never far away from a smile. She had a great laugh, a sound like water over round rocks in a cold stream. It was music from nature, not a human sound at all. Unfortunately for her, she was one of the world's shyest women. Dozens of men had courted her. But she was a self-confessed coward where they were concerned. She could be friendly with someone who had no interest in her, but she was terrified of any man who wanted her attention. She had always been very close to Skidmore for that reason, because she knew he was only interested in his wife. But their friendship had led some, in the past, to suspect that her relationship with Skid was more intimate than it actually was. Happily, those rumors had been laid to rest for several years. For some reason I was very comforted by her presence, though I could not have explained it in words.

"Why is everyone staring at me?" I asked slowly, staring at Melissa's cheek.

"You fell asleep in the middle of our conversation," Lucinda explained, rousing me from my reverie concerning Melissa.

"I did?" I realized that I wasn't sitting up anymore, and tried to clear my head.

"What's the last thing you remember?" she asked quietly.

"Stacey Chambers came into the room naked." But as I was saying the words, I realized that they weren't actually true.

Stacey appeared behind Lucinda. She was fully clothed.

"I only do that when I'm sure you're asleep," she told me heartily.

"Sorry." I might have been blushing. "The last thing I actually remember is Skid's coming into the room. And then I was dreaming about the 1920s. How long was I gone?"

"About a half an hour." Lucinda, I realized, was taking my pulse. "The 1920s?"

"Nothing," I said quickly. "Look, I guess passing out like that, it's got to be fairly normal for a coma victim, right?"

"Yes," Lucinda confirmed.

"And you knew I was asleep. As opposed to being back in a coma."

"You were talking and snoring," Lucinda said.

"I was talking?" I managed to sit up. "What was I talking about?"

"You said the name *Lisa,*" Melissa told me.

"But I'm not jealous or anything." Lucinda patted my arm.

"You were also talking in French for a minute there," Skidmore added.

"Wait." I rubbed my face with my hands. I took a few deep breaths. I tried to be completely conscious. "Wait."

"What is it?" Melissa leaned over me.

"I was talking in French." I tried to get my bearings. "I was dreaming about the 1920s in Paris."

"Yes." Skidmore leaned a little closer. He could read the look on my face.

"Jesus," I mumbled.

"What is it, Fever?" Lucinda asked softly.

"Skid," I began, "Stacey said that my house was a mess when you came to look at it—after I was shot."

"It was a mess," he agreed.

Skidmore didn't say anything else. No one did. They seemed to know that I was going somewhere with my thoughts.

"But I had just tidied up that morning. I remember quite clearly." I blinked several times, concentrating hard on fully waking up. "Lucinda was going to come over the next day, I believe."

"Yes," Lucinda said, "but the place really smelled like alcohol when I got there—after you were shot."

"Well I had been drinking that damned pastis that Andrews brought me," I admitted. "But I didn't wreck my living room. I was sleepy."

"I get sleepy whenever I drink anything," Melissa chimed in, trying to support me.

"The point is," I soldiered on, "that someone else messed up my house. I think the man who shot me was looking for something, and I might know what it is, because I've been dreaming about it."

"What do you think he was looking for?" Skid asked.

"A tin box filled with papers and letters and photographs. Did you find anything like that in my living room? Say, behind the clock on the mantel?"

"I don't remember anything about a tin box."

"He got it," I snapped. For some unfathomable reason, the thought of that agitated me greatly. "He got the box."

"What was in it?" Melissa asked. "Money?"

"No," I said. "Family photos and papers and—personal things."

"Why would he want to take stuff like that, Fever?" Skid was obviously skeptical—humoring me a little.

"I don't know," I confessed. "Maybe this man who shot me said something to me about it before he . . . I'm saying I've been dreaming about the people in it, the people in the tin box."

"The—the people in the tin box?" Melissa shot a look to Lucinda. "What's he talking about?"

"Maybe you'd better lie back down, hon," Lucinda said sweetly. "You're not quite awake yet."

"I know I'm not making myself clear," I mumbled.

"The problem is, Dr. Devilin," Stacey explained, "that when you come out of a coma like you did, you don't just wake up and everything's fine. It takes you a while to *completely* wake up."

"How long?" I asked her. "How long before I'm completely awake?"

Stacey looked at Lucinda before she answered. Lucinda nodded.

"Minimum time is usually half as long as you've been in the coma," Stacey told me, very professionally.

"I see," I responded quietly. "And what's the maximum? How long could this go on? How long could I stay in a foggy state, falling asleep in the middle of sentences? When will that be over—maximum?"

"Well," she hesitated. "Maximum time is never. Some people never get completely over it."

"Never?" I asked weakly.

"Very often," Lucinda went on, "coma patients will have hallucinations for the rest of their lives. Some continue to have the kind of narcolepsy that you've just exhibited. And sometimes they relapse."

"Sometimes people go back into a coma?" I said a little more loudly than I meant to.

"Yes." She tried to display no emotion at all.

I took in a couple of slow, deep breaths. Again, nobody said a thing.

"All right, well," I whispered, "I'm just going to ignore that information. Let me start over again. When can I get out of this bed and go home?"

"You can't go home, sugar," Lucinda said. "You're going to fall back asleep in a minute. You're going to keep doing that for a while. Some people come out of a coma with all kinds of physical or psychological problems. They need lots of taking care of. This is going to be a gradual thing—even for you. For your first few days, you might not be awake but for a few minutes at a time."

"A few minutes?" I didn't believe her. I felt completely awake.

"It gets better. I believe that sometime this year you'll get completely back to normal."

"Normal." Skidmore grinned. "Whatever that was."

"Sometime this *year* I might be back to normal," I repeated to myself. "A year."

"Could be a lot sooner," Lucinda told me.

"Coma patients usually wake up in a real state of confusion," Stacey said. "They don't know where they are or how they got there. I was very surprised you knew who I was right away."

"Some patients have acute dysphasia," Lucinda continued. "At least you don't have that."

"What is it?" Melissa asked.

"It's an inability to articulate any speech," I told her. "You can't speak correctly. Or you slur your words so badly that no one can understand you."

"Oh." Skid straightened up. He knew how badly I might take a condition like that.

"So I can't go home?" I sat back.

"No," Lucinda said firmly.

"Right." I bit my lower lip. "Then Skid, can you check my living room for that tin box? It's blue, about this big, and it has a kind of hunting scene on the cover. Lots of papers and photos inside. It's supposed to be behind the clock on the mantel."

"If you think it's important." He sighed.

"I think it's the reason I was shot," I insisted. "I just don't know why that would be the case. I don't even know the full significance of those items myself. But I know that someone thought that the contents of that box would alter the course of my life permanently. There was a letter."

Lucinda tried to tell me something, but the Chicago jazz band in the hallway began playing and I couldn't hear what she said over their version of "Wolverine Blues."

6.

"Wolverine Blues" was written by Jelly Roll Morton and recorded in Chicago in 1923. Chicago had become the capital of jazz in the early 1920s after the city of New Orleans closed the brothels in Storyville. That was important to my attacker.

Jelly Roll Morton, to the great consternation of many others, had declared that he invented jazz—on a Tuesday night in 1902. He was one of the musicians who made the move from The Big Easy to the Windy City, around 1914. There he began writing down his compositions, and in 1915 his "Jelly Roll Blues" was, at least according to him, the first jazz composition ever published. It set down on paper the kind of traditional jazz for which New Orleans had already become famous.

Unknown to Jelly Roll, a Caucasian woman who called herself Eulalie Echo also came to Chicago in 1914. She had worked in one of the brothels in Storyville. She told everyone that Jelly Roll was the father of her son, although there was no way of knowing whether or not that was true. Jelly Roll was famous and everyone wanted to be connected to him. Eulalie drank a lot, and enjoyed prodigious amounts of cocaine, which anyone could legally purchase at the corner pharmacy for about five cents a box. All the girls were using it. It didn't matter.

What mattered was that by 1914 Eulalie was living in Chicago and absolutely believed that Jelly Roll Morton was the man who had gotten her pregnant and abandoned her. Her son, Jelly Roll's son, had seemed an abomination to Eulalie. She had left his upbringing to other women in the brothel. She had dragged him with her to Chicago, for some reason, but then abandoned him on the steps of a Catholic orphanage. She tied a printed note to his hand that said, "This is the bastard son of Jelly Roll Morton. He's called T-Bone." A gangly teenager by then, the moniker was relatively descriptive. That note would later be found in a small tin box.

Eulalie had left T-Bone to the nuns because she had another son whom she loved, an entirely Caucasian child, and two children were too many to support. The father of the second child was a hog butcher to the world, a man with broad shoulders, another customer of hers but a decent Chicago native—a man whose name is lost to history. That second son's name was Chester. Chester spent his formative years in the worst part of the south side of Chicago. He grew up hearing all about the evils of the man who had raped his mother and invented jazz. Jelly Roll Morton was the devil to Chester Echo. And that wasn't the worst of it, according to his mother. The worst of it was that Chester had a half brother, a pestilence that ought to have been rubbed out long ago. But by the time Chester was big enough to do anything about it, T-Bone had left the orphanage, vanished. Some said that he had gone to France to fight in the war.

Closer to the truth was a short note from a Catholic nun who said that T-Bone had gone to Europe hoping to escape racism, fight in the war, and find jobs playing jazz. He heard Sidney Bechet playing the soprano saxophone in Paris and he took up the instrument. When most of the GIs went back home, T-Bone stayed in Paris. Some of his buddies had tried to tell him that he could become a famous musician if he would only come back to Chicago. Chicago was the capital of jazz. But T-Bone had nothing in

Chicago, and in Paris he had found music, respect, wine, great food, and the best scrambled eggs in the world. So he stayed. By 1923 he was the toast of the local Paris jazz scene.

Still, his buddies sent him letters. They tried to coax him home. They told him all about the King of Chicago jazz, Joseph Oliver, born in 1885 in New Orleans. Oliver grew up as a cornet player in the dance bands for the city's red-light district, Storyville, where T-Bone had been born. Oliver eventually became so popular there that he was able to cross all economic and racial lines. He played everywhere from the roughest working-class black dance halls to the whitest society debutante parties. Then, in 1919, a fight broke out at a dance where Oliver was playing. The police arrived, took a look around, realized that the men who had been fighting were not only white but also rich, and immediately arrested Oliver and his entire band. They said that the music had been the proximate cause of the fight; its rhythms had incited the violence in the decent rich white men at the party.

The next morning Oliver got out of jail. He packed up everything he had, got the band together, chartered a bus, and left the South forever. They were all gone by noon.

By 1922, he was called King Oliver and his Creole Jazz Band performed almost every night at Lincoln Gardens in Chicago. Everyone in town was talking about the band. Louis Armstrong was the second cornet player in the ensemble; Sidney Bechet sat in whenever he was in town. In fact, the band ended up being a virtual Who's Who of the new jazz sound, a hybrid of old style Dixieland and the more sophisticated larger dance band.

King Oliver, Jelly Roll Morton, Louis Armstrong, Sidney Bechet, and so many other superior jazz musicians were a part of the so-called Great Migration. The national press of the day, in fact, credited the popularity of jazz in the urban north to this Great Migration, which was a movement between 1910 and 1930 of some four million African-Americans away from Southern states, mostly to the North and Midwest. The idea was that African-Americans were hoping to escape racism and find jobs, mostly in the industrialized cities. And since there were more African-Americans in these urban areas than ever before, that explained the sudden appearance of jazz in places like Chicago and, later, New York. That was the somewhat confused and convoluted theory.

But this assessment also included the fact that a great many Caucasians were equal fans of the sound, and did not overlook the contribution of the entirely Caucasian Leon Bismark "Bix" Beiderbecke. He was a great cornet player and composer who was born in Iowa, of all places. After Armstrong, Bix was the most influential brass soloist of the 1920s, usually credited with helping to invent the ballad style of jazz. He taught himself to play without benefit of teacher or role model, and so he never learned the correct fingering patterns for the cornet. Some critics credit this incorrect approach to the instrument with the development of his original sound. Whatever it was, Bix's sound was timeless. Alas, Bix, the man, liked to drink, and it killed him. He died at the age of twenty-eight.

And as so often happens, the end of his life was the beginning of his legend. Once he was dead, everyone who cared about jazz had an opinion about Bix Beiderbecke. He was a saint, he was a criminal, he was a martyr in the cause of art. His Pontius Pilate was bourgeois commerce. His salvation was the invention of jazz. There were controversies about everything in his life: his true name, his actual race, his sexual orientation. It was reported that he'd been murdered by a jealous boyfriend. It was reported that he had taken his own life, leaving a note apologizing for stealing jazz from the African-American ethos. It was reported that he wasn't dead at all, that his death had been faked so that he could escape gambling debts. A story was even told that he'd been a spy in WWII, always disguised as a woman. Bix had supposedly gotten the idea from Christopher Marlowe, Shakespeare's contemporary, who had done the same thing in the courtly intrigues of the sixteenth century.

In life Bix had been a singularly gifted player and composer. In death he had become a hundred men. That is the nature of legend, of course.

These legends were more than a fascinating digression for me because Bix made a significant contribution to the Devilin family tree.

On a quiet Tuesday night early in February of 1924, King Oliver's band was playing at Lincoln Gardens. It was a huge hall, big enough for a thousand dancers. Second cornet was Louis Armstrong. Sitting in on soprano saxophone was T-Bone Morton, newly returned from Paris. It was early, around midnight. Everyone in the place was talking about what was happening in the stock market. Everyone was getting rich, things looked great, and the more gin they drank, the better things were.

After a rousing rendition of Jelly Roll Morton's "Wolverine Blues," who should walk into the place but Bix Beiderbecke. Everyone knew who he was. Everyone was happy to see him. King Oliver invited him up onto the bandstand. No one noticed the three men at a corner table in the shadows. They apparently weren't there to dance. They only drank and stared at the band.

Bix took out his horn. Oliver whispered to the musicians that they would play Bix's composition "In a Mist." The tune started up. The audience applauded. The three men stood and menaced their way toward the bandstand. One of them, obviously the leader, drew a pistol. The other two pulled long wooden clubs out of their trouser legs.

Armstrong saw the men coming. He understood what was about to happen. He'd seen those kinds of men dozens of times in the rougher dance halls in New Orleans. He stood up and abruptly interrupted Bix's solo by playing a loud chorus of "Muskrat Ramble."

Everybody in the band knew something was wrong, and when Armstrong rolled his eyes in the direction of the unholy trio, Bix was the first to react. He kicked the air, his shoe flew off, and it knocked the gun out of the leader's hand. T-Bone pulled his own pistol out of his pocket and shot another man's hat off. That got the crowd's attention and they swarmed the three troublemakers, surrounding them and containing them. At Lincoln Gardens *no one* bothered the band. And during the entire fracas, the band never stopped playing.

The leader of the three strange men, restrained by very polite bouncers, began to scream at the top of his lungs. "I know who you are, T-Bone Morton. You killed Chester! We'll kill you soon enough, even if it's not tonight! And we'll kill your little mongrel daughter, too!"

The police appeared relatively quickly and whisked the three assailants away, but not before one of the policemen identified them to King Oliver, confidentially, as members of the Illinois Ku Klux Klan. It was the nation's second largest chapter of that organization, after Indiana's. Oliver nodded. The band took a break. Everyone in the group gathered around T-Bone. T-Bone wasn't worried for his own life. He was still mourning the loss of his wife, Lisa. He wouldn't have minded dying himself, but he was concerned about his baby daughter.

"You've got to get you out of town," Oliver is reported to have told him.

After some consideration on everybody's part, Armstrong said he had connections with some shady characters in New Orleans who might just kill the three men, but it was decided that the suggestion wouldn't really solve the larger problem. If the Klan were involved, they'd keep after T-Bone no matter what.

Then Bix suggested that if the Klan was the problem, then a more Caucasian solution might be in order. Someone pointed out that appearances made it clear that T-Bone had some white heritage, and if his wife had also been white, maybe the daughter might pass. T-Bone instantly objected to this solution in a very loud voice. Passing for *anything* was out of the question.

Oliver told T-Bone that he couldn't play with the band for a while, because the band didn't need trouble with the Klan. He also observed that it might be easier for T-Bone to separate from his daughter for a short while. If someone would take care of the baby, T-Bone might have a chance to slip out of Chicago unnoticed.

T-Bone hated the idea, but he saw the wisdom of it. He began, however, to reiterate his insistence that neither he nor his daughter would ever attempt to pass for white. Ever.

Bix saved the day, supposedly, by wondering out loud why it would be necessary to say anything about anybody's race at all. He then made a suggestion that would alter the course of the Devilin family. T-Bone would hand over his daughter to Bix, who would give her to a Caucasian New Orleans family he knew. That's all. The less said, the better. T-Bone could get himself out of town and collect his daughter in Louisiana when things cooled off—maybe in a month or two.

The family that Bix had in mind was named Newcomb. T-Bone and Lisa's daughter would be given to Tubby Newcomb, who would soon, unfortunately and unbeknownst to anyone on the planet at that moment, be headed out of New Orleans. He would move quite suddenly, for reasons of his own, to a hidden place in the Appalachian Mountains that would one day be called Blue Mountain.

7.

The hospital smell woke me up, that combination of disinfectant, medicine, and angst. I opened my eyes. It was nighttime. I was alone in the room. Someone had brought a television into my room, and it was tuned in to PBS. They were playing a documentary about jazz. The narrator was talking about Lincoln Gardens in Chicago. Originally known as the Royal Gardens, the name had been changed in 1921, I was told, for unclear reasons.

Then, the narrator continued, in late February of 1924, the hall was burned, reportedly by the Chicago chapter of the Ku Klux Klan. Their complaint was that the room had become a cesspool of race mixing. Rebuilt in 1925, the name was changed to the New Charleston Café, but that only irritated the Klan, or maybe the Mob, the narrator was uncertain. In June 1927 it was bombed and closed its doors as a jazz center for the nation.

I thought then that the show's presence in my room explained the strange dream I'd been having. Later I would discover, of course, that a stranger coincidence had prevailed, but that only deepened the surreal quality of subsequent events.

I was quickly roused from my half-conscious state by an orderly bringing me something to drink. The room was dark. This orderly was not the one who'd been told to bring me soup. This was an older man, with a much more sophisticated approach to things.

"Drink it quickly," he whispered in a heavy, unfamiliar accent. "It's a very healthy green tea, loaded with polyphenols, and some extra herbal ingredients. I brewed it myself. You should be able to stay awake for a while after you get it down."

He handed me a hot white porcelain cup.

"What happened to that kid with my soup?" I rasped.

"Albert?" the old man said. "He doesn't work here anymore. And you don't want his soup, you want my tea."

Without another word, he snapped off the television and was gone.

The tea was supernaturally effective. My mind cleared and my thoughts arranged themselves in a surprisingly coherent fashion. I was able to consider, among other things, my fate.

I had gone to bed in December. Someone had shot me—killed me, in fact—maybe stolen a tin box from my house. Then Lucinda had appeared on the scene, packed me in snow, and saved my life. I'd lain in a coma for months. I'd awakened in almost-spring. Skidmore had been investigating the crime but had gotten nowhere.

My path was clear. I had to get up out of my hospital bed, go home, and solve my own murder. That was obvious to me, as was the fact that my assailant had some reason for stealing the tin box, an item of surpassing albeit antiquated mystery for me. All I had to do was ascertain the meaning of the items in the box, and my inquiries would be on their way.

If only I could remember what those items were.

Papers, letters, photographs, poems, a ring of some sort, four silver dollars—was there a pair of glasses? Or was I remembering some of the items in my mother's ancient hiding place in her room?

My mother had created many odd hiding places in and around our house, partly because she wanted to hide items she considered treasures, partly because she was possessed of a severely damaged paranoid personality. She had somehow made a fairly large chamber in one of the walls of her room at our home, the entrance to which was, cleverly, a very tight-fitting windowsill. If you lifted the sill, you'd have access to some of her treasures. I'd found the place when I was a boy and my parents were away, as they were for weeks at a time, with their traveling show. From time to time I'd opened it up, hoping to find clues as to who my mother really was. The contents of the hiding place changed often, but the effect those contents had on me was always the same. I sorted through them, never understanding their true significance, and always came away with a melancholy bordering on the suicidal.

No, I decided, the glasses were something I'd found in her hiding place, not in the tin box. My mother never wore glasses, but there you were: nothing that she held dear to herself ever made any sense to me.

I did remember that on the night I'd found the box in question, I'd also had some sort of strange experience, something I'd interpreted then as an angelic encounter. I'd later come to believe that I'd seen my own reflection in the window and imagined the rest. At any rate, my mother had fetched a letter not contained in the box, something she'd apparently kept for some time. It was addressed to me but unsigned.

I suddenly realized that I had dreamed about that night, dreams of such clarity that I'd remembered every word of the letter. Although I could not recall the exact words sitting there in the hospital bed, I felt I could grasp the gist. I was to find out who the woman was in a certain photograph that was in the tin box, but if I did, my life would change.

That's why I'd been dreaming about the people and events revealed to me in the box.

Before I could collect my thoughts any further on the subject, the telephone rang. I picked it up before I had a chance to wonder who would be calling me.

"Hello?" I said into the phone.

"Who is this?"

"Why are you asking that?" I said slowly. "You're the one who called."

"Earl?"

"Whom are you calling?"

The phone went dead. For a moment I listened to the dial tone.

I had a sudden, rising panic. How many films or television programs, I thought, used the cliché of calling someone in order to see if they might have the assurance that their prey was available. Someone had called me to see if I was in the room, then hung up when my presence had been confirmed. And there I was, trapped in the hospital room, hooked up to machines, unable to escape.

I first had the impulse to hide in another hospital room, but I was still hooked up to machines and bottles. I sat up. It took forever and required the same amount of energy that I used to need to climb a mountain.

Then, of course, I thought of the nurse's call button.

I looked around and felt around in the bed until I found it. I grabbed it up and pressed it over and over again. Seconds later I could hear someone coming down the hall.

Nurse Chambers appeared in my doorway.

"Awake?" she cooed.

"I just got a phone call." I could hear the uneasiness in my voice; I assumed she heard it too.

"Who'd be calling you?" She stepped into the room. "Everybody knows you're in a coma."

"What time is it?"

She glanced at her watch. "Not quite ten o'clock. Why you sound so worried?"

"You said it: who would be calling me?"

"Right," she agreed. "Hang on."

She turned and vanished out the door before I could stop her. I didn't know what to do. I thought about calling Skidmore, but what would I say? That I'd gotten a phone call?

As the seconds turned into minutes, I realized that I was sweating. My fists were clenching the bedsheets. I had a sinking terror in the hollow of my chest that seemed disproportionate to my situation.

When my hands began to twitch, it hit me. I'd been poisoned. The tea from the strange orderly had contained something deadly. I grabbed the nurse's call button again, fumbled it, and held it down. I felt my throat closing up and my entire head began to throb.

"Stacey!" I croaked.

Nothing.

My breathing was becoming shallow and more difficult. I was drenched in sweat. The poison was filling me up. My hands and feet were ice cold, going numb, tingling slightly.

I realized that I hadn't been pressing the call button and began stabbing it with my thumb constantly. No result.

Just as I was licking my lips and trying to take a deep enough breath to call out again, Stacey flew into the room.

"What is it, Fever?" She stopped dead still a few feet from the bed. "Oh, my God. What the hell is the matter with you?"

"I've been poisoned," I managed to tell her. "There!"

I pointed to the empty porcelain cup.

She took two speedy steps toward the bed, put one hand on my head and took my wrist with her other.

"Your pulse is racing and your head is burning up."

"Shouldn't you call a doctor?"

"What makes you think you've been poisoned?" she asked briskly.

"A strange orderly gave me tea. In that cup. That's why I'm pointing at it."

She glanced at the cup. "That's from the cafeteria."

"How do you know?" I growled.

She picked up the cup and showed me the seal on the bottom. It said Hospital in bold black letters.

"That doesn't mean anything!" I insisted, barely able to whisper.

"Can I tell you, sugar, that it's more likely you're having a panic attack than a poison tea reaction?" she said sweetly.

"Panic attack?"

"You'd have rapid heartbeat, pounding heart, sweating, shaking, choking, shortness of breath, chest pain, chills—"

"Stop," I conceded.

"You've got those symptoms?"

"Every single one of them." I exhaled. "Panic attack."

"Also weird paranoia?"

"Check," I agreed.

"Happens to some coma patients when they wake up," she said, all business. "Very common. Still, I'll find out what was in the cup."

"Thanks." But I felt very foolish.

"As to your phone call," she said, patting my shoulder, "I checked with the switchboard. You got a call from inside the hospital, from another room. Probably a wrong number."

"The call was from inside this hospital?" I blinked.

"Uh-huh," she said distractedly, checking my IV.

"What year is this?"

Her head snapped in my direction and I could hear the concern in her voice. "Fever?"

But, naturally, I couldn't answer her because I fell asleep again.

8.

Lisa Simard refused to go to the hospital. Her pregnancy was causing her a great deal of pain, but she didn't like doctors telling her what to do. She and T-Bone had argued until it was obvious that nothing could dissuade a mother whose mind is made up. During the day T-Bone was helping his friend Sylvia at her new bookstore, Shakespeare and Company, around the corner to the rue de l'Odeon. Sylvia wanted his opinion of a manuscript, a new book called *Ulysses* by a funny little man in glasses. Sylvia was going to publish it herself, since no one else would.

At night T-Bone kept the club going. But one evening Sylvia invited T-Bone to the Paris Opera's production of *Die Walküre*. It was the first Wagnerian opera staged since before the war, and Parisians were flocking.

When he came home, he sat on the bed, and Lisa woke up.

"Well, how was the opera? What did you think?"

He shook his head. "Maybe I just don't like opera."

"You love *The Magic Flute*."

"Maybe I just don't like German opera."

Lisa took his hand. "*The Magic Flute* is a German opera, but I'm with you anyway."

"That's right." He squeezed her hand. "You don't like anything German."

Her brow wrinkled. "Their food smells terrible, their wine's weak, their language sounds like a man with tuberculosis clearing his throat."

He laughed.

"They're horrible people."

"Can anything good," T-Bone agreed, "come from a people who invented the word *fart*?"

She nodded very seriously. "My point exactly."

"So I didn't like the opera." T-Bone lay down beside his wife. "How can it be great if it doesn't syncopate?"

Lisa closed her eyes. "Le Jazz."

"Oh, you can put a *le* in front of it all you want," he teased softly, "it's still going to be a one hundred percent American invention."

"Is that so?"

"Oh—it's very so. You can't get something as hot as jazz without mixing it up and melting it in a pot. And what do you think America is?"

"A big mess?"

"Very funny. You can't have jazz without African music but I'll admit you also need Irish melody and a little Jewish clarinet."

"And a French something," Lisa warned.

"I was getting to that," T-Bone said quickly. "French gypsy violins. They're hot."

Lisa sighed. The night was warm and the moon was full. It poured into their little bedroom through blinds that cut the light into neat white stripes. "Jazz must be just about the most significant thing in the twentieth century."

T-Bone nodded. "It is."

"Of course," Lisa mumbled, just about to fall asleep, "you'd have to say something about the end of war. We did that too."

"We did that too," T-Bone agreed very softly, brushing the hair from her face, petting her head. "No more war."

"I love you," she murmured. And then she fell asleep.

"Je t'aime you too, sweetheart," he whispered.

He looked down at her and wondered what he would ever do if anything happened to her. It was the end of November 1923, and Lisa would not live out the year.

In that same year Europe would first celebrate Mother's Day. Also the value of the German mark dropped to a rate of four million to one American dollar. Hitler's "Beer Hall Putsch" failed. A tri-state meeting of the Ku Klux Klan was held in Kokomo, Indiana; two hundred thousand people attended. "Yes! We Have No Bananas" was the most popular song in the world.

And in that same year the poet e. e. cummings published a book called *Tulips and Chimneys* in which there was a poem called "somewhere i have never travelled, gladly beyond." T-Bone had read the manuscript before it was published while he was sitting in Shakespeare and Company. It contained the first words that T-Bone said to his newborn daughter. "Something in me understands the voice of your eyes is deeper than all roses; nobody, not even the rain, has such small hands."

T-Bone did not speak nor read anything at Lisa's funeral. Some things are too vast—even for poetry.

I awoke with a start, sitting up. I nearly pulled one of the IV needles out of my right arm. I was alone in the hospital room with the sound of "Yes! We Have No Bananas" ringing in my ears and a great, leaping sadness that someone named Lisa was dead.

Without much concentration I saw that every single time I fell asleep I dreamed about the 1920s—or at least I dreamed about certain events as described to me by my mother. God only knew what was truth and what was fiction. My subconscious was only recalling what it had been told.

I had the distinct sensation that I had forgotten something very important. I couldn't quite get a grasp on what it was, whether it was something from one of the dreams or something my mother had told me or something that had happened the night I'd been shot. It was often said that gunshot victims don't remember much around the time of the bullet. A kind of envelope of calm, sometimes as much as a half an hour or more, surrounded the impact of the shot. But I'd been shot in my sleep, or so I'd been told. How anyone would know such a thing was not clear to me at that moment.

Long ago, Sheriff Skidmore Needle, then only a deputy, had told me that being shot in the real world was not much like what most people saw on television. For example, the mere awareness of the event could have a bearing on the victim's reaction to it. That meant, he'd said, it was possible for a person unaware of being shot to have a better chance of surviving than someone who'd stared down the barrel. There would be no fear of death, no sight of blood, no pain—all of which would play a factor in the damage a gunshot might do. There would even be an absence of preconceptions about how a person is supposed to react when shot. Finally add to that the fact that the body produces chemicals very powerful in preventing great harm, and I began to realize how lucky I'd been. And while adrenaline alone might be enough to keep a mortal wound at bay, alcohol was a powerful anesthetic and had probably kept me even less troubled by pain and shock.

I remembered that Skidmore had told me all of these facts over drinks, leading us to conclude at the time that a more or less steady supply of applejack just made good sense in the prevention of gunshot trauma. I had substituted a French country drink on the night in question, but I considered the theory proven. I was, after all, alive.

I slightly adjusted the needle in my right arm and sat back in the bed. Eyes on the ceiling, I gave stern consideration to my perennial notion of dreams: that they were always a message from the subconscious to the conscious mind.

A dream is a telegram composed in baffling poetry, I told myself. Decipher the poetry: get the message.

But these dreams were influenced by actual events. They weren't purely Freudian or Jungian. They were half-remembered stories, dim angles on true history. And how could I decode their message without the attendant facts?

I would have to start by trying to recall the historical data. I pulled the bedsheet up a little, tried to relax and dig into the world's most uncomfortable exercise: remembering things my mother told me.

The first thing that came to me, oddly, was her indignation at the very word *history*.

"Why isn't it *herstory* in my case? In my personal case? It's my story and I'm *her*."

"If the word *history* is gender biased," I had responded, "and maybe it is, then the mere word *herstory* is not sufficient to balance the long centuries of unfairly tipped scales concerning the events on our planet—to date."

"Then I think," she fired back, "that a person might be forgiven for referring to an account such as mine by using the word *mystory*."

"I see what you're doing," I told her with a growing ire. "You've done it before. I see that that the difference between *mystory* and *mystery* is only a single vowel."

"Ergo," she would conclude, "my story is in fact, a mystery."

Difficult as it might have been for most people to believe, my mother and I had indulged in variations of that same dialogue perhaps a hundred times.

Then, for no reason I could discern at that moment, another conversation came back to me.

I remembered sitting in our kitchen eating grits. I couldn't have been more than eleven or twelve. It was early morning, the lights weren't on, and ambient glow from the rising sun was rosy and gold. I was sitting at the kitchen table in my flannel shirt and jeans. The bowl was as white as the grits and they were salty; creamy from melted butter. My mother was standing at the sink looking out the window at the new light on the lawn. She had on a black dress, but I couldn't remember why. She usually wore lighter prints.

"I heard a preacher on the radio this morning," she told me. "He said that if God had wanted the races to live together, He would have made us all the same color."

Then she started laughing so much that I thought she might choke.

"It is my belief," she managed to wheeze, "that God went scrambling for His Glasses when He heard that one."

I looked up from my grits with an expression that could only have been called, even at my young age, wry. "Why would he do that, Mother?"

"Because we *are* all the same color. We're just different shades. I mean, nobody's *green*, right?"

I knew she had something else in mind. She was trying to make some other point. Whenever she mentioned God she was making a point.

"Is that preacher out of his mind?" she went on. "I believe that God adjusted His Glasses when he heard that moron, and then He took out His Big Giant Joke Book. He wrote down another couple of lines about just how funny human beings are, and then He turned his attention somewhere else. A distant star, maybe. Personally I'm not certain if He's ever going to look back this way and I wouldn't blame Him if He didn't."

And so it went, in my darkened hospital room. For hours I endured confused "gusts of memory," as Proust reports, that never lasted for more than a few seconds. Then, as he also did, I would revisit them all in the long course of my waking dream, like rooms in winter. I sorted through one image after another, lingering only long enough to be irritated, never long enough to actually absorb. My brain was a black cricket on a hot hearth, and would not stay still no matter how I tried to calm it down.

9.

At last, after a span of time longer than it took to create the Universe, seven o'clock sunrise came, and with it, Sheriff Needle.

He barreled into the room and began talking as if he were continuing a conversation instead of starting one.

"I want you to listen to this," he was saying as he pulled up the chair and sat down, "and tell me anything you can think of, no matter what."

"Morning, Sheriff," I said, sitting up.

Nurse Chambers breezed in with a paper cup and straw. "Breakfast," she said brightly.

"It's the 911 tape," Skidmore went on, "and I've listened to it about a thousand times, but you know that story. I can look for a matching sock for half an hour and Girlinda can walk by the drawer, reach in, pick out the other sock, and shoot into the kitchen without ever breaking stride."

Girlinda Needle, the sheriff's wife, twice shot, once because of me, was the strongest woman I had ever met, possibly the strongest woman on the planet. Also a superior cook and the proud owner of the largest contiguous series of burial plots in the county. She had a very big family.

"So you want me to listen to the tape," I concluded.

"Sometimes you need a fresh look," Nurse Chambers sympathized. "A new pair of eyes. Or, I guess, ears, in this case. Who knows? Maybe you'll even recognize the voice."

"Right." Skid fiddled with the handheld tape recorder.

"He had a bad night," Nurse Chambers confided to Skidmore.

"I know," he whispered back. "They told me."

"I can hear you," I said. "I'm out of my coma. At the moment."

I accepted the cup from Nurse Chambers but did not drink.

"Okay," Skid said impatiently, "here it is. This is the voice of the assailant. The man who shot you."

The static from the tiny tape recorder sounded like distant rain, and then the operator's voice stabbed the air.

"911. What is your emergency?"

"Dead man."

"Sir?"

"There's a dead man up on the top of Blue Mountain. Don't know the address."

"Who's calling? Please identify yourself."

"Never you mind who this is. I just killed that Fever Devilin. Shot him good in the heart."

"You are at the home of Dr. Devilin?"

"So you think you know who he is, do you? Well you don't know all there is to know. If you did, you wouldn't call him a doctor, you'd call him a gob of spit."

"Are you calling to report—?"

"I'm calling to tell you that he's dead!" the voice interrupted. "And good riddance!"

"Dr. Devilin is dead?"

"Yes. Damn. I shot him and I wanted everyone to know I did it! You spread it around."

There was a buzzing noise.

"Hello?" the operator said.

Skid snapped off the recorder. "That's it."

The air in the room suddenly seemed grimy because of the sound of the assailant's voice. A contagious hatred had spewed out of his mouth, into the phone, and onto the tape. Even though we were in a hospital I had the sudden urge to sterilize everything in the room.

"So." Skid set the tape recorder in his lap. "Ever hear that voice before?"

"I'd remember," I assured him. "He really, really doesn't like me."

"That's not anybody from up here," Stacey said grimly.

"Agreed," Skid said softly. "I mean, you might have made some enemies, same as I have, by rooting out miscreants, but I don't know anyone around who would feel this way about you."

"Well," I said, staring at my paper cup breakfast, "if it's someone I don't know, and I believe that's the case, then this person's feelings about me would be more about his own inventions than my actions."

"Yes," Skid said, squinting.

"Maybe it's somebody from your old university days," Nurse Chambers ventured boldly. "Winnie's always telling me that the university is pit of flesh-eating vipers."

We both stared.

"Well, that's what he says."

She was right, of course. I had heard him say that phrase on more than one occasion, and I had experienced the snake pit myself. It just sounded odd coming from Stacey.

"Didn't we make a deal about your not ever calling him 'Winnie'?" I asked softly.

"Dr. Andrews," she said to Skidmore, winking.

"Okay," Skidmore said, "but does she have a point?"

"Not really," I told them both. "Academic rivalries are personal. I'd recognize the voice of someone from the university who hated me that much."

Skid nodded. "Plus, the man on this tape doesn't sound like the scholarly type. I reckon a college professor can come up with a better insult than 'gob of spit.'"

"Possibly," I demurred. "But that particular phrase is exactly what Marlon Brando called Slim Pickens in the movie *One-Eyed Jacks*. Slim Pickens played the sheriff."

"What?" Nurse Chambers placed one hand on one hip.

"It's the only movie that Brando directed, I think," I reported. "It's a kind of Jacobean revenge drama played out in the old American west. Karl Malden is the bad guy, and his character is called 'Dad.' I mean, you don't have to be Freud to figure that one out."

"What's he talking about?" Nurse Chambers asked the sheriff.

"No idea," he answered, standing. "But I'm disappointed that he doesn't recognize the voice. That would have made things a whole lot easier."

"It's not a very good recording," Nurse Chambers told us, turning to check my IVs. "I hear myself on those things? Doesn't even sound like me. I hate it."

"Wait." Skid looked at the tape recorder. "Wait."

He fished in his pocket and withdrew another tape. He took the 911 tape out of the recorder and put the new tape in. Then he clicked the machine on and held it close to my face.

"Say something," he told me.

"I agree with Stacey," I said, smiling at her. "I hate the way I sound on these things."

Skid punched the off button, then the rewind. We listened.

"Say something."

"I agree with Stacey. I hate the way I sound on these things."

"Oh my," Stacey said softly, "that doesn't sound anything like either one of you. I just heard you record it and I couldn't identify those voices."

"Me too." Skid stared at the tape recorder. "So, basically, we've got nothing."

"Well," I began, "that tape doesn't appear to help, but—"

"What?" Skid put the little tape player in his front pocket.

"Didn't I mention something to you about a tin box?" I asked.

"You did." Skidmore looked at Stacey.

"And didn't you tell me that you didn't find it on the mantel in my living room?" I tried to clear my head, distinguish between strange dreams and waking events.

"We didn't find anything like that in our original investigation," he said impatiently.

"Look," I interrupted, shifting uncomfortably in my bed, "I realize that you think I've lost my mind, or some of it anyway. But that tin box had things in it that were important."

"Legal documents," Skid said.

"Money," Stacey guessed.

"No." I struggled with my body in the bed. "I—it was something I found out about a long time ago, and it was very important to me when I was younger. But then when I left home, and I thought I was never coming back, I forgot about it. Or I deliberately put it out of my mind. I'm still trying to piece it all together. I just can't quite remember everything."

"Fever," Skidmore began quietly. "I don't have any idea what you're talking about."

"I know." I sat back, staring up at the ceiling. "I'm not sure I do either."

"You've been having funny dreams," Stacey said, arms folded. "I've come in here when you're asleep and you talk up a storm."

"I have been dreaming very vividly," I agreed.

"That's in all the books about coma trauma: when you wake up, you have all sorts of crazy nightmares, sometimes about the things that happened around you when you were unconscious. Happens all the time."

"How many coma patients have you actually dealt with?" I asked her.

"Including you?" She jutted her chin in my direction, half flirtatiously, half defiantly.

"All right." I smiled. "Including me."

She smiled back "Exactly one. But I've been reading up on it because of you."

"Well, clearly the books are correct. But these dreams, they're very confusing. I have the idea that they somehow relate to the man who shot me. I believe that they have to do with something important about—my family."

"Why's that?" Skid's voice was filled with indulgent patience.

"That's what I'm trying to tell you. I found a tin box when I was eleven years old. It upset my mother. She showed me a letter that someone had written to me, but it wasn't signed and she hadn't written it—she told me that my father hadn't written it either."

Stacey put her hand on my shoulder. "Easy. You're getting a little agitated. Hear the heart monitor?"

One of the machines in the room was beeping urgently.

"But what I'm saying is—"

"That—what? There's something in this box that made the man shoot you." Skid was doing his best to follow my admittedly muddled train of thought.

"Something my mother didn't want me to find out. I remember that very clearly. She was very insistent on my not pursuing—something in the contents of the box wanted me to pursue—I'm trying to remember exactly, but the letter was anonymous, and my mother was worried."

"Yeah." Skid stood up. "This doesn't make much sense at all. I believe you need to rest up, get better; get out of the hospital. And when you go back home, then maybe you can start thinking about how to make a contribution to my investigation into your assault."

"But, listen, this is a contribution," I said, trying to keep him from leaving.

"Based on your mother's stories?" He shook his head. "I can't believe—just let me remind you that your mother was very— what's the word?"

"Theatrical," I suggested.

"I was going to say *crazy,*" he continued, "but have it your way: she was a very dramatic woman. I always thought there was something wrong with her, and I liked her a whole lot better than you did."

"True," I admitted. "So why am I dreaming about things she told me when I was eleven years old? All I can think about now is her strange behavior after I found that damned box. Why is that?"

"Fever," Nurse Chambers said sweetly, "sugar, you got shot in the gut, you died, you got frozen, you were brought back to life, and then you were in a coma for three months. It's kind of a miracle that you can think of anything at all. If you add in the question 'Why?' then I believe you are only asking for a whole lot of trouble that you don't really need right now."

"Amen." Skid turned and headed for the door.

I let out a sigh. "You're right, of course."

The beeping machine began to calm down.

"Good." Skid headed for the door.

"But I'm telling you that if you could find that box—"

"Look," Skid snapped, stopping in the doorway, "that's what I was trying to tell you a second ago before you interrupted me—which you always do: after you mentioned it the first time, I went back to your house and looked again. No mantel clock; no tin box."

"No clock?" I blinked.

"He took your clock?" Stacey asked.

"Why would he take my clock?" I sniffed, starting to feel a familiar sensation of drowsiness. "Why would he break into my house, kill me, and take my clock? Maybe there's something on the clock or in the clock . . . I mean, it was certainly an odd place to leave a box filled with important papers for all those years: on the mantel behind an old clock."

"How old?" Stacey wondered. "Maybe it's an antique or something, worth money, I mean."

"Well." I tried to think. "It seems to me that it came from my mother's side of the family, from my maternal grandmother, I think."

"So it was old," Skid confirmed.

"Yes," I told him, "but I can't imagine that it would be valuable enough to . . . and anyway how would the man even know about it?"

"All right." Skid started to leave the room again.

"Wait," Stacey said suddenly, remembering something. "You were going to talk to him about the phone call."

"Shoot, that's right." Skid stopped again, this time framed in the doorway. He turned and sighed. "Stacey told me that you got a call from inside the hospital."

"Oh, right," I mumbled, trying to collect my thoughts, feeling more and more drowsy. "What was that about, does anyone know?"

"They didn't say anything to you?"

"No—they said—wait, I think they asked if I was Earl. Maybe they just got the wrong room or something." I looked at Stacey. "Nurse Chambers, here, said that."

"That's what the hospital operator said when I asked about it," Stacey confirmed.

"Maybe it was just a wrong number," Skid said slowly, "but you get that call right when you come out of a coma? The timing is too coincidental for me."

"What are you saying?" I asked.

"I don't want to rule out anything at the moment. Could be nothing. Could be related."

And he was gone.

"He thinks I'm insane," I confided to Stacey.

"Skid's really tired," Stacey whispered. "You can hear it in his voice."

"I really want to go home tomorrow," I told her.

"Oh, sweetie, I don't think that's going to happen." She tucked me in a little bit. "Right now it looks to me like you're just going back to sleep."

And with that, I was out.

10.

Again the Paris streets, steel-gray, wet with rain, appeared. And with them the sound of an obscure tune I had heard many times called "The Montmartre Rag." It was the composition of early African-American jazz impresario Louis Mitchell, the only person with whom T-Bone Morton recorded before he left Paris. Mitchell's Jazz Kings had played for several years at the Casino de Paris on the rue De Clichy. Mitchell himself owned an American restaurant in Montmartre. T-Bone was the alto saxophone player on Mitchell's composition for the Pathé label in Paris in 1922. T-Bone took the place of James Shaw, Mitchell's usual sax player, when Shaw developed a toothache.

Mitchell was an important figure in T-Bone's world because he helped many African-American jazz artists establish themselves in Paris. At a time when most black musicians couldn't even walk into a restaurant on the Upper West Side of Manhattan, Louis Mitchell owned a restaurant in the gastronomic heart of Europe. He saw to it that his brothers and sisters were afforded the same opportunities. He was the man who introduced Sidney Bechet to T-Bone. He was the one who got T-Bone a job at Lisa Simard's café.

And Mitchell was the man who gave T-Bone the money to book ship passage back to America after Lisa died. T-Bone arrived at the dock with most of his belongings and all the baby's clothes jammed into his sax case. Tied to the sax case was a small bundle of Lisa's personal thing: photos, letters, and her small mantel clock. T-Bone walked onto the ship bound for America with the baby on one arm, and the sax case in his other hand. No one was there to wave good-bye, and he wouldn't have looked back anyway. He was nearly catatonic with grief. He didn't know what he was going to do without Lisa.

Mitchell had wired King Oliver in Chicago. He recommended T-Bone. Mitchell said in the telegram that T-Bone was one of the greatest saxophone players he had ever heard, the equal of Sidney Bechet. That's how T-Bone came to be at the Lincoln Gardens on a quiet Tuesday night early in February of 1924. That's how T-Bone found himself in the company of Bix Beiderbecke, who subsequently came up with a plan to save the life of T-Bone's infant daughter. Bix knew people, Caucasian people, in New Orleans—a strange family, but wealthy and decent enough in their own way—who would take the daughter for a while.

Unfortunately, no amount of exhaustive genealogical study would ever reveal what happened after that night in Chicago. T-Bone Morton vanished from history, and only confusing half references exist concerning the infant daughter.

That time when I awoke there were angels in my room: streaks of blurred light racing all around me, humming impossible music. I thought for a moment that I wasn't awake at all, still dreaming.

But as the light slowed down, I was clearly in the hospital room.

Still, I could see faces; hear voices that belonged to the streaks of light. I might have been able to decipher what they were saying if I'd had a few more uninterrupted seconds with these creatures, but unfortunately, Nurse Chambers opened my door and they all vanished.

"Dr. Devilin?" she said softly. "Are you awake?"

"I am awake," I sighed, "and you are a person from Porlock."

She came into the room quickly, frowning. "No, I'm Stacey Chambers."

"I know who you are."

"But I'm from Blue Mountain," she said hesitantly, "not from—"

"When Coleridge was writing his poem 'Kubla Khan,'" I explained, "he was interrupted by a person on business from Porlock who kept him from his work. After the interruption, he couldn't remember the vision or the rest of the poem. But the phrase 'person from Porlock' has come to represent any interruption thrown in the way of inspiration and vision."

"Okay I don't know what that means," she said briskly, checking one of the dozen wires going from my body to some machine, "but you had a big spike in your blood pressure while you were asleep and I had to come in and check on it."

She busied herself with the device, her back to me, while I tried to think of the right way to apologize to her.

I finally decided on, "You're a kind of angel, really, Stacey, and I genuinely appreciate what you've done for me."

"Oh for God's sake," she said without turning around, "you fall asleep for a few months and you turn into a girl? It's confusing because you used to be a whole lot more—look, if you're too nice to me, I can't flirt with you and make Lucinda jealous. And we both like that."

"Both?" I smiled. "You and me or you and Lucinda?"

"Well." She finally turned around. "Your pressure is completely normal now. Maybe you were having a bad dream."

"I was. A little short one." I decided against telling her about the angelic streaks of light.

"Your voice is back, have you noticed?"

I hadn't, but when she mentioned it, I realized that my throat wasn't raw anymore, and the sound of my voice was more normal.

"Good," I said, locking eyes with her. "Does that mean I can go home now?"

"Now?" She just laughed. "No. Not hardly."

"Stacey," I began once she quieted down, "last autumn— which I remember as if it were yesterday because, to me, it was yesterday—I was in the doldrums. I had come to a midwinter wood, like Dante. I needed some shaking up. And presto, as my father used to say in his magic show: I got shot. Something shook me up—shook me up a great deal. Now all I can think about is the past. I'm obsessed with it in my dreams. If I don't get out of this hospital bed and back into my home so that I can start figuring all this out, I might lose my mind."

She stared back at me. Finally she muttered, "Your daddy never said the word *presto* in his life."

"I want to go home."

"Of course you want to go home. And that's a good sign. When a patient wants to go home, it means they're feeling better."

"There you are," I said. "I'm feeling better."

"Make a deal with you," she said, folding her arms. "If you can walk from here to the sunroom and back, and then stay awake for two hours after that, I'll talk to Lucinda about getting you out of here."

"No, no," I insisted. "Not Lucinda. I want to talk to the doctor."

"What doctor?"

"The *doctor*," I answered. "The one who took the bullets out of me. The one who saved my life. My attending physician."

Nurse Chambers shifted her weight onto one leg. "Sugar, Lucinda is the one who saved your life. And the doctor who took out the bullets, Dr. Mercer? He's gone. He retired on Valentine's Day. He's in Italy with his wife."

"I don't have a doctor?"

"You don't need one." She smiled sweetly. "You have Lucinda."

No arguing that. Lucinda Foxe was more qualified than most MDs in America.

"Fair enough," I said at length. "So, now, what's your challenge? Make it to the sunroom down the hall, get back here, then stay awake for two hours."

"Righty-o," she confirmed. "That's all you have to do."

"Well unhook me from all these machines and watch me work."

I don't know what she did next because I fell asleep.

The next time I woke up, Lucinda was in the room. She was sitting in the chair reading an old *Time* magazine. I opened my eyes. She didn't look up.

"Did you know," she told me before I could say anything, "that eighty-seven percent of Americans say they believe in angels?"

"Hm?" I mumbled, rising toward consciousness.

"I'm reading an article about angels."

"Does it say there how many also believe in the Loch Ness monster and Bigfoot?" I sniffed.

"Right about the same percentage of hospital patients who get to go home when they say they want to." She closed the magazine and set it in her lap.

I stared at the cover of the magazine. There was a picture of an angel on it, a Pre-Raphaelite-looking woman with wings and very nicely done-up hair.

"Here's my plan," I announced. "I get up, go home, and solve my own murder. That's what they call incentive. I have a really good reason for going home, for staying awake, for getting to work. Plus, I've had *no* coffee since I came out of my coma, and, as you know, coffee is my bread and butter."

"Then what's bread and butter?"

"Bread and butter is my cream of wheat," I fired back. "Let me go home."

She stood, dropped the magazine onto the chair, and smiled devilishly. "Stacey told you the test. If you can make it to the sunroom and back, then stay awake for two hours, we'll *talk* about letting you go home."

"Done." I scrambled forward. "Unhook me from these machines."

She did in short order. I sat up. I put my feet on the floor. I made it almost all the way to the door before my legs gave out.

Nine days later, with more than three-dozen failed attempts behind me, I finally passed the test. My muscles hurt all the time, cramped significantly. I was dizzy for an hour after I walked. But I had passed the test.

Thereafter ensued the most vociferous series of arguments in which Lucinda and I had ever participated. She actually took a swing at me the first time I tried to put on my shoes. But in the end, I convinced her that I would heal much more quickly if I could get my muscles working and my brain waves cresting. At least I would like to think that's what happened. Closer to the truth: I wore her down. She kept saying *no* and I kept getting dressed. She was spending all her time in my room trying to keep me from climbing into my jeans. Ultimately, she just had to get back to her real work at the hospital and let me do what I was determined to do. Oh, there were long speeches about how stubborn I was, and how angry she was—and I agreed with everything she said. But I was going to go home no matter what.

Her final volley had been that I couldn't go home without clothes. They'd thrown away the things I'd been wearing when I'd been shot, and her argument was that I'd be arrested for indecent exposure if I tried to head home in a hospital gown. Then, out of nowhere, a pair of my old black jeans and my favorite green flannel shirt appeared under my pillow. I assumed that she had simply, and sweetly, relented after I'd passed the "walk and wake" test.

So I was already dressed when Skid barreled into the room. It felt good to have my old green shirt on instead of the humiliating hospital robe.

"I just got word from Nurse Chambers," he began without a hint of salutation, "that you think you're going home. I don't know who you paid off or what you did, but I'm against it."

"Against what?" I asked without looking at him.

"You know what," he raved. "You're going home so you can butt into my investigation. You're going home so that you can save the day, solve the crime, figure something out."

I turned to face him. "I got shot. I want to know who did it." The simplest answer is always the best.

"I get that," he said, "but you're not really in any shape to—I talked to Lucinda."

"Then you probably know that she did everything short of shooting me again to keep me from going home," I responded, "and as you can see, I'm dressed."

"I brought my sidearm." He wasn't smiling.

"Look," I sighed, "I know you're here to talk me out of going home because Lucinda told you to do it."

"Lucinda didn't tell me to do a damn thing. I'm doing this on my own recognizance. You're not ready to investigate your breakfast choices, so I don't know how you're in any shape to look into your own murder."

"People keep referring to it as my murder." I finished tucking in my shirt. "It makes a nice dramatic effect, but I feel I ought to point out the very salient fact that I'm not entirely dead."

"Yet," he intoned.

"Yet," I affirmed. "So could we segue gently into some other phrase? Would that be all right?"

A slow wave of dizziness took deep hold of my body, surging from my sternum then back to my spine and upward to my cheeks and eyes. It was the kind of sensation some people have just before they drop off to sleep. I used my new secret trick, something I'd discovered a few days earlier. I had a small wood screw in my hand and I pushed the point into my leg. The pain was instant, and chased away the drowsiness. I'd hidden the screw, stolen from one of the drawer pulls on my hospital nightstand, under my pillow. It had kept me from fainting several times each day.

"Fever?" Skid took a few quick steps toward me.

"I'm okay." I held up my hand, warding him off. "The muscles in my legs cramp every once in a while. They're still not quite used to being in action again."

That was true, but it had not provided my impetus, on this particular occasion, to stay awake. What kept me from falling asleep was a little metal screw.

Unfortunately, staying upright and conscious was not my only problem. Even with the biting pain, I still lost concentration and comprehension. I needed to cover that. I used another trick for that, something I'd learned in graduate school. Often then, when I hadn't known the answer to some question I'd been asked, I simply asked another question. For example, I'd been asked the question, "Mr. Devilin, could you give us an example of Spinoza's determinism?" by one of my colleagues bent on proving that the folklore department was not a sound intellectual investment for the university. I had responded, "Wouldn't Spinoza have as much in common with the Stoics as with the Determinists?" Thereafter ensued a debate for which I received praise from the very professor who had tried to embarrass me, whose question I never answered. Of course, I'd been correct in that both philosophical schools had made efforts to provide a therapeutic approach toward a human achievement of *eudaemonia* or happiness.

"You look like you're about to fall asleep, to me," Skidmore said, obviously suspicious.

"I'm thinking." I dug the screw into my thigh a bit deeper, winced, and turned to face Skidmore. "Just what is your real objection to my investigating this—crime?"

"Your health," he insisted. "Damn."

I finally took a good look at my oldest friend. His sheriff's uniform was wrinkled; there was a smudge on his tie. His eyes were bloodshot. He sported at least a dozen small cuts on each of his hands. His boots had been muddy, but he'd taken the time to scrape them off before coming into the hospital.

"Not to mention the fact," he continued, "that Lucinda Foxe would hurt me bad if anything happened to you and she thought it was my fault."

"I agree with that. Lucinda is the one to be afraid of."

"You must have had some kind of an argument when you told her you were going home."

I stopped torturing my leg with the screw and slipped it casually into my pocket.

"No," I told Skid. "We had a deal. I passed her test. She had to agree."

"It can't have been that easy."

"All right," I admitted. "I may have worn her down."

"I can believe that," he said flatly. "But she's not happy about it."

"I know." I stood. "Now. Sheriff. You look terrible. What in God's name have you been doing today?"

"Oh." He smiled. "You remember Truevine Deveroe, right?"

"Of course." I smiled to think of Truevine. She was a dark-haired, strange, shy girl whose family lived back in a remote part of our community. She had been taunted, as a teenager, by bullies of both genders who enjoyed calling her a witch.

She had once saved my life under mysterious circumstances. That kindness had, in turn, caused me to write a short article called "The Witch's Grave" concerning folk remedies for certain health problems that were once considered occult.

"Well, you know how she loves her dogs," Skid went on. "One of them took off yesterday afternoon, and she came to me for help."

"You've been chasing one of Truevine's wild dogs through the woods? Really?"

"Well," he said, avoiding eye contact, "when you hear the reason her dog took off, I think you'll be a little more understanding."

"All right." I folded my arms, waiting.

"She and the dog, they were trudging through the blackberry thicket on the downslope from your house when they both saw somebody coming out your back door. The dog took off after the intruder, and hasn't been seen since. Truevine and me, we been tracking him most of the night."

"Someone was going through my house last night?" My voice had come out much higher than I'd hoped it would.

Skid grinned. "Still want to go home?"

He looked toward the door but all I could do was stand there and try to stay awake.

11.

A half an hour later I discovered that my house was a disaster. One of the windows was broken. The front door lock was torn up. The porch was muddy and covered with old leaves and twigs and new pollen and bird droppings.

I pushed in the broken front door to find that the front rooms, usually neat as a pin against the advent of surprise company, were an irritating clutter. The kitchen was musty and smelled like a nursing home. Papers and tapes and all sorts of books and records were everywhere on the floor.

The worst of it for me, though, was the obvious ambience in the rooms: the feeling that no one lived there. The exposed rafter beams looked dusty. The wood floors seemed stained. All the furniture was musty. The rugs were askew. The walls seemed a bit moldy. And all windows were the dull, heavy-lidded eyes of a corpse.

"The guy left this mess," I said softly to Skid as we stood near the doorway, "and there's no evidence? No fingerprints or fibers or shoe prints?"

"None."

"No hair or dried sweat or greasy residue?"

"Not even snot," Skid answered. "You want to stand here and talk about that or you want to clean up?"

"I can clean up?"

"Fever," he reminded me, "the crime happened over three months ago. We've been over everything seventeen times. Please. Clean up your house. Damn."

I bent over and picked up a book and was immediately disheartened by the prospect of a cleanup. Facing my first night back home without the comfort of hospital personnel or the benefit of intravenous food, that also seemed suddenly daunting.

As if hearing my thoughts, Skid headed into the kitchen.

"Girlinda was worried about your eating, so she made enough food for ten people to live off of for a month. It's all in the ice box. She didn't know how you'd be with solid food yet, so she made some awful good soups. One's a cream of turnip and parsnip that's just as sweet as candy, and my favorite is a white bean soup with little bits of Benton's bacon in it."

Then, without any fanfare at all, came a sound from upstairs that filled me with a kind of celestial gratitude. I heard Lucinda's voice, singing softly.

I looked over at Skid.

He blushed—actually blushed. "Well, you didn't think we were going to let you be alone on your first night home, did you?"

"In the final analysis," I answered, not looking at him, "I don't deserve friends like you."

"That's true, you really don't." He patted my arm. "But that's me: I'm a good Christian. Everybody says so."

"Hallelujah." I smiled.

"Plus," he went on as he opened the refrigerator door, "you got a fiancée who's a nurse and Girlinda for a cook. Cussed as you are, you're lucky you don't live on the side of the road somewhere, let alone in the lap of luxury."

"'Let alone in the lap of luxury,'" I repeated. "That's fun to say."

He shook his head. "You know, if I wanted to," he said heavily, "I could worry about you all the time."

"All right." I took in a deep breath and headed for the mantel.

I knew the tin box I was looking for wouldn't be there. I knew that Skid and plenty of other people had exhausted every possible effort to discover clues of any sort. I knew that I would feel worse after I looked and discovered the same thing. Still, I couldn't help staring at the empty spot over the fireplace where the old clock and the mysterious tin box should have been.

I heard a noise on the stairs and turned to see Lucinda watching me. She was wearing a light blue sweater and old jeans and looked a little like an angel.

"That's where your tin box used to be?" she asked, still standing on the steps.

"Right, yes." I smiled. "I wish I could tell you how happy I am that you're here."

"And I wish I could tell you," she returned, taking the last few steps down and into the living room area, "just how unhappy I am that you're here—and not in a hospital bed."

"Which soup you want?" Skid called from the kitchen.

I looked into my kitchen, and the incongruity of a man with a gun strapped to his waist holding a pink Tupperware container in each hand made me laugh.

"This is my new money-making idea," I told Lucinda. "A reality television show called *Sheriff Chef!* With an exclamation point. Law officers from small municipalities would compete—"

"Don't." Lucinda sighed. "The title says it all. Don't explain it."

"I really liked the sound of that white bean soup," I told Skidmore.

"It's puréed?" Lucinda asked.

"Yes, ma'am," Skid answered.

"All right then," she told me. "But just one cup."

"I heard," Skid allowed. "Just one cup." He went to work pouring some soup from one of the Tupperware containers into a bowl and heating it up in the microwave.

"Have you eaten?" I asked her.

"Look," she said sternly, "you should emphatically *not* be up. You should be lying in bed or at the very least sitting in a big old chair with your feet up."

"I feel fine," I protested.

And, of course, just then a crashing wave of exhaustion hit me. I reached quickly into the pocket of my jeans, found the little metal screw, and shoved it into my thigh. I did it so quickly that my leg reacted with a will of its own, as if I'd been stung by a bee.

"What?" Lucinda said instantly, seeing me twitch.

"I just remembered something," I lied.

"What is it?" Lucinda said, a little alarmed. "Sit down."

"Yes." I collapsed onto my sofa.

"What did you remember?" Skid called from the kitchen.

"How much have I told you about these dreams I've been having?" I asked, mostly to cover my dizziness.

Lucinda sat next to me on the sofa. Skid came into the living room area and took the big chair next to the sofa, setting a small bowl of soup down on the coffee table between us. There was a tablespoon in the bowl, and the soup gave off lovely steam and an even more inviting aroma.

"These dreams," I continued, "are directly related to the crime that took place in this house."

They were both staring at me, and it was obvious that they were much more concerned with my current state of consciousness than my theories about crime and the unconscious.

Then another great surge of dizziness threatened to capsize my brain and I saw, quite clearly, my mother standing beside the fireplace. I knew I was seeing a memory, but it was as solid as any reality. It was as if two pieces of film or two slides were being projected onto the same screen in my living room.

Unbidden, a sudden memory leapt into my mind, and I found myself, almost in a trance state, relating that memory to Lucinda and Skidmore.

"In the early 1960s my parents left Blue Mountain," I began. "They went to Atlanta to change the world, and my mother volunteered to be the den mother of a certain local Cub Scout troop. It had been formed somewhat illegally in an Episcopal church and included two Mexican brothers, a Jamaican child, and three Caucasian sons of various ministers in the area. It was an obvious attempt to challenge the Scouts' mentality concerning integration in the South of that time, and my mother rose to that challenge with great fervor."

Lucinda put her hand on my shoulder.

"So my mother's first idea was a field trip to the Wren's Nest. That's a house in West End where Joel Chandler Harris wrote the 'Uncle Remus' stories. She marched the boys in, slapped her purse on the counter at the entrance way, and took out the several dollars' worth of fee, the price of admission."

"Fever?" Skid began.

But Lucinda shot him a look, and he continued to listen to my story.

"Behind the counter was an ancient woman who had worked at the Wren's Nest forever and she stared at my mother indignantly.

"'You can't bring those little colored boys in here,' she whispered to my mother.

"'I can't do *what?*'

"'We don't allow Negros.' The woman apparently had a very difficult time pronouncing the last word correctly.

"'If you aren't the most ignorant cracker bitch in this entire world,' my mother is reported to have responded, 'then I don't know who would be. First, two of these children are from Mexico and one is from Jamaica. Second, you're telling me that Negros aren't allowed to *pay* to come into the house of the man who stole their stories, made money from them, got famous from them, and never gave them a dime in return? Is that what you're telling me?'

"'You'll have to leave,' the old woman said, picking up the phone to call the police.

"'You couldn't pay me to stay,' my mother told the woman.

"Then my mother kicked the counter that lay between her and the old woman. She kicked it so hard that the glass cracked. She marched the Cub Scout troop out of the house, onto the porch, down the steps, and they all went half a block to the Gordon theater and saw a Tarzan movie—one with Gordon Scott."

Skid and Lucinda stared at me. Several silent seconds slipped past.

"What are you talking about?" Skid finally said.

"I don't know," I confessed. "But there's something important about that memory. You have to believe me."

"Who's Gordon Scott?" Lucinda wanted to know.

"I have to piece together these memories and strange bits of dream," I mumbled, "and if I do, I somehow—I'll figure out why the tin box was so important, what my mother was trying to tell, or trying not to tell me. And why my assailant would take that box and an old clock, and nothing else."

"Skid," Lucinda whispered, "I don't think we're going to need that soup right away."

And with that, I dropped off into peaceful slumber, slumping down on the sofa.

When I woke up I was lying prone on the sofa with a blanket over me, and it was nighttime. Eyes closed, I heard familiar voices from the kitchen. I sat up.

Three sat at the kitchen table, talking quietly.

"Where's my soup?" I called out, sitting up.

"Well, look who's decided to wake up." The accent was unmistakable.

"Dr. Andrews?" I scrambled to get my legs over the side of the sofa and lean forward.

"Your soup's right here in the microwave," Lucinda said, turning. "Why don't you come and eat it at the table?"

"Who let him in?" I stood and inclined my head in the direction of Winton Andrews, the world's most unlikely Shakespeare scholar. He was a rugby player from Manchester, England; tall, blond, and bony, the sort of person who would bet strangers he could drink them under the table in any neighborhood bar—and win that bet. He was also quite capable of directing plays at the New Globe Theatre in London to rave reviews. He had been my best friend in Atlanta before I'd left the university, and we'd remained close enough for him to become inextricably involved in my little Blue Mountain community. Especially now that he was, apparently, quite enamored of our Nurse Chambers.

"What do you think you're doing here?" I asked him.

"I came to Casablanca for the waters," he said with a completely American accent.

"Waters? What waters? We're in the desert." I headed toward the kitchen.

"I was misinformed." Andrews grinned.

"What the hell are you boys talking about?" Skid asked.

"*Casablanca*," we both said.

"It's a scene from the movie." Andrews winked at Lucinda.

That was new. I'd never seen him wink before. In fact, as I examined him, several things were new about our boy. His hair was shorn. He was not wearing a loud Hawaiian print but a muted polo shirt. And he was wearing his glasses, which he never did.

"Did you just wink at my fiancée?" I asked, going to the microwave.

"What makes you think she's still your *fiancée*?" he replied, luxuriating over the final word, giving it the full French treatment.

"You've been out of commission for a while. And I do have, as you know, a way with *les femmes.*"

"God," I mumbled, pushing the timer on the microwave. "Here's what I know. I know you have to figure out a way to keep Stacey Chambers from calling you 'Winnie.'"

"I think it's cute," he protested.

"Here's what I'm worried about," Skidmore interrupted, a little more vociferously than was necessary, I thought. "Now that Andrews is here, I'm worried that the damn Hardy Boys are going to ride again. And I don't want that. (a) Fever's not up to it, and (b) it just gets in the way of the actual police investigation."

"When you were a deputy I never heard you curse," Andrews said.

"I've pointed that out to him," I told Andrews. "I think it's the pressure of the sheriff's job."

"I'm serious with you both," Skid said louder. "Last thing I need in this mess is a visit from the Two Stooges."

"Are we the Hardy Boys or the Stooges?" Andrews said. "You've got to make up your mind. I have costumes to prepare. I'd rather be the Hardy Boys, the Stooges are too physical."

"Stop it," Lucinda piped in. "Skid's right about your not being up to anything much, Fever."

"I'm fine," I told Andrews lightly.

Lucinda turned to Andrews. "I told you: he falls asleep in the middle of a sentence. He can't be out and about."

"I haven't done that so much in the past couple of days," I insisted.

The microwave sounded its alarm, and my repast was ready. The cup was very hot, but I didn't care. The soup smelled heavenly. I took it and sat at the last available chair around the old chrome and Formica dinette table.

Lucinda looked me in the eye. Without a word, she held up her fist, then turned it and opened her hand. In her palm lay a small metal screw.

"You think I don't know every trick?" she sneered. "You think I don't know my job? I saw you put your hand in your pocket, and then I saw you jump. You think you invented that, the idea of staying awake by—I mean, my God, you never heard the expression 'pinched himself to stay awake'?"

"That's an expression?" Andrews wondered. "It sounds more like a phrase."

"You shouldn't be out of the hospital at all," Lucinda went on.

"Nothing to worry about," Andrews announced. "I'm here."

"Lord," Lucinda swore. "That's *just* what I am worried about." She reached across the table and tapped Skid's arm. "Can you arrest them both—like on suspicion of something or other?"

"Yes, ma'am," Skid said right away. "It is my suspicion as the sheriff of this county that these two boys are idiots."

"Serious as a crutch," Lucinda said sharply to Andrews, "he needs rest. He's not right. He has dire health issues. You understand me?"

"Yes, ma'am," Andrews answered very sincerely.

"And while we're at it," Skid added, "there are about a hundred legal reasons why you two are not permitted to pursue the matter of Fever's assault. Is that also clear?"

His voice was so strong, so filled with iron, that Andrews and I both nodded solemnly.

The conversation, greatly subdued, turned to the magnificence of Girlinda's culinary accomplishments, and that might well have been that: a fine place to end our story.

12.

Again, I might have continued in a happy state of suspended animation, carelessly falling asleep at a moment's notice, living as much in dreams as in reality for the rest of my life. Some people do indeed have that sort of luck. My lot was more tragic, or, to put it a little less theatrically: more complicated.

Lucinda stayed with me in my room that night; Andrews passed out in the guest room. Skidmore went home to report to his wife that her cooking was, once again, a treasure greatly to be prized by everyone within sight or smell of any dish she had created.

I, only, alone, escaped sleep, thinking to wander the house in search of clues, like Ishmael trying to find reasons for Ahab's murderous obsessions. I couldn't say that I had harbored any hope of finding physical evidence, but when I threw my legs over the side of the bed at 3:00 a.m. and patted Lucinda's arm as she slept, I did see something that no one else had mentioned.

The clock, my father's clock, was ticking loudly on the night table beside my bed—the clock that should have been on the mantel.

I hadn't noticed it when we'd come to bed but I had barely noticed the bed itself before I'd collapsed onto it. Sleep had been instantaneous.

Yet there it was, that clock, the missing, stolen clock, ticking as if it might explode at any moment.

I sat staring at it, trying to think how it had gotten there, and why no one had told me it hadn't been stolen, and—not the least mystery—who had wound it up during my three-month absence? I always forgot to wind it and sometimes went for months without hearing it tick.

Thanks to those questions, I was wide-awake, blood pounding in my ears. I was trying to bring my mind to a focus it hadn't known in quite a while, even before my assault. It didn't take long for me to assemble a preliminary theory. The killer had found the tin box he was looking for behind the clock on the mantel. He had pocketed the box and brought the clock upstairs. He'd shot me in my sleep, then watched the clock for a certain span of time he deemed sufficient for me to be dead. Then he'd called 911. He'd called to gloat, to brag. He'd called so that someone would know right away that he had done his work.

It was a strange theory, but one that fit all the facts, I thought. It did, however, create almost as many questions as it answered. It didn't explain why he had stolen the box. How had he even known of its existence? Why had he been so bent on killing me? Who was he?

It was clear, at last, that the box was his only prize. He had not stolen the clock. Skid, the deputies, even Lucinda hadn't noticed it—which seemed natural, really. Why would they? I'd gone on and on about the box, not the clock. And how were they to know that the clock ticking in my room was supposed to have been on the mantel downstairs? But nothing explained why the clock was ticking. Who had wound it?

That thought prompted a much more disturbing fear, and it took hold of me. I suddenly realized that the killer had come back into the house. Maybe that's what Truevine and her dog had seen. Or maybe the killer was even in my house that night as we all slept. Maybe he'd come in, wound the clock, and put it on the nightstand beside my bed. He was waiting somewhere. Maybe in the shadows in my room, maybe on the stairs, maybe down in the kitchen.

Just then, to confirm my terror, there was a soft scraping downstairs, the sound a kitchen chair would make.

Just as I was about to wake Lucinda, a worse possibility reared its scaly head: what if this were another one of my nightmares, my truer-than-life dreams? I began to doubt that I was awake. I felt awake, but I had felt quite conscious in a dozen recent dreams. I had seen Nurse Chambers naked, and watched Bix Beiderbecke play his cornet.

There was another noise, something on the table, a heavy piece of metal, perhaps a gun. I thought better of waking Lucinda. If this were a dream, it wouldn't matter, and in any other reality, I wouldn't want to endanger her.

I stood silently. The cold wooden floor stung my bare feet. I made my way quickly toward the door with as little sound as possible. On the back of the door I found more than saw my old bathrobe. The room, the hall, the stairs were all pitch-black. I slipped into my robe. It smelled musty. I instantly thought about sneezing. Still, robe wrapped tightly around me, I glided over the icy floor toward the wooden stairs, clutching the banister.

I could hear the killer clear his throat softly. There were more metallic sounds. He was loading or perhaps even cleaning his gun. He had a gun. But I had several advantages. The light switch in the kitchen was close to the last stair step, so I could turn off the light without his seeing me. My eyes were more used to the dark. I also kept a burled walking stick, solid as a baseball bat, in a stand at the bottom of the stairs. And if those two elements were not enough to exaggerate my courage, I could rely on the increasing, giddy feeling that I was not awake at all, that I was dreaming.

Slowly down the stairs, avoiding the steps and places that creaked, keeping to the inside edge, I made my way to the final step. My hand floated out toward the stand on the floor, and I felt the heavy wooden walking stick. I took firm hold, but didn't move it yet. It would certainly make a sound when I pulled it out of the holder and alert the monster in the kitchen.

Then, he sighed and belched.

I used the moment to lurch forward, grabbing the stick and flailing out at the light switch. The kitchen was plunged into darkness. The man cried out. I jumped into the kitchen, swinging the stick in front of me like a rabid blind man, making involuntary noises that sounded like a wounded animal.

"Jesus Christ!" the killer yelled. He had an English accent.

He shoved a chair in my direction. It hit my stick and then my leg. I cursed, raised the stick high and lumbered forward, growling.

"Fever?" the killer said in a very familiar tone.

Two seconds later, I realized that I was about to bludgeon Andrews to death. I could see his startled face quite clearly in the moonlight.

"What the hell?" Andrews whined, staring at the very large stick that was poised over his head. He was dressed in a sweatshirt and pants, and holding a fork in front of him, his only defense.

"What are you doing down here?" I asked, still unwilling to lower my weapon.

"I'm eating! Damn." He relaxed a little. "What are you doing?"

"Um," I let go my breath. "I'm defending my life. From my killer."

"I haven't killed you," Andrews mumbled. "Yet."

"No, but I mean . . ."

"Put down that walking stick, all right?" He took his seat once more.

He'd been eating some banana pudding from the pan, another of Girlinda's superb culinary creations. I stared down at it.

"That looks good," I admitted.

Andrews shook his head wearily. "Can I finish it in peace?"

"You know that this is no packaged pudding, vanilla wafer concoction," I told Andrews, lowering my weapon. "Girlinda starts by making a gram flour and brown sugar pastry. Then she makes a vanilla custard with egg yolks from her own chickens and cream from her own dairy cows. She's sliced a half dozen organic bananas into wafer-thin discs and nestled them artfully in that custard. The egg whites were whipped with confectioner's sugar until they turned into some kind of supernatural version of meringue. Baked until the topping was golden and the custard was still creamy, this is a holy confection. This is something to rival any great invention from the finest gustatory minds of France or Italy or anywhere else on the planet."

"I know," he said, continuing to eat. "It's Girlinda's banana pudding."

I leaned my stick against the stove and sat down with him at the table. I realized then that my hands were shaking a little, and my hairline was wet.

"Sorry," I stammered, "I mean, about the whole bludgeoning thing."

"Any particular reason you wanted to kill me?"

"No." I longed for the pudding, but I heard the warning voice of Lucinda in my mind's ear, telling me that my stomach wasn't ready for it.

So I contented myself with more vicarious pleasures. I took in the lovely aroma. I allowed myself to recall other puddings from other times. I finally had to ask the question of Andrews.

"How does it taste?"

"It is," he managed to say with his mouth full, "beyond description. I've had world-class crème brûlée that wasn't this good."

"I know," I sighed.

"Too bad you can't have any," he mocked. "So go on. Tell me

what's the matter. I don't think you've ever tried to bash in my brains."

"Not that I haven't thought about it," I contended.

"Of course," he freely admitted.

"But here is the trouble," I continued. "I thought you were my assailant, the man who shot me, returned to finish the job."

"Why would you think that?"

"I woke up," I told him, "and found the missing mantel clock—did we tell you about that?"

"Skidmore told me that the only things missing from the house," Andrews answered, "were a clock and a tin box. You found the clock?"

"On my bedside table, ticking to beat the band. And then I heard a noise downstairs, and my sleepy, paranoid brain did the rest. I was absolutely convinced you were the killer."

"Well," Andrews opined, "in the first place you understand that he didn't actually kill you, and I thought you wanted to stop thinking of him that way. And in the second place, how would he know you weren't dead? He was confident enough in his efforts the last time that he called 911 and reported your demise."

"He's had three months to discover otherwise."

"Good point." Andrews scooped up another forkful of Girlinda's creation.

"I can't work out this clock business," I went on. "Has it been there the whole time? Why is it on my bedside table? Did it just get there? Who's been winding it for months?"

"Why is this important?" Andrews asked, setting down his fork.

"How much have you been told about the tin box?"

"Only that you're going on and on about it," he answered, "and nobody can figure out what you're talking about."

"Yes, I know everyone thinks I'm confused about it," I said softly. "But there's something very important about it."

"What is that?"

"I don't know."

There was a sudden commotion at the top of the stairs.

"Fever?" Lucinda called.

"Yes," I answered. "I'm up. Andrews is eating banana pudding."

"You're not having any of Girlinda's heart-attack desserts!" Which warning was followed by rapid footfalls on the stairs and Lucinda's sudden appearance in the kitchen.

She was wrapped in a quilt and her eyes were sleepy. She looked fantastic.

"No," I assured her. "But I did think that Andrews was the murderer come back to my house wreaking mayhem."

"Whereas I am a simple academic," Andrews inserted, indicating the banana pudding with his fork, "wreaking only dessert."

"Lord," she sighed. She pulled up a chair at the table and stared at the banana pudding as if it might explain itself further.

"I was just asking skinny, here," Andrews said to Lucinda, inclining his head my way, "what was so important about this tin box with which he is so obviously obsessed."

"All right," she responded, sitting back, "I could hear about that too."

I tried to clear my mind. I tried to separate the dreams from the fears from the genuine memories. I tried to understand the answers myself.

"I saw an angel," I blurted out.

Andrews and Lucinda exchanged a glance.

"When I was young," I went on, avoiding their eyes. "Or I saw something. I saw my own reflection in the window, maybe, or a flight of geese. Wings were on my mind. Or flying was on my mind, at least."

"He really shouldn't be out of the hospital," Lucinda said to Andrews, as if I weren't sitting at the table with them. It was her nurse's voice, a tone and an approach I had often heard when she was talking about a patient who was unconscious, or barely cogent.

"If you'll just let me push through the weird images," I protested, "I promise this will all assemble itself into something resembling coherence."

"Should we get him back into bed?" Andrews asked Lucinda, ignoring me.

"I may have been dreaming," I went on. I could hear the sound of my voice edging toward desperation. "The point is that I suddenly was aware of a tin box behind the clock on the mantel in the living room. I'd seen it a thousand times, I suppose, but it had been nothing more than an adult decoration, something that was just there. It had become almost invisible in its ever-presence, especially to a child's eyes. The point is that, quite suddenly, I wanted to know what was inside it when I was eleven. My mother reacted so strangely to the request—I remember it to this day. I mean, she acted so strangely on *most* occasions that if this particular one stood out, it was significant in some way or other, wouldn't you think? The point is—"

"Stop saying 'the point is,'" Andrews snapped. "No one at this table thinks you know what your point is."

"I saw things in that tin box that scared my mother, silenced my father, and baffled me." I closed my eyes, trying to see the objects in question. "Letters, papers, documents; several photos. In a seemingly unrelated series of monologues, my mother subsequently attempted to explain things to me by telling me stories about strangers in Paris and Chicago after the First World War. Those stories are now consuming my dreams and many of my waking moments. Everything in my brain and body is trying to tell me that the contents of that box, and those stories, mean something. They mean enough to someone that I should be killed because of them."

I could hear that my voice had grown freakishly high-pitched and abnormally loud even for me. Andrews and Lucinda were staring at me as if I might suddenly leap up from the table and destroy the room.

Then a remarkable thing happened. Andrews set down his fork and ignored his dessert. He leaned forward, clasped his hands, and turned into a university professor—right before my very eyes.

"All right," he said calmly. "Let's examine that."

It wasn't the reaction of an indulgent friend or a professional analyst. He was a colleague preparing to examine ideas and facts in order to arrive at a conclusion that would improve understanding.

Lucinda saw it. "Oh, no," she said firmly. "You two are not going to take this on. This is a police matter. Skidmore is very capable. And Fever's in no condition to sit up let alone gad about."

"We're not going to gad about," I told her, staring at Andrews. "We're going to sit right here in this kitchen and talk."

"What was the photograph?" Andrews asked, already playing the academic game.

"It was—I think it was a picture of a woman. From the 1920s. She looked exactly like my mother. On the back the name *Lisa* was written. This Lisa, I believe, owned a nightclub in Paris."

"The resemblance to your mother was striking?" he assumed.

"It was almost exact."

"But your mother didn't say, 'Oh, that's my grandmother or great-grandmother,' or something."

"No. Instead she avoided the photo in all her explanations." I bit on my lower lip. "There was also some kind of letter. A letter that she gave me or showed me the very first time I looked at the contents of the box. I don't remember it exactly at this moment, but I've dreamed about it too. It was anonymous and it admonished me to pursue something that seemed to upset or frighten my mother so much that she spent a good deal of time talking me out of it."

"Why haven't you ever mentioned any of this to me before?" he asked.

"Or me," Lucinda chimed in.

"I just—I never really thought much about it as an adult. I mean, it happened when I was so young. It was strange for a while, but there were so many more strange things about my parents—I let it go. My mother's infidelities, my father's increasingly strange behavior, the very odd life and livelihood they'd chosen: I hated my childhood. The last thing I wanted to do was dwell on it. I wanted to escape it. I left when I was barely sixteen. I had no intention of ever returning here. And by the time I did, so many other things were important to me, I just didn't remember much about— and then, as you both know, things were fairly active for me when I first arrived. My old college professor tried to kill me, a witch brought me back from the dead, an itinerant minister and an albino dwarf menaced my home—"

"Please." Andrews held up his hand. "Let's not reexamine old plots. We've got enough to deal with right here, right now."

"Except that all of the clues to this incident may very well lie in the past," I insisted. "So 'right now' may not, in fact, be the most important time in my life, currently."

"All right." He sighed in agreement. "What do we do?"

"Nothing until morning," Lucinda said instantly. "Andrews, eat your pudding. Fever, go to bed. I—will be up directly. I have a few things to say to young Dr. Andrews."

I heard her voice. There was no arguing with that voice. It was the Law—with a capital L.

"Good night," Andrews and I said at exactly the same time.

I stood. I smiled at them both, and I felt they understood everything that was in my smile—the gratitude and affection, the kinship.

Then, as I turned and headed toward the stairs, I tried not to dwell on a sudden uncomfortable realization. For a moment when I'd come downstairs with a club in my hands, I had genuinely not been able to separate my dreams and fears from my reality.

And in that moment, I might have killed Andrews.

13.

Lucinda departed early the next morning for a long shift at the hospital. She left simple, stern instructions. I was to be watched at all times, never allowed out of the house, not given solid food.

As luck would have it, she had given those directions to Andrews while he was still in a banana pudding stupor. I'd seen something like it many times before. He appeared to be perfectly awake. He even responded to easy questions. But Lucinda made the mistake that I had stopped making many years earlier: she believed that Andrews had heard her. She left my house secure in the knowledge that she had threatened and encouraged him in just the right amounts, and that I was in safe hands.

Of course, nothing could have been further from the truth.

I was making soft scrambled eggs when he stumbled into the kitchen sometime after nine. The sun was well up, and my day was several hours old already. I'd dressed in a new dark green turtleneck shirt—something that Lucinda had gotten me, apparently, for Christmas—and the typical black jeans. I'd slipped on some cheap slippers with thick wool socks, intending to get boots a little later.

"Mmm," Andrews murmured. "Smells good." He sat at the table. He was still in his baggy T-shirt and dirty sweatpants.

"These eggs aren't for you," I said. "They're fairly plain, I'm afraid. No salt, a little runny. Closest thing to liquid food I can get and still eat something that doesn't go 'glug.'"

"Okay." He was staring at the espresso machine.

He'd passed my first test: no acknowledgement of the notion that I could only have liquid food.

"Would you like some espresso?" I asked.

"More than life itself." He nodded, but did not otherwise move.

"I'll just get it then, shall I?"

He rubbed his eyes. "Did you really try to beat me to death with a walking stick last night," he yawned, "or was that just another one of my seven hundred nightmares last night?"

"You had nightmares?" I turned off the fire under the eggs and stepped up to the espresso machine. I'd already had five cups, and the machine was well warmed.

"I dreamed that I was a blackbird in a cherry pie."

"'Four and twenty blackbirds,'" I quoted, "'baked in a pie.' From your banana pudding experience last night?"

"God only knows," he said.

I slid a small cup under the nozzle of the espresso machine and pressed the button. Steam hissed, aroma arose, and a fine beverage was made. I set the cup on the kitchen table and Andrews grabbed for it as if it were a lifeline to a drowning man.

"Once you're completely awake," I told him, returning to my eggs, "how would you like to have a look around the yard?"

"What for?" He yawned.

"I don't know. See if there's anything in the way of a clue that the legal establishment might have missed."

"Oh." He sipped his espresso. "Okay. I'm in."

Test Number Two was passed: I could get out of the house.

"Good." I scooped up my eggs, sloshed them into a small bowl. Grabbing a tablespoon from the silverware drawer, I sat at the table beside him.

"After I finish these," I told him casually, "I'll just nip upstairs and see if there's anything else strange that I didn't notice before. Aside from the old clock being up there, I mean. Didn't want to do it while Lucinda was asleep. You'll be all right down here for a moment or two?"

"Of course," he answered, slightly more sprightly. "This espresso is saving my life."

"It's good," I agreed.

And Test Number Three asked and answered: I didn't have to be watched all the time. It appeared that Andrews hadn't heard a word of Lucinda's instructions.

I finished my eggs and regretted them immediately. My stomach instantly rebelled against the unrecognized, invading food I'd given it. I moved slowly, hoping to keep it fairly calm, carefully placing my bowl and spoon in the kitchen sink.

"Get something to eat if you want," I told Andrews, pointing to the refrigerator as I left the room. "Girlinda made a lot of food."

He didn't answer.

The steps were harder to manage than I might have hoped. A bad night's sleep had affected me adversely. Still, once I was in my room and my heart stopped pounding, I was fairly steady. I took a full five minutes, steadying myself by holding on to the foot of the bed, just surveying the room with a critical eye.

Everything seemed in order.

With a dawning awareness, I realized that my bed had been cleaned—the entire room must have been cleaned. I tried not to think of the blood—what the scene must have been like for Lucinda when she'd found me there in December. Or course the room smelled different than I remembered: less dusty; more sanitized. Not just the bed, but the desk, the lamp, the rug, even the pictures had been gone over, wiped off, sprayed with some faintly lemon-scented cleaner. The room didn't feel freshly cleaned, though it was impossible to determine how long ago it had been tidied. Skidmore could have had the place scrubbed by a service after all the searching for evidence had been done. But he had said that he was continuing his investigations. That left my mind to consider another option: my assailant had done this work himself, in an effort to eliminate evidence.

Just as that thought was sinking in, I heard heavy footfalls on the stairway.

"Hey," Andrews called. "I'm not supposed to leave you alone."

He appeared in the doorway with a piece of cornbread in his hand.

"You're not?" I asked him innocently.

"And you're not meant to go outside, either," he answered, taking a huge bite of the cornbread, raining crumbs on his shirt and my floor.

"Unless you're with me," I said. "You know you'll have to clean that up."

"What?"

I pointed to the floor.

"Oh." He stooped immediately and began picking crumbs off the floor and popping them into his mouth.

"You're eating off the floor." I shook my head.

"Have you tasted Girlinda's cornbread? It's like you're eating a fresh ear of corn. If that corn had been planted and tended by buxom angels."

"Buxom angels?"

"Besides," he went on, standing up again, "these floors are cleaner than my kitchen counters at home."

I nodded. "I thought so too."

"Who's been cleaning up while you've been away?" He finished the cornbread in one impossible bite.

"Who indeed." I brushed past him. "I'm going outside. Do you want to change or will you be wearing your pajamas?"

"These aren't pajamas," he objected, staring down at his dirty shirt and sweatpants.

"All right." I sailed down the stairs and headed toward my front door.

"Wait." He clambered down after me.

I shoved the door open and greeted the day. The mud and old leaves on the porch were decorated with yellow pine pollen. It was a porch where nobody had lived for a while.

"The same person who cleaned my bedroom," I said, really to myself, "didn't seem to feel a similar compulsion to tidy up out here."

"My room—your guest room's a little musty too," Andrews observed, coming through the doorway.

Past my front steps, the day had turned to gold. The sun was up, the sky was clear, the air was crisp. Spring's wanton suggestion hid everywhere: trillium under brown leaves, rhododendron buds about to open, mountain laurel yearning to show white cups instead of snow.

"Looks like winter's done," Andrews said softly. "You slept through winter. Like a bear."

"It'll snow tomorrow, or the day after," I assured him. "Winter looks finished, but a part of its plan is to lull you into a false sense of spring."

"Winter is not an anthropomorphic malevolence," Andrews said, kicking at the leaves on the porch. "It doesn't mean to be cold. It just *is* cold. That's its essential nature."

"You invoke Aristotle's *Metaphysics*, 'what belongs to a thing in respect of itself belongs to it in its essence.'"

"I refer, rather, to Aquinas," he corrected, "'essence is itself the very thing that exists.'"

"Or do you misunderstand Hegel," I went on, "when he tells us that 'essence is mere Identity.'"

"I've really missed you." Andrews was grinning.

I nodded, avoiding looking at him. "Well, I'm not entirely back yet. Winter's not gone, and I might slip into hibernation again at any moment. So let's have a look around the yard while I can still walk."

I charged off the porch. Andrews followed.

"What are we looking for?" he wanted to know.

"Yes," I admitted. "I don't know. But in the same way that it's curious for my room to be so clean when the rest of the house is as it should be after months of neglect, we may find such anomalies here in the yard."

"Except I'd just reckon that Lucinda cleaned up your room because she knew she'd be sleeping there last night."

"I don't think she had time," I told him, kicking random sticks and stones on the ground, looking for anything out of place. "I'll ask her, of course, but I don't know when she would have done it."

Andrews sat down on the steps. "Well, she did come to your house before you got here."

"Did I tell you that Truevine Deveroe was up here day before yesterday with one of her dogs and saw a man coming out of my house?"

"What?" he asked, louder than he meant to. "Truevine, the witch girl?"

"The dog ran off after the man," I went on, "and Truevine called Skidmore."

"Did they—they didn't find the man?"

"Not so far," I said, "but I have the idea that he came here to put the clock up in my room."

"Clock?"

I stopped poking around and looked back at Andrews. "I didn't mention that to you last night?"

"The clock on the mantel." He nodded. "Right. The reason you almost bludgeoned me to death. That clock."

"That clock."

"Why in God's name would a man break into your house to

put that clock in your room?" He shook his head. "You're really shot, brain-wise. You know that, right?"

"I don't know *what* I know."

"You're obsessing over this clock, I'll tell you that." He locked eyes with me. "And you're doing it to avoid thinking about something else. I don't know what, but this is a thing you do: sometimes you fixate on something innocuous in order to eschew more germane matters. You do this, I believe, because you have a brain that won't admit that it can't figure something out. You have a vain brain."

"I have a vain brain?"

"You heard me." He shrugged. "So we can rummage around in your yard if you want to. We can talk about the clock or the brand of cleaner some mysterious maid used on your bedroom floors. We can even indulge in some operatic version of your own post-coma trauma. Or you can cut out this crap and have a look at whatever it is that's really important here."

"And what would that be?" I asked.

"I don't know," he answered. "But you do, your brain does, your dreams do."

"Look, Dr. Freud," I began.

"That's Dr. Jung, boyo," he corrected.

"Look, damn it," I snapped, "I want to spend *less* time in my subconscious, not more! I'm struggling here, to—you know, to stay awake; stay out of my dreams."

"But you said . . ." he objected.

"I know I said I wanted to figure out what the dreams were about," I admitted, hopelessly. "But I want to—I don't know what I want to do."

I heaved myself over to where he was sitting on the steps and collapsed beside him. I surveyed the yard. Old leaves and new growth fought each other; helped each other. The decaying leaves from seasons past were turning into sustenance for the new crop of March's bounty, but the spring shoots had to struggle upward through those final remnants of last year's autumnal glory.

I found a lesson in that observation.

"You know," I said slowly, as much to myself as to Andrews, "everything new is born out of everything old."

He turned to stare at my profile.

"Have you been reading those books again, that Buddhist monk, what's his name?"

"His name is Thich Nhat Hahn," I sighed, "and I haven't read him since I woke up. I'm talking about something a lot more organic and, I guess, genealogical."

"Thich Nhat Hahn? That's fun to say. Thich Nhat Hahn."

"Stop it. I'm trying to tell you that I've had an insight."

"Thich Nhat Hahn."

"I'm realizing that my mother was trying to tell me something about my heritage," I went on, ignoring Andrews as best I could. "Or, rather, trying not to tell me something. Trying to avoid telling me something. Encouraging me not to pursue the matter."

"Your mother was trying to tell you not to investigate something?" He nodded. "Under ordinary circumstances, that would be the fastest way to get you to do it."

"Exactly," I agreed. "So did I do it and I just can't remember it now? Or did something prevent me from doing it, and I just let it go in favor of a thousand other things she told me not to do?"

"And I care about this because . . . ?"

"I have to find out about my mother's family." I stood up. "This is about her and her family. I'm positive of that."

"You think that the man who tried to kill you," Andrews realized, "did it because of something in your maternal genealogy!"

"Though why that would be the case I have no idea." I got to my feet and headed back into the house. "But I actually believe that if you find the motive, you have a better chance of finding the man."

"And sometimes the motive is the man." Andrews stood up.

I opened my front door. "I don't know what that means."

"Good, you're going back inside," he said, following me in. "I knew that walking around out here was a bad idea."

"No, I'm getting my keys," I told him. "We're going to Fit's Mill."

He swallowed the last bit of his cornbread and stopped dead still.

"We're not going anywhere of the sort," he insisted.

"You can come with me if you want to." I lumbered through the door, heading up the stairs to collect my keys and wallet. "But if you're joining me, you should put on some shoes."

"We're not going anywhere," he repeated, still standing on the porch. "And what is Fit's Mill?"

"It is, believe it or not," I called down to him from the stairs, "the final resting place of my mother's remains. I think."

"You don't know?"

I heard the mantel clock—it was ticking on my bedside table. "I can't even be certain she's dead."

"What?"

I could hear that Andrews was headed up the stairs. I had every hope that he might soon be changing out of his pajamas.

"With my parents," I called out, steering myself into my room and pocketing keys and wallet, "you never can tell. I thought my mother was dead once before, and then I found her quite alive and well. I talked with her in June Cotage's kitchen, and had the opportunity of telling her good-bye. And, of course, my father always claimed that he *couldn't* completely die. Simply refused to. His ghost is still around. So is hers."

Everyone in Blue Mountain could still tell stories about my

parents and their odd traveling performance group, The Ten Show, though it had been disbanded for nearly fifteen years. Rumors still circulated about my father's bizarre magic act, and my mother, his lovely assistant. They were quite well-known in the world of professional magicians—a world about which I knew absolutely nothing. My father's work was often mentioned around town, especially if something odd or unexplained had happened. When a seven-month-old baby had fallen from a second-story window and escaped unharmed, someone told someone else that the child had been caught by the ghost of my father, who had always been interested in protecting innocents. On the other hand, if a young girl in our town got pregnant without benefit of husband or wedding ring, my mother's name would be invoked—the patron saint of sinners, if such an oxymoron would be allowed in any decent religion: a patron saint of the promiscuous lover, the unfaithful wife.

I traded my slippers for hiking boots and headed down the stairs. I didn't turn around when I heard him behind me, but I could tell he'd put on heavier shoes, at least.

"What do you mean your mother was 'dead once before'?" he asked.

"You don't remember? One of the main reasons, seven or eight years ago, that I first came back to Blue Mountain to live in this house was because both of my parents were dead."

"I can barely remember seven or eight days ago."

"I thought my mother was dead," I said as I stepped around him, heading out the front door, "but there she was at June and Hek Cotage's place: Dolores Devilin, older, no wiser, trying to offer me some kind of favor."

"I don't remember anything about that. And frankly, I'm always a bit uncomfortable whenever I hear you talk about your mother, so—"

"I'm telling you that if my mother is, in fact, dead, she's buried at Fit's Mill."

I turned to face him. He had not, in fact, changed clothes. He was still wearing sweatpants and his dirty T-shirt. He had only added chukka boots and a light blue jacket.

"Well if we're going," he announced, "I'm driving, so give me your keys. Now."

"You don't know where it is." I looked him up and down disapprovingly, and then headed out the door.

"You'll guide me," he insisted, following me, "if you don't fall asleep too much on the way. Keys!"

I very deliberatcly locked my door—an uncharacteristic gesture in my community—before I held up the entire key chain.

"This is certainly the blind leading the lame," I mumbled.

"Amen," he intoned, grabbing the keys from my hand and heading for my truck.

14.

It felt good to be rolling down the road. The day had opened up nicely. The cool air rushed all around us as Andrews drove my big old beat-up green truck through the clean spring morning. The inside of the truck was a comfortable mess, poorly folded maps, half-read paperbacks, and a little straw. I loved my pickup truck. It was as much my home as the kitchen table. We were headed faster than we should have been down the highway and away from Blue Mountain. I directed Andrews toward a trail I knew, a back way that was, I admitted, more footpath than thoroughfare.

As we turned off the paved road and onto the trail, I allowed myself to be distracted by the beauty of the woods. Light flirted and flashed and darted through new green and old shadows. Nothing in this part of the landscape was entirely free of shade and soot and shadow, but spring light blasted and shook and stemmed in every direction. I was mesmerized by the patterns.

"Did anyone tell you," I said hazily, beginning to slip away, "that your bottle of French pastis may have had a hand in saving my life?"

Andrews responded by swerving the truck in a violent S shape and coming to a halt.

"What the hell?" I snapped, startled back to complete consciousness.

"This isn't a road," he explained. "Plus: you were drifting."

"I was not."

"Look." He slowed the truck. "If you're not going to be any more aware of your state of mind than that, I'm turning the truck around and the only place you're going to investigate is your bed."

"No." I sat up. "You're right. I was drifting. It won't happen again."

"You were drifting."

"I was gazing at the dappled—what's that Hopkins poem, 'Glory be to God for dappled things'?"

" 'For skies of couple-color as a brinded cow' " he quoted. " 'For rose-moles all in stipple upon trout that swim; Fresh-firecoal chestnut-falls; finches' wings'—then something, something."

"That's the one," I affirmed. "That's where I was."

"Drifting along in a Gerard Manley Hopkins semi-erotic frenzy of alliteration," he warned, "is still drifting, when all is said and done."

"It won't happen again," I repeated.

"We'll see," he said. "Now, where do I go? I mean, this isn't a road."

I surveyed the flora ahead, and it appeared as dense and impenetrable as a fortress.

"Right." I blinked. "I think I might have told you the wrong place to turn off the road."

"Damn it, Fever."

"Wait." I squinted. "I think that's it right there."

I pointed to a fallen pine, long dead and mostly decayed, not twenty feet ahead, barely thirty feet from the road.

"We have to go over a tree?" he asked.

"We have to go around a tree." I motioned to one side of the tree. "See? Over there to the left of it?"

"Ah." He saw the place I meant.

There was a narrow opening between the rotted top of the fallen pine and a hard row of maple trees. It didn't seem big enough to allow my truck through, but I'd been on this road several times over the years. Fit's Mill, among other wonders, was a secret Eden for the Plumleaf Azalea or *Azalea Prunifolia*, an endangered variety of the sweet-scented, deciduous shrub, and among the most beautiful. I had once bought one to plant beside June Cotage's grave site because she loved them so much.

"We're not going to fit through there," Andrews insisted.

But he urged the truck forward.

"We'll make it," I assured him.

We did not.

Something in or under the rotted pine tree punctured my left front tire. It exploded like a shotgun blast, and the steering wheel shivered as Andrews lost control. We ended in a soggy pine-scented mush, the engine still sputtering.

"I hope you don't have a spare," he said calmly, "for two reasons. (a) It would serve you right. (b) I don't feel like changing a tire."

I grabbed the handle and shoved my weight against the door. "I would deserve it," I agreed, "but alas for you: I do have a tire. And a jack."

It took a bit of doing to set the jack, with much attendant grunting and cursing. At first it kept sinking into the muddy ground. I had to find a dry log to set it on. Andrews had decided at first that he would not, in fact, lift a finger to help me.

"I think part of the problem might have been that you were thinking of the wrong poem," Andrews finally observed as he stood watching me work. "You should have come up with e. e. cummings. You should have said, 'in Just-spring when the world is mud-luscious.'"

I looked up at him, sweating. "You can be 'the little lame balloonman,' isn't that what's next in the poem? I'm currently thinking of you as a little lame balloon man. Among other things."

"I'm not helping." He folded his arms. "You got us into this."

"Fine." I stood up unsteadily. "I've been in the hospital for three months, for God's sake."

"Which is why you shouldn't be out and about *at all,*" he answered me, raising his voice. "Lucinda said you should stay home, and now you can see why. You nearly fell asleep in the truck, and then you told me to turn at the wrong place. Now you're paying the piper."

"I'm paying the piper?"

"I'm attempting," he assured me in his best upper-class accent, "to wear you out so that you'll fall back asleep."

"You are?" I asked, every muscle in my body screaming out for sleep. "Why?"

"So that I can change the damn tire, and take you home."

"How's that working out?" I mumbled, going back to work.

"Suit yourself." I could almost hear him shrug.

Before I could make any sort of response, a car pulled up behind us on the paved road. I turned to see a perfectly restored black and chrome 1962 Lincoln Continental, all sleek rectangles and Kennedy-elegant.

The driver's side window lowered slightly. The way the sunlight slanted onto the car and the road, it was impossible for me to see the driver, but his voice was thick with an odd accent.

"You boys need help? Making quite a racket. Heard you half a mile up the road."

"Thanks for stopping," I called, turning my head his direction.

"We don't need any help, though," Andrews rushed to answer. "Everything's under control here. He actually likes doing this kind of thing. Not to mention that this was all his fault. So you are witness to his just deserts."

"I see," the voice drawled. "You all headed over to Fit's Mill, I wager."

I leaned against the trunk, breathing hard. "How would you know that?"

"You started down the shortcut. It's the only place that trail goes. They got some unusual azaleas over there in Fit's Mill, I hear. Pretty."

"They do." I squinted, trying to see inside the car.

"Some like to put the Plumleafs close to a grave site," he said cheerfully, "because they smell so much like honeysuckle. Makes you feel better when you're standing over a loved one."

"What?" I asked.

"Well, if you're certain you all are fine," he said, and the driver's side window began to close. "*Ça va?*"

"That's some kind of New Orleans accent you've got there," I suddenly realized.

But the window closed and the car took off. Seconds later, I couldn't even hear the sound of the engine.

"That was unusual," Andrews allowed.

"That was a New Orleans accent," I muttered.

"It's an unusual accent, all right," Andrews said, "but I was referring to the fact that you don't see that many African-Americans up in these parts."

"He was black?"

"What?" Andrews took a step closer to me. "You didn't see that he was—"

Before he could finish, he slipped in the mud and ended on his backside.

"God. Damn. It," he said slowly, in carefully separated syllables.

I couldn't help grinning. "Kind of lost your balance a little bit there."

"I landed really hard."

"I've seen you land harder on a wooden bar stool than you just did in that nice soft mud." I didn't bother to help him up.

"But as long as you're down here, why don't you help me with this tire."

He grumbled, but inside of ten minutes we were back in the truck, our shoes and pants and hands caked with mud. We'd made it beyond the fallen tree and were bouncing down the old logging road that was the shortcut from Highway 76 to Fit's Mill.

The trail was, in general, two deep ruts in a sea of weeds and grass. On either side of the path there were thick holly and red cedar and tulip poplar and loblolly pines. Yellow jessamine and scarlet trumpet honeysuckle perfumed the air and decorated all that new March green.

"You really don't see that many black guys up here, do you?" Andrews said, eyes glued to the trail for any sign of further trouble. "Why is that?"

"Migration patterns."

"I beg your pardon." Andrews laughed.

"Settlement of these mountains happened pretty early in American history," I explained, "with predominantly Scots-Irish stock. The English settlers stuck to the lowlands. Everybody else chose something farther up the Eastern seaboard."

"Your own great, great however-many-*greats* back grandfather was from Scotland."

"Exactly," I said. "I'm impressed that you remember."

"He killed a man and had to flee his country, change his name, and hide out in the hills," Andrews responded with glee. "I delight in knowing that's your heritage."

"On my father's side," I agreed.

"And not many black folk migrated the same way," he assumed.

"There were African-American patterns, of course, but they had to wait until the early twentieth century, in general. And when that occurred, roughly between 1910 and 1930—the so-called Great Migration—it was a movement of some four million

African-Americans away from all the Southern states to the North and Midwest."

We hit a dip in the trail and Andrews gripped the wheel.

"Well, sure," he said. "You'd want to get as far away from that racist crap as you possibly could."

I nodded. "That was the idea, at least. Of course, in reality, there was no escaping—*is* no escaping it. I mean, part of the idea was that there would be industrial jobs in places like Chicago and Detroit and Milwaukee, and everyone could make money. But the money was minimal, and everyone would agree that poor is poor no matter what your geography is. The Scots-Irish immigrants in these mountains discovered that there was no money here; the African-American workers in Chicago fell afoul of the same foible."

"Nice alliteration, in the continuing vein of Gerard Manley Hopkins."

"But as far as that man in the Continental goes? The one we just met?" I went on. "He wasn't from around here, so your point is moot. He was from New Orleans."

"So you're trying to tell him," Andrews said.

My next comment, whatever it might have been, was obliterated. The back window of my pickup truck exploded. Glass spewed in every direction, clipping my left ear and the side of my face, bouncing off the windshield and ricocheting back at me. Andrews slammed on the brakes and we skidded nearly sideways, and hit a tree.

"What the hell?" he shouted.

"Shotgun!"

I grabbed his collar and forced his head below the window level. Glass was still clinking out of its frame. Head low, I searched the woods and the trail behind us, eyes darting here and there wildly. I thought I might catch movement or reflection. The shooter would have been close.

"What do you mean?" Andrews whispered. He did not struggle to get up.

"I mean," I answered, sotto voce as well, "that someone shot at us with a shotgun. And they were close."

"How do you know?"

"I only heard the window breaking, not the blast from the gun."

I glanced upward at the roof of the cab. There was a hole the size of a small dinner plate not two inches from where my head would have been.

The engine was sputtering. Andrews still had his feet jammed down, one on the brake, the other on the clutch. I looked out at the front of the truck. Despite slamming into a tree, it was barely dented.

"You should turn off the engine," I said.

"Oh." His hand flew up and he turned the key.

The engine coughed and then everything was suddenly silent: no birds, no wind, and no movement.

"He was kneeling or lying on the ground," I announced.

"What?"

I pointed to the roof. "The shot went through the back window and up, out through the top."

"Jesus." Andrews sat up, staring at the hole.

"It was the guy in the car," I said. "The guy in the Lincoln Continental."

"Why the hell would he . . . what are you talking about?"

I opened my door and climbed out of the truck, heading back behind us on the trail.

"What are you talking about?" Andrews repeated, leaping out his side and following me. "Where are you going? There's a man with a gun out here!"

"There's a *coward* with a gun out there!" I shouted, hoping the man would hear me. "He waited until we passed and then tried to shoot us in the back!"

I was hoping to draw the man out, make him show himself. If this was the same man who'd shot me in my sleep, I felt he'd be somewhat intimidated by confrontation.

"But," Andrews stammered, "the man in the Lincoln Continental?"

"Too coincidental, don't you think?" I asked him, eyes still trying to look everywhere at once. "A stranger stops, and a few minutes later someone tries to kill us. Kill me."

Andrews stood next to me, slightly crouched, waiting to dive for the ground at the first sign of trouble. "You really are paranoid. I mean I understand why you would be, but I think that an elderly well-dressed man in a town car is your least likely suspect in an event like this around here. Isn't it some kind of hunting season or other?"

I had to think for a moment. "Most of the seasons close in February, at the latest. But I think turkey season starts in March and goes until May."

"There you are."

"And, of course," I went on, "it's always feral hog season. There's no closed season for that."

"Feral hog?"

"Wild boar," I answered.

"In Georgia?" He didn't believe me. "Wild boar like Beowulf killed?"

"Yes," I answered absently, still scouring the brush for any sign of our assailant.

"How in God's name would there be wild boar—?"

"Oglethorpe," I snapped.

He stood silent for a moment. Then: "What?"

"Oglethorpe, along with a little more than a hundred other people from England, came to Georgia in 1733. Most of them were tradesmen and farmers who were used to the old usufruct rights: letting their cattle and hogs run loose."

"Like in England."

"Like in England," I assured him. "And a favorite food of the day was salt pork, usually fried with cornbread, sweet potatoes, and molasses. But hogs got away, as hogs will do. And then they multiplied."

"As they will likewise do," he added.

"Now they're everywhere in these woods, bristled and tusky and great for a barbecue."

"So why couldn't your shattered window be the result of some drunken yahoo out looking for—?"

"Because my truck doesn't look anything like a hog," I interrupted, "no matter how drunk you are. And look."

I pointed to a place in the ground where the grass had been flattened and the earth was indented. There was a red shotgun shell casing.

"Okay." Andrews looked around, searching the darker part of the woods. "So—somebody took a shot at us."

I nodded.

"Then why did he leave?" Andrews continued. "If he wanted to kill you, why didn't he just reload and come over to the truck?"

"Good question."

"And, PS: where in those woods could you drive a Lincoln Continental?" he wondered. "That old guy didn't follow us on foot, not chasing your truck."

"You really got a good look at him in that car?" I asked. "You said 'an elderly well-dressed man.'"

"Yes."

"Could you identify him if you saw him again?"

"Oh." He realized what I was asking. "Well—yes. I think I might at that."

I stood for a moment, trying to hear, see, smell anything that might indicate where our attacker could be. Alas: nothing.

"All right," I sighed. "Let's go brush out the glass and get on over to Fit's Mill."

"You still want to go there now? After this?"

"Well I certainly don't want to stand here in the woods while someone with a shotgun has a chance to get another bead on me."

Immediately Andrews headed back toward the truck. He was nervous, but wouldn't want to admit it.

"How is it that we escaped being sliced to ribbons by flying glass?" he asked casually.

"Safety glass," I answered as if he were an idiot. "You have it in your car, every car in America has it."

"I don't have a car anymore," he said absently, not really thinking. "I ride my bike. I'm environmentally responsible."

"Ah, well, thank God for that, the planet is saved," I responded, striding behind him. "Now all I have to worry about is a stranger from New Orleans trying to kill me."

"The guy in the car didn't try to kill you," Andrews shot back, irritated. "And I heard that 911 tape Skidmore has. The man on the tape didn't have the same accent as the man in the car. Not even close."

I stopped walking. I felt dizzy. I tried to breathe.

"No," I finally managed to say. "The man in the car had the same accent, the same voice, in fact, as a hospital orderly who gave me some strange tea a few nights ago."

15.

For the rest of the drive to Fit's Mill, twenty minutes or so, I did my best to determine if the orderly who had given me tea in the hospital had been real or another dream hallucination. I didn't want to talk about it, and, as luck would have it, Andrews was willing to travel in silence.

The shortcut, overgrown as it was, spilled out onto a back dirt road near someone's tiny farm. The farmhouse on that land was a wreck. Paint was peeling off in wide strips, like river birch bark. Part of the roof had caved in and was covered with a cheap blue tarp. The front porch had become nothing more than a pile of rotted lumber blocking access to the house through the door. Chickens and weeds ran rampant in the yard. Three old rusted cars sat in various states of impossible decay not ten feet from the house. A litter of indigo crocus, royal blue scilla, and yellow daffodils bore witness to better days, or at least days when more care had been lavished on the place. An ancient woman was moving at a glacial pace between the back of the house and a nearby lawn chair. She stared at us and I waved. She did not wave back.

The dirt road was not as muddy as the woods had been, but the sky had become seriously overcast, and it threatened to rain and create more mud. It wasn't long before we were on the only real street in town.

The town of Fit's Mill had always been odd and small. Few young people stayed. Most older people were too poor to leave. Why my mother had chosen to hide out there during the last years of her life was a mystery that I had given up solving. She knew no one there. No one liked her, as far as I could determine. Her reputation had preceded her, and most of the old-timers only felt sorry for me when they discovered that I was her son. A man named Ramsey who worked in the town's only gas station had showed me her grave—for five dollars. He claimed to have slept with her. I had heard that he'd died, recently, of alcohol poisoning: too much of the homemade stuff.

"Jesus, what a depressing little place," Andrews said, taking in the heart of Fit's Mill.

The street was white top that hadn't seen repair in decades. It was as cratered as the moon. Emerging pokeweed and kudzu were everywhere. The only identifiable buildings were the post office, the gas station, and a diner that was actually a front for illegal liquor sales.

The post office was a corrugated tin facility that had been unused since 1951. An increase in the number of rural delivery routes had lead to a decrease in the number of small post offices. The gas station had two pumps, but only one worked. The diner never looked open, and there were never any lights on, but there were always a few people inside, and smoke invariably rose from the outdoor grill in back.

"I may have mentioned barbecue a while back?" I suggested when Andrews gawked.

"Yes?" he barely answered.

"Well, right there is a place where we could get some of the most amazing wild boar barbecue in the world."

He eyed the building with great suspicion. "I don't know."

"You can also get a shot of something resembling whiskey that might make you go blind."

"Well, then." He grinned. "I'm in."

He nosed the truck in the direction of the diner and parked in a patch of weeds near a new black Ford F-150. When we got out we both took a second to brush the worst of the auto glass from the seat and the rest of the cab, but without a broom and dustpan or, better, an industrial vacuum, we really didn't have a hope, so we gave up.

"All right," I warned him softly, "you have to expect the coldest shoulder treatment you've ever experienced. When we walk in the place, everyone will stare, all conversation will stop, and someone might ask us to leave."

"But you'll take care of it," he assumed.

"I'll take care of it."

I began trying to brush the caked mud off my hands and my pants, with only moderate success. Andrews didn't even bother.

The front of the diner had one door, no sign, a large, dark, dirty picture window, and was nearly covered by old and new kudzu vines. The door had once been painted blue, but time and neglect had nicely antiqued the finish. Its handle was black from dirt and car grease, the patina of unwashed years.

I grabbed it, tugged it, and stepped inside. Andrews was right behind me.

Two men in black Sunday suits sat at one of the five tables. Another man—someone with whom I had a vague acquaintance—leaned behind a counter in front of completely barren shelves. Everyone stared. All conversation stopped. The man I knew, the one at the counter, spoke up.

"We're closed." His eyes were bloodshot and his demeanor was darker than a junkyard dog's. He was dressed in a white shirt buttoned to the neck, no tie.

"Ramsey sent us," I said, staring him in the eye.

"Ramsey, he's dead," he answered immediately.

"I know." I stood still and let all three men have a good look.

"How you think you know Ramsey?" the man at the counter asked after a moment.

"He claimed he went to bed with my mother," I answered tonelessly.

"That would be Dolores," one of the men at the table said. "He never talked about no other woman. You'd be her boy Fever, then."

I didn't move.

"What is it you think you want here, Fever?" the man behind the counter asked, pronouncing my name as if it were a private joke.

"You know exactly what I want," I said plainly. "Five country back ribs, two whole ears of corn, some pinto beans, slaw if it's fresh, and a glass of something wrong to wash it down with."

Silence.

Then the other man at the table smiled. "I wouldn't trust that coleslaw, but the pig is been done since sunup and it's fine."

I nodded. "And my friend here comes from England. He's never tasted anything like your barbecue, or the—specialty of the house."

The man behind the counter managed something like a smile. "Specialty of the house. I like that."

He drew his right arm from behind the counter and brought up a very clean shotgun. He set it on the counter.

"We were just having us a little enticement ourselves," one of the men at the table said, bringing a paper cup out from under the table where he'd been hiding it, "before we went over to Wednesday morning service."

"Church service on Wednesday?" Andrews blurted out.

The man shook his head. "Damn, boy. You *are* from England. Say something else." He turned to his companion. "You hear that?"

"Say something else," the second man encouraged.

"God save the Queen," Andrews obliged.

All three men laughed, and with that, the place thawed to a slightly more comfortable level of tension. In short order, Andrews and I were seated at our own table, the man behind the counter had gone out back to pull pork from a steaming pig, and another one of the men had gone somewhere else with the assurance that he'd be right back with the "specialty of the house."

"How do these men know who you are?" Andrews whispered. "Do you know them?"

"I went to elementary school with the owner, the man behind the counter. His name is Travis. I haven't seen him in a long time. I had no idea he'd be here. We don't care for one another."

Before Andrews could worry further, Travis appeared with plates of food to distract him, and set them down in front of us. I gazed at the meal before me. The pulled pork smelled like an autumn fire, burning leaves, rosemary, and sweet vinegar. The ears of corn were still in their husks; I could feel the heat from them. The pinto beans were the color of chocolate, in bowls of their own. I knew from previous experience with this food that those beans had been grown on a little farm close by during the previous year, picked late, dried, stored over the winter near the smokehouse out back. A few days earlier they had been cooked in bacon, bacon fat, bacon drippings, and anything else having to do with bacon that Travis happened to have on hand. I had once found a small tooth in a bowl of these beans. I had always convinced myself that it was part of a pig's tusk.

Andrews was watching me, uncertain as to why I was just staring at my food.

"Are we going to eat this?" he asked, still whispering.

"Wait," I intoned.

Seconds later, the other man returned with two large Mason jars that, at first, looked empty. But he carried them with such care that even Andrews soon realized they were filled to the brim with an absolutely transparent liquid.

"Ah," Andrews said, nodding. "Specialty of the house."

"Kick your ass," Travis assured us.

The jars were set before us, and the three men all stood back. They were apparently very curious to know what reaction Andrews might have to their local cuisine and brew.

The only thing that gave Andrews pause was the fact that there was no silverware of any kind on the table and no napkin. Seeing his dilemma, I quickly picked up a piece of the boar between my first two fingers and thumb and began eating. He understood, and followed my example.

We ate for a moment in silence. He scooped up the bowl of beans and drank some down as if it were a thick soup. I began husking the corn gingerly, burning my fingers.

When Andrews stopped to breathe, he glanced at Travis. "This is the best pork I have ever eaten in America or in England."

"Damn right," one of the men agreed, shifting his weight.

They were still watching, anticipating Andrews's reaction to the liquor we'd been given. I saw that our conversation with them would go no further until we tried, reacted to, and praised the drink. I finished husking my corn and picked up the jar, holding it steadily so as not to spill a drop. Andrews saw and copied.

As one, we sipped.

I closed my eyes. First a fire touched my lips, but the scent of September apples and hickory smoke made it bearable. Then my tongue lit up, first with a kind of smoky poblano pepper heat, then with a rich, bitter vanilla. I swallowed, and the finish of that first taste went on for thirty seconds: elderberries, charcoal, pipe smoke, more vanilla, and then, just when I thought it was over, a final volley of lavender.

I opened my eyes. "Best ever, Travis," I said, as if a holy event had just transpired.

"God in Heaven," Andrews agreed.

"Why is there a little taste of lavender in this?" I asked him. "That's new."

He nodded slowly. "Damn if you don't have an exceptional pallet, Doctor. That batch was cooked over hickory wood and lavender stems. I believe it lends a bit of sophistication to the finish."

"Agreed." I took another sip. "Goes perfectly with the pig."

"That pig was one I got myself—about a week ago." Travis smiled genuinely for the first time since we'd walked into his place. "They're everywhere this year."

"Cold winter," one of the other men said sagely. "Extra snow."

"What does your boy, here, think of the brew?" Travis wanted to know.

Andrews, not one for sipping, gulped five huge swallows without reacting at all. I knew that he'd done it to impress the men.

"It'll do," he pronounced lightly, "if you don't have anything stronger."

That did it. All three of the men laughed; one patted him on the back.

"He's okay," the man told me, grinning. "I seen this particular batch make a grown man cry. And he drank it like it's water."

"Holy water," Andrews corrected. "Where I come from? A man could be knighted for creating a liquor this fine."

Everyone liked that. Everyone sat down at the table with us.

"We got to get to our service in a minute," Travis said, taking a seat right next to Andrews. "But I know you'uns did not come into my establishment just for this kind of breakfast. It's fifty dollars, by the way. Each."

"Prices have gone up," I observed, staring Travis in the eye.

"Well," Travis said politely, "the food is on the house, because you mentioned Ramsey, rest his soul. The hooch is five dollars a jar but this is a test batch, and since you correctly guessed the secret ingredient, I can let that go too. The hundred dollars is for the answer to your question."

"What question?" I asked, still staring him down.

"You want to know who shot up your truck a couple of minutes ago." He didn't blink. "I'll tell you, for a hundred dollars."

"That seems fair," I said immediately, reaching for my wallet. "Unless of course it was you who shot at me. Then it seems like cheating."

"Well, it was a shotgun," he responded, not offended in the least. "But it wasn't mine."

"And actually," I went on, "I really did want Andrews, here, to taste your food and this fine drink. The only questions I came in here to ask were about my mother."

"Oh." Travis sat back.

"I know she lived here for the last several years of her life," I told him, taking out too many twenty-dollar bills. "What a surprise to me when I learned that. I thought she died long before I came back to Blue Mountain. So I'm wondering if you ever talked with her, or knew anyone who did. I'm trying to get in touch with some of her relatives—that side of my family."

Travis nodded, not looking at the money. "Why's that?"

Something had made him tense up more, but questions about my mother often had that effect on people.

"As I get older," I answered, "I discover I'm more interested in genealogy. I want to know where I came from. I have a lot of information about my father's family, but almost none about my mother's. We, I'm sure you can understand, did not get along, my mother and I."

"Dorrie was a mess," he said. "I am not unsympathetic. What I am is uninformed in this regard. She came in here to have supper almost every Tuesday night for a couple of years. She sat by herself, didn't talk to anybody, didn't look around. She came here every Sunday morning for a gallon of the good medicine and never made conversation. Just set down the money and smiled. I don't believe that Ramsey ever got into her bed, but he did like to talk about it. I hope you will not be offended if I observe that your mother was a handsome woman even as she traveled into her fifties, and she did have a somewhat enticing reputation."

"All right." I patted the money on the table between us. "Who would know? About my mother's family, I mean."

"Couldn't say," he admitted, staring down at the bills.

"You know who might could have some information?" one of the other men began.

"Shut up, Wade." Travis gave the man a cold stare.

Wade nodded and lowered his head. All cordiality was gone from Travis's face. The room grew darker. There was a thunderhead rolling in over the mountains to the north.

"What is it?" Andrews asked before he realized that the conversation had turned strange.

Travis locked eyes with Andrews. "Wade misspoke."

Andrews glanced around and read the situation. He held up his jar, already half-empty. "Okay. But he serves a right mean breakfast beverage, doesn't he?"

Travis relaxed. Wade exhaled. The third man cleared his throat.

"It's about time for us to get to the meeting, boys," the third man announced.

Travis put his hand on the money but didn't take it. "You care to know who shot your truck?"

"Why not?" I assented.

Travis scooped up the money and jammed it into his pants pocket. "Hunters."

I shook my head. "That's not worth a hundred dollars."

"It is when I tell you why they did it." Travis stood up. "They're from this town—this piece of crap little town—and they still know they're better than you are. They want you to get on back to Blue Mountain, get married to that nurse, and settle down. Stay away from here."

The three men began to exit and avoided looking at me.

"They don't want me here in Fit's Mill," I said.

"They do not," Travis confirmed. "We got to get to our meeting. You'uns finish eating. When you leave, just flick this little button on the door and lock it behind you, hear?"

I nodded.

"I really enjoyed this drink," Andrews called out affably.

Travis did not turn around as he left the building. "Hope not to see you again," he answered back.

I sat back in my seat. Andrews continued eating. The men did not start a car or a truck, so it was clear to me that their meeting was close by.

"Do you think I should follow them to the meeting?" I asked.

"No." Andrews shoved a huge bite of food into his mouth.

"You think we should just finish this and leave?"

"Yes." He took a swig from his jar. "You didn't get the information you came for, and it doesn't seem likely that you will."

I folded my arms and nodded. "All right, then. At least let me go over to my mother's grave site, as long as we're here, and then we'll go home."

"Right."

"Grave, then home." I leaned back, not moving at all. I'd barely touched my food and most of my liquor was still in its jar.

Andrews continued eating.

The yard where my mother was buried was a sad affair. Dead weeds and leftover leaves littered the ground and the gravestones. There were, perhaps, thirty such sites as hers. Some of them had only simple markers. None of them had been attended. Ever.

The wild azalea next to my mother's grave was doing its best to add color and scent to the sullen air, but it was scraggly and sick, and might not see another spring. Several tortured shrubs were scattered about in no pattern whatsoever, and I finally realized that they were chestnut remnants. They served as the perfect metaphor for Fit's Mill. Until the beginning of the twentieth century, the American Chestnut was one of the most prevalent trees in the mountains. But chestnut blight fungus destroyed most of the old growth around 1900. After that, the species existed mainly as low shrub. The town had been a hub in the nineteenth century, the only gristmill in three counties. Before World War I it had been a relatively thriving metropolis with a bank, a restaurant, an ice-cream parlor, several other stores, and a Nickelodeon. The trip from other places to Fit's Mill was an occasion, and often whole families would come along.

Now the town belonged to kudzu, and the cemetery was practically a vacant lot.

A single red cardinal cried out in what seemed to me an attempt to invigorate the gloom. I saw it sitting like a rose in its jagged, barren chestnut bush. Close by was its nest: empty and in disrepair.

The thunderhead blocked out all sun, and gave a chill to the wind. I found myself wishing I'd worn a heavier coat. I moved, almost drifted, toward my mother's grave. As I did, I felt myself weakening. My legs were heavy and unmanageable, my eyes struggled to stay open; my breathing was very loud in my head.

I took one more step, and there was my mother, sniffing the honeysuckle smell from the azalea beside her grave, and smiling.

"The Olympics were held in Paris in 1924," she said. "It was quite a celebration. Sonja Henie was there. She was only eleven. After that she was a movie star in America. Also that year: Hitler was sentenced to prison, Robert Frost won a Pulitzer Prize, and Gandhi was fasting in India."

"Mother?" I whispered.

"And I think you'll find this interesting: the first mass murderer of the twentieth century—Fritz Haarmann was his name—he was sentenced to death in Germany. So he was in jail at the same time as Hitler. And after he died they put his head in a jar so that scientists could examine his brain. Haarmann, not Hitler."

"Why are you telling me these things?" I managed to mumble.

I heard Andrews, somewhere in another world, say, "What?"

My mother sat down on her grave. "He was a sick man, Fritz Haarmann. A child molester put in the insane asylum. There's no telling why he was like that. Of course, everybody will tell you it was his mother's fault. Everybody always blames the mother. She raised him with poison. She's the one who told him to go to France and kill T-Bone."

"Fever!"

I heard Andrews shout as if he were standing at the mouth of a deep tunnel in which I was buried.

Then I hit the ground, and everything was gone.

16.

I woke up on my mother's grave. Andrews was sitting beside me, talking on his cell phone. I knew he was speaking English, but I couldn't quite make out what he was saying. I seemed to have something stuffed into my ears. I was shivering, and it was raining. The overgrown azalea bush beside the grave did little to keep me dry. I tried to sit up, but my muscles wouldn't cooperate.

"I'm wet," I mumbled.

"Hang on," I heard Andrews say into the phone, "I think he's awake."

"I'm awake."

Andrews listened to the person on the other end of his telephone conversation and then handed the phone to me.

"Hello, Lucinda," I guessed, finally managing to sit up.

"If I had a gun I'd shoot you myself," she fumed. "What the hell do you think you're doing?"

I knew I was in trouble then. I couldn't remember ever hearing her curse.

"We just went to Fit's Mill," I began, hoping to convince her that the issue was distance. "It's only ten minutes from my house."

"It's a half an hour," she snapped.

"Not if you take the shortcut," I said, but instantly regretted it.

"You cut through those woods? When drunk boys are out there

shooting at wild hogs? You listen to me. I am going to get a pair of handcuffs from the sheriff of this town and I am going to lock you to your bed."

"Not that I wouldn't enjoy certain aspects of that," I answered, rubbing my forehead, trying to clear my mind.

"Shut up."

"Okay."

"Put Andrews back on."

I held out the phone. Andrews shook his head.

"Tell her I'm not here," he whispered.

"I heard that!" the tinny voice on the phone shouted.

"You called her," I told Andrews.

He sighed and took the phone. He listened. Then he listened some more. He closed his eyes. He wiped rainwater off his face.

At last he said, "Right." Then he closed the phone and put it in his shirt pocket.

"Did you know," I said to Andrews, trying to stand up, "that the first mass murderer of the twentieth century was a German named Fritz Haarmann?"

"Mm-hmm," he answered. "That movie *M*? With Peter Lorre? Supposed to be about that guy."

I shook my head. "How do you know these things?"

"I am astonishingly knowledgeable about a ridiculously high number of things," he assured me, "and incredibly erudite about same. Plus, I love old movies and you happened to hit one I've seen seventeen times."

"You've seen a Peter Lorre movie seventeen times?"

"I've seen *that* Peter Lorre movie seventeen times. I've seen *The Maltese Falcon*, like, maybe fifty. And that's got Peter Lorre in it too."

"Okay but did you know that this Haarmann was in prison the same time as Hitler?"

"Wow. Did not know that. And you bring this up now because—?"

"I didn't bring it up." I stepped off the grave. "My mother told me about it."

Andrews stood. "Ah. Another piece of the puzzle. Glad to know Hitler figures into your current situation. He's behind the plot to kill you, is he?"

"That's not what I said at all," I fired back.

"Still. Nazis do make the best bad guys, really."

"Laugh all you want to," I said, doing my best to head back toward my truck. "These are the only clues I've got."

"Clues from your dead mother?"

"Some of them are from other sources."

"I'm taking you home," he said, some of the humor gone from his voice. "You might be used to Lucinda being mad at you, you certainly deserve it. But I don't care to hear that sound in her voice ever again. I'm taking you home. I'm not letting you leave your house ever again. For any reason. We'll grow old together and die there. You'll go first, of course, because I'm in much better shape."

"And that's what makes you think you can keep me from going wherever I want to?"

"That's part of it." He'd caught up with me and had the truck keys already in his hand. "But to really keep you from going any-where all I have to do is run you around a little bit, feed you solid food, and then wait for you to pass out."

"Yes." That's as far as my thinking went before I bent over and threw up what little lunch I'd consumed, and every bit of illegal liquor I'd drunk.

The rain was letting up by the time we turned off the dirt road and into the woods. The ramshackle farmhouse that was the path marker seemed deserted. The lawn chair was gone. No animals, no people, no sign of life existed anywhere on the grounds. I began to wonder if I'd really seen anyone there at all when we'd gone by the place earlier.

The mud in the woods was difficult, but not impossible. The darkened sky gave a certain luster of despair to the forest that it had not known when we were traveling in the opposite direction. The only good thing I could think of was that pig hunters would most likely be under a tree or in a car or on the way home owing to the rain. Still, I kept a sharp eye out for any movement in the trees.

As we neared Highway 76, Andrews slowed down.

"Left up here," I said, still scanning the woods for men with guns.

"Sh," Andrews whispered. "Look."

I turned to see the black 1964 Lincoln Continental parked on the shoulder of Highway 76. It was impossible to tell if anyone was inside. I had the sensation that it was a mythically huge crow, waiting by the roadside for something dead to eat.

"What should we do?" Andrews asked, still whispering.

"Act as if it's not there," I told him. "Maybe it's not."

He stopped the truck, shifted to neutral, and turned his entire body so that he could stare me down.

"Maybe it's not *there*?" He poked my arm. "Did you hit your head when you fell down?"

"Yes." My gaze was locked on the black car, waiting for any movement, any indication that someone was inside it.

"You are *very much* not ever going out of the house again ever," he mumbled, barely coherently.

He turned back and shifted into first gear, eased the truck forward. Suddenly every sound was alive to me: mud shushing, wet twigs creaking, wind in the upper branches, individual drops of rain on the truck's roof and hood. Just as the front tires of the truck hit the pavement of Highway 76, the lights of the Lincoln came on.

"Keep going?" Andrews asked.

"Yes," I urged him impatiently. "Only faster."

Andrews hit the gas, and the rear wheels of the truck spun wildly. We fishtailed and were unable to gain purchase of the road. The Lincoln moved calmly forward, an almost stately wafting, and came to a stillness once again right in front of the truck, its driver's side door only a few feet from our front bumper.

The truck sputtered and coughed. Andrews realized, too late, that he'd taken his foot off the clutch. Our engine went to silence, and the sounds of nature prevailed.

The driver's window of the Lincoln lowered slowly.

Andrews watched the window go down and asked very casually, "Did you know that Lincoln Continental was one of the first cars to have electric windows?"

"What?" I asked distractedly, straining my eyes to pierce the darkness inside the car that was nearly blocking our way.

"It was cool, I'm just saying." Andrews sniffed.

Then, a voice from inside the car: "You boys all right?"

"You were in my room!" I called out sharply. "My hospital room. At the hospital."

"Yes," was all he said. "I see you got the clothes I left for you."

"You were pretending to be an orderly."

"Naw, I didn't pretend to be a thing in this world. But I did bring you some tea. Made you feel more better."

"You were dressed like an orderly," I said accusingly.

"Damn," he said, laughing. "Did the tea make you feel better or not, boy?"

I exhaled. "Well, yes. It did. But that isn't really the point."

"Can't agree. It was the very exact point of that tea. So."

"Ask him what he wants," Andrews whispered.

"Fever Devilin." The man in the car leaned forward a bit so that I could see his face. It was a radiant face, the face of an angel or a mystic—or a lunatic. "I came to help. Came as soon as I heard you in the hospital. If you can get that damn truck out the mud, let's go back to your place and talk about it."

"You know my name," I said, "but I don't know yours."

He smiled. "That's right. Can you get onto the highway or not?"

I turned to Andrews. "Can you?"

He started the truck, slipped it into first gear once more, and eased forward. "I guess so."

The Lincoln shot forward so suddenly that I thought my eyes were tricking me. In seconds it was gone down the highway, vanished past a bend nearly a quarter of a mile away.

"Whoa," Andrews said, staring in the direction that the car had gone. "That was fast."

"Did he see something?" I frantically checked the woods around us, but there was nothing I could see.

"He's going to beat us back to your house." Andrews nudged the truck up onto the highway, turned left, and we were on solid blacktop. "Wait. How does he know where you live?"

"Right." I started sweating, even though I didn't feel hot. It was difficult for me to tell, but I was afraid I might have a high temperature. I felt my forehead. It was clammy.

"So," Andrews said, urging the truck forward, "go home?"

"I think I really did hit my head," I complained. "Or maybe there was something wrong with that food we just had."

"You threw up because you haven't really eaten a meal in three months. There was nothing wrong with that food. The liquor, on the other hand, is apparently affecting my motor skills. My arms feel disconnected from my body."

"And you stalled my truck out back there. That doesn't usually happen."

"Even when I'm drunk," he agreed.

I grabbed the dash and gripped it. "God!"

"What?"

"We've been poisoned!" I leaned forward suddenly. "Those men in the restaurant gave us poison."

The truck slowed, barely perceptibly. "Poison? Poison barbecue? They keep that on hand, do they? Just in case?"

"No, but," I sputtered.

"There is really something wrong with you." But he was smiling.

"Are you losing feeling in your arms or not?" I couldn't stop the rising panic.

"No. Jesus. I'm just not used to that brew, and I drank the whole jar. Also: I didn't throw up, I didn't pass out; I didn't hallucinate my dead mother. That's *you*. It's not poison barbecue or bad liquor. This is you being you. You're very odd. Seems to me that you'd know this about yourself by now. The unexamined life is not worth living."

"Listen," I objected, struggling to catch my breath, "if the unexamined life is not worth living, my life is worth a trillion dollars. I spend most of my waking hours every day wondering what the hell is wrong with me."

"Well, I can tell you that one of the things *not* wrong with you is poison." Andrews shoved the truck into gear and we sped along up the highway. "Stacey told me that you had a panic attack in the hospital. Was it sort of like what you're feeling now?"

I exhaled. As I did I tried to imagine that poison was panic and both were a black smoke pouring out of my mouth and into the sky, mingling with the charcoal clouds there. I had to admit to myself that I was feeling exactly the way I'd felt in the hospital. And I'd been certain that I'd been poisoned then too. The only thing that kept me from completely relaxing about the idea was the fact that the strange man with the New Orleans accent appeared to be the proximate cause of my panic both times.

"Fever?" Andrews pressed.

"Yes. I'm okay. I'm feeling better. Let's get back to the house."

"I have to admit that I'm very curious about this guy," Andrews said affably. "Cool accent."

I spent the rest of the trip back to the house trying to calm my breathing, quiet my mind, and prepare for a conversation with the stranger.

The Lincoln was parked very neatly in front of my house. There was no sign of its driver. Andrews parked my truck close to it and we sat for a moment without talking.

"So." Andrews was staring at the empty front porch. "Where is he?"

As if cued by those words, my front door opened and the man appeared in the doorway, waving.

"Come on in," he called. "I put on some water for tea."

Then he disappeared back inside.

Andrews turned to me. "Well. If there's tea. You didn't lock the door?"

"I did," I said slowly, "although I hardly ever do."

"I think you should start doing it all the time."

"For all the good it does," I pointed out.

We both extracted ourselves from the muddy truck without further comment and made for the house. I realized after a quick examination that we were both a mess: soaked to the bone, caked with mud, and Andrews was still a bit drunk.

We clomped onto the porch. I could hear my guest humming softly in the kitchen. The melody was beautiful, but I didn't know the tune.

As I opened my door the aroma of lemon and ginger nearly overcame me. The tea was apparently very potent.

"Come on in," the man beckoned, as if it were his own house.

He stood comfortably in the kitchen. He was dressed, as I had partially seen, in a sharp black suit from another era: thin lapels, three buttons. His bone-white shirt was starched. His dark maroon tie was also thin, nineteen-fifties style, with some sort of tiny crest at one place on it close to his heart. I realized I had seen the same outfit on Miles Davis in a black and white photo somewhere.

"I've got to get out of these clothes," Andrews insisted.

The man gave us a quick once-over and agreed. "Good. The tea be ready when you come down."

"What's in the tea?" I asked, well aware that suspicion edged every syllable.

"Angelica root and van-van," he said proudly.

"I don't know what that is," Andrews said slowly, "either of those things."

"Gris-gris," the man assured us. "*Angelica archangelica* is the botanical name of the root, and van-van is made from lemongrass, citronella, palmarosa, gingergrass, and vertivet."

"All right," Andrews complained, "but you realize that I didn't recognize a single noun you said."

"Naw." He laughed. "I expect not. You got no gris-gris in London. None at all."

Andrews turned to me. "What is he saying?"

"Gris-gris," I answered quickly, eyes still on my guest, "is Creole voodoo." The man laughed so heartily that it was a little frightening. Combined with the low, fast-moving clouds and the distant rumbling thunder, it was quite effective as a portent to voodoo.

"You're Creole," I said steadily. "Not Cajun. I thought your accent was Cajun, but it's not really. It's a little outside my area of expertise, so I think I can be forgiven the confusion."

"Oh I don't think much about either one of those two words," the man said. He moved to the stove and stirred the pot he had put there. "Heritage, lineage, family history—it's all a whole lot more complicated than a single word can handle. Needs a whole lot more than that to tell the story. My mother came from France. Her mother came from Belgium. Somewhere in there we even got German and Dutch, but my skin is pretty dark so I have to assume they bumped into an African or two. You never can tell. It's all very confusing."

Andrews headed up the stairs. "Well, I'm changing. These clothes are disgusting."

I continued to watch the man in my kitchen.

"Take your mother for another example." The stranger went on stirring his tea, not looking my way. "You may not be perfectly acquainted with all the facts about her genealogy."

It only took a second for a few of the pieces to fall into place.

"You know something about my mother," I said quietly. "About my heritage. Something important."

He nodded once. "That's why I'm here."

"Who are you?" I whispered.

"Well." He grinned, staring deeply into the tea. "I think you might find the answer to that a little funny."

17.

The tea was, despite my suspicions, delicious. A bit of sourwood honey took the edge off, and it was very enlivening. Andrews and I sat on my sofa sipping it while our guest stood by the empty fireplace humming quietly. I was watching his every move, ready to jump, ready to dodge. Andrews was slumped down with his eyes closed, smiling.

Without warning, the man stopped humming. The sudden silence was so startling that Andrews opened his eyes and I jumped enough to spill tea onto my shirt.

"You all used to keep a clock on this mantel," the man said softly.

Instantly it was clear that this was the man who had tried to kill me. He had snuck in the house in December, he knew about my mother; he'd moved my clock. He was back at that moment, lulling us into calm, readying to finish the task he had begun before Christmas. I set down my teacup and stood in the same motion. I planted my feet, balled my fists, and prepared for anything he might do.

"Andrews," I said, deadly calm. "Would you please hurry into the kitchen and call Skidmore? Tell him my assailant is here and ask him to get here as quickly as he can to arrest him."

The man smiled. "Hang on a second, Dr. Andrews. The man who tried to kill Fever is not in the house at this moment."

Andrews blinked several times in rapid succession. "What?"

"If you would just simmer down a bit," the man said softly to me, "I'll tell you what you want to know."

"I want to know about you," I insisted.

Andrews sat forward, still groggy. "Do I call Skidmore or not?"

"No," the man said in a very deep voice. "Finish your tea."

Instantly Andrews sat back, took a sip of his tea, and closed his eyes again.

"Look," I began.

"You want to know who I am," the man said, his voice a rumble of thunder. "Take a deep breath in and then blow it out, you hear the words I'm about to say. You got to have ears that can hear. You got to have eyes that can see. So go on and breathe."

Without even thinking about it, I drew in a tremendously deep breath, held it for a second, and then blew it out as if I were blowing on a coal to make it flame up. I did, in fact, feel more relaxed.

"Have a seat," he whispered.

I sat.

"I told you it might sound funny," he continued, "but here it goes. This is a part of my story. Now, you might not know this, but the very first elected official in the New World, before all this was even America, was a man named Edward Wingfield. He was born in Stonely, Huntingdonshire. That's in England. He ran Jamestown because he was a big financial backer. He was the only shareholder in the group to sail from England, so it was no surprise that he was elected president of Jamestown. May of 1607 it was. But nobody liked him. From the beginning he was all wrong. He hated the native population, and made his men set up the colony on a miserable plot of land just because it was easy to defend from attack. It was no good for farming. Wingfield was also against having Catholics, non-Europeans, and women in the colony. How the hell he thought you could get by without women I have no idea. But it didn't take long for everyone in the colony to send him back to London and take up with John Smith. From there on, you probably know the rest."

I squinted in his direction. "I have absolutely no idea what you're talking about."

"My family," he went on, as if I had not spoken, "as I mentioned, some of them came from France. And way back, one of my kin went by the name of Guichard d'Angle and he was the earl of Huntingdon in the fourteenth century. That's the same place that Wingfield's family was from. My kin was a Knight of the Garter and when he was older he was appointed the tutor of Richard the Second, who was just the Prince of Wales at that point, you understand. When Richard became king, he named my great-great kin, Guichard, Earl of Huntingdon. Since then, we've felt kind of responsible for anything that goes on with the folks from the old homeland."

"No, but seriously, what the hell are you talking about?" I growled.

"Heritage. Responsibility. Self-knowledge." He shook his head.

"I mean how does any of this remotely affect me?"

"I am the Earl of Huntingdon," he said.

I waited, but he said nothing further. He seemed to be watching me to see what I was going to do or say. It seemed to be some sort of test.

"Andrews," I finally said, "are you getting any of this?"

"Hm?" Andrews mumbled. "What? Sorry. I wasn't listening—this tea is really good."

"Leave him be," the stranger snapped. "This is only for you."

"*What* is only for me?"

"I am the Earl of Huntingdon," he said again. "I wrote you a letter when you were a child. It used to be in a tin box on this mantel, behind a clock. Your mama showed it to you. Now it's gone and you're in trouble, bad."

I felt a tingling in my arms and heard a buzzing in my head. I began to realize that I might be in my half-dream state again. Or maybe, I thought, it was all hallucination, no reality. I could hear the words that the man was saying, and I could understand that they were perfectly good English words, but I couldn't make them coalesce into anything remotely resembling meaning or sense.

"You didn't stay in Fit's Mill long enough," the man went on, his voice increasingly hypnotic. "You didn't find what you should have found. You got to go back. You got to go to the meeting place, get up with those men, hear what they say."

"No." I tried to move, but found I could not.

"I tried to warn you about all this," he told me. "And so did your mother. But it's too late now. They found you out. They tried to kill you."

"Who tried to kill me?" I had to struggle for every breath.

"But I won't allow that." His voice was fierce, but it was also the most soothing sound I had ever heard in my life. "Because we take care of our own."

An instant calm flooded my body, as if the tea were warming all my blood, and I felt more relaxed than I had since I'd come out of my coma. With that, I closed my eyes and fell dead asleep.

When I awoke, Andrews was gone and I was stretched out on the sofa. The sun was going down, the sky was red, and the storm clouds were gone. Crickets' black tapestry hung in the eastern air and night birds sang out so loudly that I thought they all might be perched on my front porch.

It was delightful to hear one sing out, but it was better when that call was answered, an echo a little way off in the distance. Singing alone is beautiful. Singing together is holy.

Just as I was about to muster the strength to sit up, I heard Andrews clanking around in the kitchen.

"I had a little nap," I called out sleepily.

"You had a hibernation," he answered back. "Do you know it's almost seven?"

"Are you making dinner?"

"God, no. I'm foraging. Somewhere in here is Girlinda's fried chicken."

"All right, but we have to go back to Fit's Mill."

"No!" He appeared in the wide archway between the kitchen and the living room. "I told you: you aren't ever leaving this house. Not ever again. (a) I don't want you to die but more importantly, (b) I don't want Lucinda to kill me. And she would."

I sat up. "Oh, you really don't have to worry about that. She'd be too busy killing me to bother with you. She'd kill me once, take me to the hospital, bring me back, *just* so she could kill me again."

"And you want to risk that because—?"

"The man told me to go," I said, easing up off the sofa. "You weren't, by any chance, awake when he left?"

"No, and I assume you weren't either."

"Right," I said, "but he was clear that I have to go back to Fit's Mill."

Andrews leaned against the archway. His hair was at war with itself, and his face still betrayed a spot of barbecue sauce here and there. He'd changed back into a T-shirt and sweatpants and he was clearly settled in for the evening.

"Now, who was that guy again?" Andrews asked, scratching his arm.

"No idea." I stood.

I made my way past Andrews, into the kitchen, and opened up the fridge. It was packed to the gills with translucent Tupperware containers. I was familiar enough with Girlinda's cooking to suss out most of the contents. I put my hand almost immediately on the large maroon-topped rectangular trove that held her famous fried chicken, renowned in story and song.

She used a bird from her own yard, one that had wandered for all of its life anywhere it wanted to go, eating bugs off of her squash plants, pecking at seeds and berries on the ground. It had roosted in trees and laid, perhaps, a thousand eggs in its lifetime. It had stepped lightly through a dozen winters, leaving hieroglyphics in the snow as it went. It had slumbered peacefully under harvest moons, safe from red foxes and wild dogs inside a coop made from old barn wood. And when its time had come, it had given its life quickly, without anticipation. Then Girlinda lovingly bathed the pieces of the bird in buttermilk and salt for twenty-four hours, until it was silken and tender and soft. Each piece was dipped in flour, then in egg wash, then in cornmeal. The cornmeal had been cut with sage and tarragon and crushed black peppercorns. Then each piece was deep fried individually in duck fat. Nowhere else on earth was there a better piece of fried chicken than the one I was about to eat from Girlinda's maroon-topped Tupperware.

"Found it," I called.

"The chicken?" Andrews actually leapt toward me.

Seconds later we were both eating, chicken in one hand, napkin in the other. Andrews tried to talk, but he was unwilling to keep the chicken out of his mouth long enough to finish a sentence, so nothing was coherent. I gathered that it had something to do with my staying indoors for the rest of my life.

I chewed each bite of chicken very carefully, savoring as well as rending, and we both took our time finishing the meal.

"I'm going to Fit's Mill." I stood up.

"Now?" he managed to say.

"No. Now I'm looking for iced tea and potato salad."

"Oh." He settled back into his chair. "Good idea."

A happy fifteen minutes later, we were sipping the last of the iced tea and staring at empty Tupperware containers.

"Now," I sighed, "if I don't throw up, I might be ready to travel."

Andrews didn't move. "Because the man told you to. The man with the accent."

"Yes."

"But you have no idea who the man is?"

"Right." I nodded. "No idea."

"Well, as you so clearly know what you're doing, count me in." He slumped in his chair.

"The thing is—" I began.

"The thing is," Andrews interrupted, "that you thought the man tried to kill you in the hospital, then you thought he was the one who shot up your truck, then you told me to call Skidmore because he was the mysterious person who tried to kill you in December. And now you want to follow his advice."

"That reminds me," I responded, "I have to get my back window fixed."

"I'm serious with you," he shot back. "I think you might have suffered some kind of oxygen deprivation or something while you were in a coma. I think that it's affected your cognition. Your mental acuity is very skewed—even for you. Which is saying something. You're not going to Fit's Mill tonight."

I stood. "With or without you."

"Wait." He reached into his pocket and produced a nice shiny object. "I have your truck key."

I did likewise and showed him my key ring. "You have a *copy* of my truck key."

I headed for the door.

Somewhere in my mind I knew that what I was doing was ridiculous, and dangerous beyond stupidity. But, as with any compulsion, I felt helpless to resist. The urge to find out who had tried to kill me, what my coma-dreams meant, why I had not felt completely awake and aware since I'd left the hospital—a dozen other impossible questions about my mother and my family—all overwhelmed me. And so I felt my body marching through my front door, onto my porch, headed toward my truck.

"Damn it!" Andrews shouted.

I heard his kitchen chair bang backward onto the floor; heard my front door slam and his feet stomping across the porch.

"I'm driving," he hissed. "At least that."

He passed me, loping toward the truck. Night was coming on. The last of the sunset was gone, and the wind had turned white-cold, a sure snow-sign. The stars, winking on one by one, looked like dots of snow frozen into the Parrish blue sky. Even the moon, low behind black tree silhouettes, was made of ice, late winter's rage. The air had hardened, refusing to allow sweet showers that might pierce the drought of March to the root. Dark clouds were gathering behind the mountains, and snow was on the way.

18.

The drive back to Fit's Mill happened in the kind of silence that is worse than any storm, an unspoken argument that festered and made matters worse. Andrews was livid and I was crazed. We went the longer way around, eschewing the shortcut through the woods. Andrews merely followed the signs on Highway 76. All the way, he had gripped the steering wheel so tightly that his knuckles had drained of color, and the moonlight through the windshield made him a ghost.

Cold air bullied us from behind, pouring in through the broken back window, and small sheets of crackled auto glass littered the floor, the dash; the seats with ice crystals that neither one of us was willing to acknowledge.

All I could think of was that the men in the restaurant had warned us not to return to Fit's Mill. Instead of making me feel sensibly frightened or at least intelligently cautious, the very thought of their threats made me red-faced with anger. For unknown reasons I possessed the confused, righteous indignation of a man unjustly accused.

It was somehow my intention to teach these men a lesson, to show them who I was, what I was made of. Just by presenting myself before them I would teach them that they could never keep me from finding out something that I really wanted to know. I would make it clear to them that no one could come into my own house and try to kill me. I would demonstrate that I had absolutely no fear.

I had no idea what Andrews was thinking. As he edged the truck into a parking space in front of the now-abandoned restaurant, he spoke for the first time since we'd left the house.

"And where do you think you'll find these men now? What do you think you're looking for here?" He didn't turn off the engine.

"They might still be meeting," I suggested, knowing how ridiculous it sounded.

"How would you even know where this meeting is?" he fumed. "And, PS: it started hours ago. It won't still be going on. Do you see that this town is rolled up? That everyone has gone to bed?"

"Maybe they took a break and came back. I mean, what else is there to do in this town?" I cast my eye about the sad street. There were no lights except for the headlights of the truck, no sounds, nothing but the shabby bondage of leafless kudzu stems holding half the town in place. The air continued to chill, and the clouds had come over the mountain, silent and mythically gigantic.

"I know it seems insane," I began.

"Seems?" He banged his forehead on the steering wheel. "Seems insane?"

"But I have intuition," I continued.

As if on cue, we heard singing begin down the block, a large group in a minor key. The lyrics were as foreboding as the storm clouds: "I chanced to look and there I spied a curious book: of past days where sad Heaven did shed a mourning light upon the dead."

"What the hell?" Andrews whispered.

"I've never heard that hymn before," I admitted, opening my door as quietly as I could.

"It's not a hymn," Andrews said, still sitting in the truck, his voice hushed.

"What?" I turned back to face him. "What do you mean it's not a hymn? Can't you hear them singing?"

"Those words," he said, his voice still very soft. "Those are metaphysical lyrics by Henry Vaughan."

"Who?"

"He was a Welsh physician and a poet in the seventeenth century. He had a weird twin brother who was a hermit and an alchemist. They were both nuts."

"How on earth would you know?" I began.

"I had to teach some of their work once," he interrupted me impatiently, "in a course that was mostly about Herbert and Donne."

"Well," I sighed, "that makes me very uncomfortable, and I don't know why."

Still, my legs swiveled out of the truck and began to carry my body toward the sound of the singing.

"Wait," Andrews urged. "How can we just barge in?"

"I don't know," I admitted. But I didn't stop.

Andrews shut off the engine and the lights, and instantly the night grew darker. The snow clouds suddenly overtook the moon. Even its light was gone. My eyes weren't adjusting to the pitch, and I had to stop, unable to see a thing.

"Andrews?" I whispered.

"I can't see," he answered back.

There wasn't any light coming from the direction of the singing. There didn't appear to be any light on earth at that moment.

"You have a flashlight in your truck, right?" he asked.

"Of course," I told him, "but I'm not positive we should alert everyone to our presence."

He snorted. "Yes, well, when we bust into the meeting hall, I think they'll know we're here."

With that we were flooded with blinding light: three or four high-voltage night torches.

A recently familiar voice responded to Andrews. "Oh, they already know you're here."

"Hello, Travis," I said lightly.

"It's Devilin and that English boy," another voice shouted toward the direction of the hall.

Oil lamps illuminated the inside of the small meeting hall. It didn't appear that the room had electricity; there was certainly no heat. The wooden floors were so worn that they looked like dirt. The smoke from hundreds of other nights' lamp flames smudged the walls. The exposed rafters were delicately laced with spiderwebs and the ceiling was nearly black. There were wooden benches and folding chairs scattered without pattern. Andrews and I stood in the double doorway. At the other end of the room there was a battered podium that had been painted long ago with a large, plain letter W. There were no windows.

"Go on in," Travis said from behind.

Andrews and I stepped into the room. There were, perhaps, fifteen men standing around, and one older man at the podium. The lamps made shadows, and some of the faces were completely obscured. There was a tall, thin man in a black suit near the back door. He looked familiar. I thought I might have seen him before, but it was hard to tell.

"Come in, come in," the man at the podium said warmly. "All are welcome here."

"This here is Fever Devilin," Travis said, his hand on my shoulder. "And his friend is from England."

"England?" The older man sounded impressed. "Well, that is something."

"They were told to stay out of town," another voice from behind said loudly.

"Now, now," the older man said, smiling, "I think it might be important to Dr. Devilin to hear something about our society."

Several men laughed. It was not a pleasant sound—more like the noise of crows on carrion.

"Let's all take our seats, then," the older man said, "and I will start again from the beginning."

"Have you been meeting since we saw you this morning?" Andrews was apparently compelled to ask.

More laughter.

"We have a morning service and an evening prayer," Travis explained, "on Wednesdays. Gets us through the week, you might say. We just got here when we heard your truck. They sang. We came to get you. Understand?"

"I see." Andrews took the nearest folding chair.

I found an empty bench; Travis sat beside me. He had his shotgun in his hands. Everyone else sat, and the older man at the podium closed his eyes.

"I am Elder James," he said in a strong voice, "and we are the Sons of Wingfield."

Everyone except for Andrews and me answered as one: "All are welcome here."

"Brother Travis," said Elder James, "please tell our new friends the illustrious origin of our order."

"Gladly," Travis answered, standing, shotgun by his side. "We are the spiritual Sons of Edward Wingfield, the first president of America, born 1550 in Stonely, Huntingdonshire; died in 1631, a member of Parliament. He chartered Jamestown from King James in the year of our Lord 1606 and came to Virginia in 1607. He had recruited one hundred and five good white men, all of whom took the Oath of Allegiance and the Oath of Supremacy. We take those oaths to honor his ways as the first American."

Travis sat down.

I could tell that Andrews was squirming to say something, and I was doing my best with glances and some attempt at telepathy to keep him from speaking up. Luckily, Elder James took the floor in a decidedly dramatic way.

"Lord!" he shouted from the podium.

Nearly everyone in the room jumped.

"Hear me!" he went on, top volume. "We are beset on every side by the heathen, the Godless, the colored filth, the aberrant faith, the wayward, the wicked, and the lost. For over four hundred years we have worked to keep our land free of this contamination. We continue to labor, ridding this world of pestilence and fraction. Wading in the waters of our cankered blood we pull out the disease and purge it from the body of our state. Let no unclean thing touch us, Lord. Let no rank contagion foul our soil. Let no sore, no sickness, no salt of silt betray our skin, our bones, or the purity of our fiber. Snow is white, Lord; moon is white. Sun white hot, and sea-tops white. Rain is cleansing, wind is raking: silence in our footsteps and our single-minded purpose. Bring us the storm, and let us use the thunder. Bring us the storm, let lightning be our sword. Bring us the storm, and let us bend the wind for You, toward your terrible Word, Your awful reckoning. Bring us the storm, Lord, Thy will be done."

The crowd roared as one. "Thy will be done!"

Travis leaned close to me and whispered, "You can see why they didn't want you here."

I nodded, but I had no idea what he was talking about. I had certainly seen lots of church services in small towns and hidden mountain halls. Often they were dark, and filled with the Wrath of God rather than the Love of Jesus. This had been different. There had been no Bible verse, no mention of Christ, no admonition against sin or accusation of the group's danger from satanic influences.

This was a political rally.

Andrews saw that Travis had spoken to me, though clearly hadn't heard what he'd said.

"Someone named Edward Wingfield, from England, was the first president of America?" he whispered.

"He was elected," Travis said in ordinary tones, "as the president of the Jamestown colony in 1607, in May of that year. He would have continued to rule, except for the fact that he made the men work too hard, and they resented it. They got rid of him and Smith took over, kissed up to the dark-skins, the forest monkeys all over there, and got us headed in the wrong direction right away. Don't you agree?"

Andrews smiled. "I'm not even certain I understand what you just said. Maybe it's the accent. I sometime have a hard time understanding certain American dialects. Same thing happens to me in Minnesota."

Of course, Andrews had lived in Georgia for more than twelve years. He was engaging in a kind of deliberate irritation often used to provoke anyone he felt might be guilty of possessing an inferior IQ. I knew I would have to put at stop to it, or Travis would become dangerous. And Andrews was wrong. Travis wasn't stupid.

"I'm more interested in the society," I interrupted. "I've done a significant amount of research in these mountains for years, and I've never even heard a whisper of this group."

"That could be," Travis allowed, "because your interest is primarily academic, as opposed to participatory. I believe it's true that when people around here see you coming, they know you want to study them. That very relationship can produce a certain behavior that alters your findings. The very act of observation can change what is observed. A lesson we learn, for example, from even a casual examination of the study of subatomic physics."

I glanced at Andrews. "Travis is possessed of one of the most remarkable minds I've ever come across," I said quietly.

"Thank you, Doctor," Travis said. He exhibited no false modesty.

Andrews nodded. He instantly realized his mistake, and, to his credit, had decided not to talk.

"I've known him," I continued, "or, heard about him, at least, for most of my life. He and I were the only children in our elementary school who were reading on a college level by the third grade. After that I believe that Travis became home-schooled."

"My parents," he explained to Andrews, "did not have faith in the local school system. They instilled in me a certain secret knowledge the likes of which could never be taught in a government-run educational situation. Most people do not remotely have the ability to absorb a vast awareness of the human condition."

Andrews nodded again, avoiding eye contact with Travis. I had also seen that behavior in Andrews. He appeared to be submissively deferential when, in fact, he was preparing to attack. I'd seen him behave exactly that same way in several rugby matches—just before he'd beaten a referee into the ground. I wasn't certain why he felt such ire toward Travis, unless he had rightly ascertained that Travis was, to a very large extent, insane with barely contained rage.

So I spoke up quickly once more. "You mentioned an Oath of Allegiance and—"

"Anti-Pope," Travis snapped, eyes locked onto Andrews. "Our allegiance is to our own."

"Yes," I answered uncertainly.

"I was raised Church of England," Andrews said proudly. "We started all that."

"You know, Travis," I said instantly, "your observation is very interesting to me—that I might influence the behavior of my folk informants just by the very fact that I think of them as *informants*. Of course, I've worried about that for most of my so-called academic career. Or, not so much worried about it as realized it was a problem. Until, that is, I came to the conclusion that any conversation between any two people carries with it a certain degree of that gestalt. The idea that I'm observing the conversation from my own point of view as well as participating in it, and the other person is doing exactly the same thing, renders any conversation a dilemma. That concept can drive you mad, or it can make you decide that all conversation is futile, or, as I finally decided, it can redouble your effort to genuinely listen to another human being—in every conversation, large or small. So—"

"Dr. Devilin," Elder James interrupted from his podium, "I sense that you are a confused man."

All eyes turned toward Elder James.

"You are a man who suffers from deep inner conflict," he continued. "A man who wants so badly to know himself, but is, at the same time, terrified of what he will discover."

Andrews couldn't resist. "Someone's been reading your diary," he whispered.

"Did our friend from foreign shores have a question?" Elder James boomed, glaring at Andrews.

Before I could stop him, Andrews stood.

"Yes I do." He glanced in Travis's direction. "Do you people meet all the time? We were here having barbecue this morning, and some of these men were going to a meeting then."

"We are in special meetings," Elder James responded, working hard to demonstrate his patience. "Several groups of brothers have gathered. We have visitors from far and near with us today, with many more services to come. But that really isn't your question, is it, brother Englishman?"

"Dr. Andrews is currently full of questions," I mumbled, mostly to Travis.

"I can see that on his face." Travis nodded, and then called out, "Ask the one question that's on your face, Dr. Andrews."

"It's not a question so much as an observation," he said thoughtfully, as if he were in a graduate student discussion group. "I am actually familiar with Edward Maria Wingfield. He was born in 1550 at Stonely Priory in Huntingdon, which is now Cambridge. He was the son of Thomas and Margaret, and was raised Church of England. The middle name, pronounced mah-RYE-uh, derived from Mary Tudor, sister of King Henry the Eighth. The father had renounced his calling as a priest, and died when young Edward was seven. As a young man Edward was admitted to Lincoln's Inn, the law school, and by 1593 he was a member of Parliament. And in 1605, his money got progress toward the Jamestown Colony moving."

Many of the men in the room were nodding. Elder James began to smile.

"You speak like one of us," he said, clearly surprised. "You have some of our knowledge, and, perhaps, share our convictions."

Andrews held up his index finger and spoke rapid fire. "Not quite. I am merely an Englishman who knows his country. Wingfield was a paranoid idiot who nearly destroyed the Jamestown Colony because of his terror of the indigenous population in this country. He set the buildings in a place that he felt would be easy to defend from attack but was, in all other ways, useless. The land he chose could not grow crops and people began to starve to death. His solution was to work the men harder until many grew sick and died. He was eventually deposed from his position and sent packing, back to England, never to return to the New World again. If that had not happened, there would likely be no America at all. No English-speaking America, at least. So when I say that you are extremely wrong-headed—"

I flew to my feet. "I see absolutely no reason to listen to this foreigner tell us about our own country!"

Travis only smiled. "Nice try, Fever."

He took hold of his shotgun, but did not point it at me, or at Andrews.

Elder James was still smiling. "Dr. Devilin, I believe the time for all prevarication is at an end. You were warned not to come here. Your truck was shot. Travis told you to clear out. And still, here you are. Are you determined to be the author of your own undoing?"

"Aren't we all?" I asked. "But I hope you will believe me when I say that I do not have the same disrespect for your enclave as does Dr. Andrews. He has disdain for every organization on the planet. That is the truth. He despises all religions equally, all forms of government, all systems of economics and, as far as I can determine, every sporting rule ever written."

"I do." Andrews nodded enthusiastically.

"I, on the other hand," I went on, "would very much like to know what I've done to this august assemblage to provoke such ire as evidenced by a shattered truck window, and such rejection at the hands of my old school chum Travis."

A silence hung in the hall, a winding sheet of nameless fears and unspoken accusations. It muffled my ears as if I'd been deafened.

At last Elder James spoke up. "Could we all take our seats, and continue with the meeting?"

Everyone sat, some more reluctantly than others.

"We were about to catalogue our accomplishments since the last meeting," the Elder continued, "but that is not for outside ears. So I will, instead, encourage our members to witness. Anyone who wishes to do so may tell our guests why he has joined our group. This is our practice whenever strangers, potential new members, or women are present."

Some of the men looked down at the floor, clearly uncomfortable at the prospect of speaking in front of the rest. Travis, as I might have suspected, stood once more, laying his shotgun on the bench beside him.

"As you all know, my father helped to start this particular chapter," he began, avoiding my gaze, "but Sons of Wingfield would be considered the oldest fraternal organization in America. And we have chapters all over the country. All part of this nation. We're made up of autonomous groups that work in their own communities. Each club raises its own funds and chooses its own projects to improve the lives of all community residents. Members must be of legal age and believe in a Supreme Being."

"So this is like a Rotary Club," Andrews interjected, "or the Rosicrucians."

Travis smiled and turned his way. "You'd best not make light of the group, Dr. Andrews."

Andrews closed his mouth immediately and his face went white. I have no idea how Travis managed it, but his sentence had been one of the most threatening group of syllables I had ever heard. Clearly Andrews had felt the same.

"We derive from the original settlers of the Jamestown Colony," Travis went on. "When John Smith took over, several of our founders kept, in secret, to Wingfield's precepts and dictates."

"And those are—?" I asked as politely as I could possibly manage to.

"That our country was meant for certain people," he said immediately, "and not for others. The rest of our pledge belongs only to the initiated."

"Yes." I looked down. "I see."

"You think that you know us," Travis snapped viciously. "But you don't."

"Hang on a minute," Andrews chimed in, unwisely, I thought. "Why did you make such a point of telling us that you have chapters all over the country? You said it twice."

"I did?" Travis asked.

But he asked in such a way as to make me realize that he knew he had mentioned it twice. He was trying to tell us something.

"Travis," Elder James said softly, "I think you might could tell your friend who shot up his truck."

It seemed an odd turn of events, although not much of what was happening in the small, strange hall made sense to me. I assumed, at the time, that I was continuing my flirtation with divided realities: some of what I saw and felt was real, some was imaginary.

"A hunter did it," Travis said to the Elder. "I already told them that."

"But he was not from around here, Dr. Devilin," Elder James said, leaning down hard on his podium. "People come from all over America to hunt wild boar in Georgia. Some even come from as far away as Chicago."

"Chicago." Travis nodded.

"I bring it up, son," the elder continued, "because I want you to know how seriously we take pride in our local families. It does not matter to most of us what your mother did, or how your father made a living, or even that you yourself left us for such a long while. You and your family are deeply troubled, wrong about most things, and too odd to ever be close to most of us. But you're one of ours. You're our trouble. You're our mess."

Andrews nodded, clearly reading things in the words, and in the room, that I could not. "The man who shot at us," he said, "was from Chicago. He's been hunting. And he's a member of your society."

"What?" I asked, hushed. "Chicago?"

Andrews turned my way. "That's why there's such a palpable air of ambivalence in this hall. One of their members shot at you, for some reason, so they have allegiance to him. But he's a Yankee and an outsider, and they also have some obligation to you as well."

I cocked my head, not quite certain I'd correctly heard what he was saying. "If I weren't brain-traumatized would I have come to the same conclusions as you've just done?"

"Honestly?" Andrews asked. "Probably before I did."

"I feel a little light-headed," I told him.

"We're going to continue with our meeting now," Elder James interrupted. "It might be time for you all to leave on back home."

Andrews stood immediately. "Excellent."

He grabbed my arm before I could speak, and in dizzying seconds we were out the door and into the night.

19.

We were on Highway 76 before we spoke again.

"Am I still hallucinating," I finally asked, "or did you actually have a better insight into what was going on in that hall than I did?"

"Sorry." He smiled. "You can't be Holmes every day of your life. Sometimes you have to be Watson."

"Then tell me, Sherlock," I sneered, "what did I miss?"

"The main thing," he said instantly, as if he'd been holding his breath waiting to tell me, "is that you don't seem to read this Travis person."

"In what way?"

"You don't trust him, that's obvious. I mean it's obvious to him, too. So you see everything he does through a filter of suspicion. That colors your reaction and you miss the subtleties of his communication. You and he have some sort of subconscious connection that you don't seem to recognize—but he does."

"You've been reading too much Jung again." I slumped a little in my seat.

"As it happens," he said, "*The Red Book* has just come out in a very lovely hardback coffee-table edition."

"*The Red Book*?" I tried to focus. "That's Jung's diary after he broke up with Freud?"

"It's the Holy Grail of the Unconscious," he answered, "but that's hardly the point. The point is that you can't see Travis the way I can. First I'd like to know why that's true, but second and more important: I think you ought to fix that. Because he just told you, as best he could, who tried to kill you."

I let that sink in. I allowed certain buried memories to rise to the surface, like letting old ghosts out of a crypt.

"Travis was from one of the families that delighted in torturing my parents when I was little," I began. "Travis himself was a member of the bully enclave that impelled me to leave Blue Mountain as soon as I could. He's very smart, I know that, but his intellectual abilities don't do him any good because of his disposition toward bile. He hates almost everything. And it's a kind of white-hot sickness; it festers his blood and boils his brain. He's the all-American psychotic racist, he loathes women and revels in degrading them, and anyone who doesn't see things his way is supposed to be exterminated while he swears and screams and spits at them. He's the primary pestilence on the green tree of our nation and I wouldn't mind if he sank into a pit of flesh-eating vipers."

Andrews sat in silence for a moment, letting my tirade permeate the air in the truck, despite the chilly wind roaring in through the back window.

Then he cleared his throat and said, as casually as he could manage to, "Don't hold back. Tell us what you really think."

I exhaled. "I suppose I do have a bit of pent-up something-or-other where he's concerned."

"Which is my point." He continued to watch the road.

"And you feel that my attitude toward him may be incorrect."

"I don't know about that," he dismissed. "He could easily be the next Hitler, I see that, but it's just possible that you're misjudging him based on your past association with him—a time when you were both boys, children. Personally, I'd hate to be judged for the rest of my life on my own schoolyard behavior. And my point is that your attitude toward him clouds your ability to see who he really is, or at the very least, what he's really trying to say."

"And what, please tell me, is he trying to say?" I glared at his profile.

"He gave you every kind of clue in the book," Andrews answered accusingly, "and you didn't pick up on a single one."

"Clues about what?" I felt impossibly thickheaded.

"He was trying to tell you who shot you!" Andrews blasted. "Jesus. He had everything but charts and a hand puppet!"

I sighed again, and looked out the window. I slowly began to realize that I had not been especially observant in the meeting hall. Andrews was correct in his assessment: I had dismissed nearly everything Travis had done or said because he was, in some ways, invisible to me. I had the idea that I already knew everything about him, about who he was and what he was doing in this lifetime, so I casually, even deliberately, ignored everything about him.

"This is a problem," I said, still staring out at the road.

"I know," he responded.

"No, I mean, this is a problem that most people have. A problem of the human condition. We get ahold of some kind of shorthand in understanding people, and we think it works, and we use it to assess, categorize, and then, very often, dismiss people. It's the basis of stereotyping, and profiling, and several other very sorry words that end in *i-n-g*."

"Not sure I follow," he said.

"People hear your accent, for example," I explained, "and they think, 'Oh, he's an English guy.' And they think that means they know you, know who you are. So they don't have to think any more about it. That's the shorthand: English guy, got it, now I don't have to think anything more about him, don't have to make any more genuine contact with him. All the rest is based on that."

He nodded, but his brow was furled.

"All right," I sighed, "I personally feel that the worst case of this sort of thinking has to do with race, with skin color. People look at something so facile, so obvious as the color of a person's skin and think that they know something—know a lot, in fact—about that person. I think it's the worst propensity of the American nature."

"Well," he said, hesitantly, obviously struggling to understand, "racial problems—it's not just an American thing, right?"

"Right," I agreed, "but I don't know other countries, I only know this one, because I live here. And I'm telling you it's one of the worst qualities we have, the notion that we can figure out everything about a person on first glance, as if that first look could give you every bit of information you would ever need. It's the poison of racism at its root: instant judgment, instant dismissal, without any actual thought whatsoever. It's destroying the nation."

The truck slowed a little. Andrews continued to appear deep in thought. The moon broke from behind the clouds and suddenly silvered the road ahead, the pines, even the roadside weeds.

"I don't believe I've ever heard you discuss this sort of thing," he finally said. "Not in all the years of our association. And it isn't as if our primary concern here is, you know, racism in America. I mean, where the hell did all that come from, Fever?"

I stared out at the white, white road. "I don't know."

"Well, you're pretty worked up about it."

"No I'm not," I protested. "I'm just thinking out loud."

"Really?" he asked." Look at your right hand."

I glanced down. My hand was clutching the door handle so hard that it looked like a ball of snow. All of the blood was gone from it. I took a deliberate moment to loosen my grip, trying to calm myself. Then, without knowing why, I felt like crying.

"Chester did it," I said quietly. "Chester made this happen."

He nodded as if he understood, then slowed the truck a little more, and looked right at me. "Who the hell is Chester?"

I avoided looking at him. "One of the monsters from my dreams, or from my memory, or from something that my mother told me that's mixing in my dreams and my memories. Or a figment of my imagination. Or a desperate hallucination because I was in a coma for three months. Take your pick."

"You know," he ruminated philosophically, "you were pretty messed up before you died, but since you came back? You're absolutely gone around the bend."

"Yes, all right," I grumbled, "but here's what I know about Chester."

"Now *he's* the man who tried to kill you."

"No," I answered, "he's the man who killed T-Bone Morton."

"Well then," he mocked, shaking his head, "now we're getting somewhere. Who the hell is T-Bone Morton?"

"A jazz saxophone player from 1926."

"I'm going to run the truck off the road now," he said casually, "if it's all the same to you."

"T-Bone Morton is a jazz saxophone player from Chicago."

"Chicago."

"Look, don't run this truck off the mountain just yet, do you mind?" I sat up, suddenly revitalized by something of which I was not quite conscious, something that felt very much like the first moment of a new day. "I actually think I might be—I'm beginning to see the connection between my weird dreams and my, well, equally weird life, actually."

"Okay." Andrews cleared his throat.

"And it has to do with the relationship these dreams have to some strenuously buried memories, things my mother must have told me."

"Jung's idea, of course," he began hesitantly, "is that dreams are a kind of window to your unconscious. And when you can look through that window clearly, you can find solutions to things in your waking life."

"Exactly," I agreed. "I have to be a kind of psychic archaeologist."

"I'm very uncomfortable with that phrase," Andrews allowed.

"Be that as it may," I assured him, "I'm going to excavate certain memories, dig into the images. Like Theseus."

"Wait. Like Theseus?"

"Haven't we talked about this before—the theory of the Minotaur? The labyrinth on Minos is actually a metaphor for the human subconscious. Everybody is Theseus. Everybody has to dive into the caves of the mind and slay the Minotaur, the monsters that live there, the troubles that lead to psychoses."

We were nearing my home, and I was feeling more awake than I had since I'd come home from the hospital. The cold air rushing through the cab was like a plunge into freezing water. I felt astonishingly invigorated. Just as I was about to tell Andrews that I had turned a corner where my health was concerned, it started to snow very hard, and suddenly the entire world turned white.

20.

Back home, safe in my living room, we sat for a while watching the snow and thinking. I had started a fire, made espresso, and settled into my chair close to the flames.

Andrews had collapsed onto the sofa, shoes off, feet toward the hearth.

"I should probably remind you," he said, raising his head to take a sip from his cup, "that the mythological Minotaur was a product of a mixed relationship: the queen of the island mated with a beautiful white bull. Her love for the bull was a punishment from the gods. And whom the gods would punish they first make mad. I bring it up because—"

"Half of what I'm saying seems insane," I interrupted, "the product of scattered images and half-conscious concepts. I know that. I know that I'm not right. I was afraid of this state of mind when I first woke up. I can confess that now, to you and to myself. But I've had a few experiences that I thought were hallucinations but turned out to be real, as confirmed by your perceptions. I've taken a bit of courage from that. But mostly, something seems to be falling into place."

"Okay," he sighed, obviously exasperated. "First: what do you mean about the hallucinations that turned out to be real? I mean, I haven't seen any bats or green lizards."

"The man from New Orleans," I said softly. "He's pretty strange, and he could easily have been a phantasm of my troubled mind. But he really was in a Cadillac and then he really was in my kitchen, right?"

"I'll give you that," he admitted. "That guy's very odd. So, to continue: what's falling into place?"

I stared into the fire. The sparks rose up like red stars, shooting upward, all the way to the top the chimney, I imagined, and into the snow-blurred sky. "I think I'm beginning to remember something important that my mother told me when I was a child. And if I could remember everything entirely, I believe that I could not only solve some questions concerning the person who shot me, but I could also slay a few of my own very serious minotaurs."

"Oh." He set down his cup, lay back, and folded his arms across his chest. "Well, that is something."

"Yes, it is," I insisted. "I might be able to shake loose from a couple dozen difficulties that have kept me on the strange side of life for most of my born days. The demons that have kept me off balance and odd. I mean I might be waking up from *that*."

"Only an unstable individual," he countered, "suffers from the illusion that he can escape his basic nature. That's my belief."

"But what if being 'off balance and odd' isn't my basic nature after all?"

"Look, Fever," he sighed, "you've had a rough time of it recently. I mean, you got shot, you got dead, and you came back. You're in a bit of limbo now, don't you think? I wouldn't make too much of any insights you think you might be having in this condition. Things will shake down. You'll get back to normal soon enough. What you want is rest, good food, Lucinda—and my scintillating company."

"I remain undeterred by your little speech," I told him briskly.

"What if I could find documentary evidence? That is, what if I could find something like proof of my theories?"

"What *theories*?" he snapped. "You're just rambling."

I leaned forward, more energetic than ever. "I'm saying: what if I could find tangible facts about Chester and T-Bone and their connection to me and my family? What if I could prove to you—and what if this very unusual man from New Orleans—"

"Enough!" Andrew sat up and glared at me.

I exhaled. His face was so tense I thought he might hurt himself, and his eyes were rimmed in red. Clearly there was more to his current state than I understood.

"Why are you so upset?" I asked.

He ran his hand through his hair, massaged his forehead, and then tugged absently on his earlobe. "The truth?"

"Of course the truth."

"You're scaring me." He shrugged.

I think I cocked my head a little like a dog.

"You're not the same person you were, Fever." His voice cracked. He swallowed. He was clearly very upset. "I'm afraid something is really wrong with you. I'm trying not to demonstrate my alarm to you, but there you have it: I'm scared."

I had no idea how to react. I couldn't remember another time in our entire acquaintance that Andrews had spoken so emotionally.

"Everyone's concerned," he went on, managing to collect himself a little. "Lucinda more than anyone, of course. You have to . . . you should reel yourself in a bit, is all I'm saying."

I shook my head. I wanted to reassure him, but I didn't want to lie. "I don't think it would be the right thing to do if 'reeling myself in' means not being honest about what I'm going through. And you have to give me a little leeway, don't you, given that I was—that all those things happened to me: shot, dead, coma, everything. And then someone took another whack at me in the woods, blew out my truck's rear window, my beloved truck, and then I was threatened with *barbecue*, for God's sake."

That made him smile. "You weren't threatened *with* barbecue, you were threatened *by* barbecue."

"I stand corrected."

"Well, you'd think I'd be used to your very strange peregrinations by now." He sighed. "But you always seem to find new and different ways to worry me."

"It takes a lot of planning," I agreed. "I make charts and everything."

"So what is it that you think you need to do now?"

"I guess we could go to sleep now and talk about the rest in the morning," I answered, "if you're tired."

"I'm beat with a brickbat." He slumped back into the sofa. "I may just sleep here. What I don't understand is how you're so energetic."

"I know," I marveled. "I feel the same way I did a long time ago when I had a near-fatal allergic reaction and they gave me steroids and Adrenalin. I think I could lift up this house. Oh, and let's take my truck in tomorrow morning first thing to get a new rear window."

"*Rear Window*," he mumbled. "I love that movie. Why couldn't you do that, be like that: the grouchy Jimmy Stewart–style invalid? Just sit around your house all day."

"Because you don't have that kind of luck," I assured him. "Are you really going to sleep right there?"

He didn't answer, which I took to mean *yes*.

I felt increasingly more manic, so I eased out of my chair as quietly as I could and tiptoed upstairs. I wasn't really thinking about anything in particular when I headed into my mother's room. I simply seemed to drift in that direction. I flicked on the light and passed through her doorway into another world.

The smell of it took hold of me, the ancient dried lavender and rosemary, the dust, the ever-so-faint presence, after all those years, of an Avon perfume called Unforgettable—her favorite, or so she'd told me when I was seven or eight. I'd saved up money from chores and odd jobs nearly half a year to buy her a small bottle of it for Christmas. Clearly the bottle was still somewhere in the room, though I'd never found it.

I suppose I was hoping that I might stumble upon some secret, mystical trove of information about—about what, exactly, I didn't know. I had spent so many hours in that room when I was a child and my parents had gone—off touring their show. I had always hoped, in those days, to find out something more about my mother, something that would explain her to me. I had thought, then, that hidden somewhere in things might be the key to perfect under-standing: why she seemed to think of me as the price she'd had to pay for something wrong she'd done. When I'd first learned about sex, I'd come to the conclusion that she'd had sex with my father, gotten an unwanted pregnancy, and had the child because of the straightlaced community in which she lived. It only took me a short while to realize that my mother cared about the moral dictates of our little community only marginally more than she cared about German opera, which she hated. She would often actually spit at the mere mention of Wagner's name.

So I knew at a relatively early age that guilt had not made her treat me like penance instead of a person. She had no guilt gene. She cheated on my father several times a day when she thought she could get away with it. He either didn't know, which seemed unlikely to me, or didn't care, which seemed incomprehensible to me. Either way, I remained baffled about their relationship even long after they were both dead and buried.

Still, sitting down on the floor in my mother's room was an ex-periment in nostalgia and regret bordering on madness, as usual. A gaggle of salamanders gyred in my gut. I did my best to battle the melancholy ghosts, one by one, as they seeped into my pores from the very air around me. Then, a bit less commonly, my heart began to beat faster and my breathing grew shallow. My eyes stung and my lips dried. Something in my stomach threatened to return to my mouth, and sweat beaded at my hairline. The pounding in my chest grew more profound, and I could hear it in my ears, suddenly louder than thunder. All I could think, for some reason, was, "True! Nervous, very, very dreadfully nervous I had been and am; but why will you say that I am mad?"

I realized that I was glaring at the floor in front of me as if I might be able to see through the wood, and it suddenly occurred to me that the quotation from Poe might be another gift from my unconscious: there might be something buried underneath those planks. I considered that my feeling of nausea might well be more existential than gastronomical.

I leaned down, trying to see if there was any clue anywhere that some of the planks might not be battened down. Nothing presented itself immediately, but just the thought of investigation made some of my uneasiness abate. I reached into my jeans pocket and found a quarter. I used it as a pry, inserting in first between one floorboard and another to see if anything felt loose. The first couple of tries were fruitless, but the fifth time found a bit of a disjunction. With only a little effort, a three-foot section of wide, well-worn plank came up. There, underneath, in a dark wooden hollow: a small metal box. It was another antique candy box like the one that had been stolen from my mantel. This one was red with silver outlines and seemed to depict a great oak tree under which two lovers were kissing, but the box was so dented and dirty that the tree could have been a waterfall, and the lovers might have been two great fish.

I reached in, collected the box, sat back, and set it in my lap.

Before I opened it, I took a second to let the wonder of it sink in. Hundreds of times before, in the home where I grew up, I had spent so many lonely hours waiting for my parents to return, searching all over the house for any hint as to who and what they really were. After all those years, I could still unearth something so significant as this hidden treasure. Or was it that I had half-remembered something my mother had told me when I was young? It seemed unlikely, as I took in a few deep breaths, that I would have come up with the idea to tear up floorboards unless I had already known, somewhere in the dark wilderness of Mnemosyne, that something was there. And I would only have known about it if my mother had told me. So, I reckoned that I had accessed some hidden switch that had illuminated another maternal land mine. Only this one was still ticking. It hadn't exploded yet. And while a part of me desperately wanted to return the tin box to its hiding place, put the board back, and forget the whole thing, the worst part of me had to see what was inside. I even heard my mother's voice echoing in ancient air. "Don't do it, Fever. Don't run after this thing. Forget all about it."

Against advice from the dead and my own better judgment, I snapped open the lid. Inside the tin box there were three documents. The first one appeared to be an article from a very old newspaper. I read it slowly.

"Anonymous parties are seeking the last known location of the possible son of Ferdinand Joseph LaMothe, known as 'Jelly Roll' Morton. LaMothe was born into a Creole community in downtown New Orleans, Louisiana. He became Ferdinand Morton by Anglicizing the name of his stepfather, Mouton, and took up the nickname 'Jelly Roll' as a piano player in the Storyville district where he invented jazz in 1902. His 'Jelly Roll Blues' was the first jazz composition ever published, in 1915. His parents were never married. He himself had several children out of wedlock, but our concern is with one of his sons, the musician called T-Bone Morton, a major, though little-known exponent of the Sidney Bechet style of soprano saxophone playing. T-Bone (no Christian name is known) lived for a time in Paris where he served well in

WWI and subsequently became a minor Parisian celebrity in the hot jazz scene of the early 1920s. He returned to America after the death of his wife, said to be the radical daughter of the winemaking family Simard, with their infant daughter. After some trouble in a Chicago dance hall, reportedly at a King Oliver concert, T-Bone Morton and his daughter disappeared. No further record of T-Bone Morton or his daughter can be found at the present time. Any person or persons with information as to their whereabouts should contact Edwin Cross at the Clayton *Tribune*."

The second document was a letter dated 1937.

> *Dear Mr. Newcomb,*
>
> *Thank you for your interest. It was not generally the custom of this hospital to keep records concerning the prostitutes some twenty years ago, but you are in luck. The person about whom you inquire was called Eulalie Echo, but happily for your search, was in fact the daughter of the prominent New Orleans business family Zatarain from Gretna in the Parish of Jefferson. They sent a rather sizeable money contribution to the hospital and the woman was treated here as a normal patient. She did indeed have a son, named Chester in our records, though no birth certificate survives. You may wish to know that the mother was a drunkard and that the baby suffered some brain damage. The patient was prescribed cocaine by her attending physician to help with the drinking problem. I pray this information suffices, as it is the entirety of our knowledge on the subject.*

The letter was signed by a hospital administrator.

The final bit of gold was a wrinkled black-and-white photograph. It was a picture of a beautiful young woman, dressed for church, standing in front of a 1930-something maroon Hudson Terraplane, the kind with a waterfall front grill—a fairly expensive automobile for our part of the world in those days. On the back, in my mother's handwriting, it said "Birdie, 1943." Our house, my house, was in the background.

I strained to remember any hint of a conversation or a speech from my mother that might have been hidden somewhere in the locked box of my own familial recollections. Nothing came to me, but it seemed obvious that these things had been hidden with a purpose, and that I had been told about them sometime in my childhood. The fact that I had proof for Andrews, only moments after I had vowed to procure same, was a bit too eerie for scrutiny, I thought.

So, instead, I simply put everything in the box, closed it, clutched it to my chest, replaced the floorboard, and got to my feet.

As soon as I stood, I felt a wave of exhaustion threaten to knock me back down to the floor. I had a moment of panic, afraid that I would fall asleep again and somehow forget what I'd just found. I thought it would be a good idea, then, for me to bang the tin box hard on the back of my hand. It really hurt, and I made a very strange sound.

Apparently it awakened Andrews, and he called out from downstairs.

"What the hell are you doing up there?" he wanted to know. "And shut up while you're doing it!"

"I found something," I answered him. "Come up here, would you?"

"No!"

"Andrews, seriously, I found something important. Proof of everything."

There was a moment of silence.

"Everything?" he said.

"Well, not everything in the world," I admitted, staggering unsteadily out of my mother's room. "But proof of some of the things we've been talking about."

I made it out of my mother's room and into the hallway a few steps toward the top of the stairs. I could see that Andrews was sitting up, rubbing his face, trying to wake up. How long had I been sitting in my mother's room, I wondered. It seemed like minutes, but Andrews had been deeply asleep.

"I don't know what you mean," he mumbled, "and/or I don't believe you. Plus, what the hell time is it?"

I had no idea what time it was.

"Fever?" Andrews said as he stood up. "Are you still there?"

"Sorry," I answered. "Right here."

"That's it." He stumbled toward the stairs. "Time for you to go to bed!"

"No—hold on." I made it to the first step at the top of the stairs and sat down, my head still a bit fuzzy. The knuckles of my left hand where I'd banged it were red and beginning to swell.

Andrews finally saw me and got up the stairs in three or four great leaping steps. It was very touching, I thought.

"Look." I held up the box.

"What did you do to your hand?"

"In this box," I went on, "I have proof of T-Bone Morton, Chester, and someone named or called 'Birdie.'"

"What?" He glared. "You need to put some ice on that hand."

"No," I protested drowsily, "but this box—"

"I see your little box—wait, is this the thing you were going on about in the hospital? The one that was stolen?"

"No," I told him. "This is another tin box. It has buried treasure."

"You had this hidden up in your room all the time? You really are a genuinely troubled individual. Dangerously twisted."

"I did not have this in my room," I whined. "I found it up in my mother's. Under the floorboards. Like 'The Tell-Tale Heart.'"

"Oh. Okay." He reached down and took my arm. "Let's get you to bed now. You've had a big day."

"Don't you want to see this stuff?" I nearly shoved the tin box into his face.

"It'll keep," he said patiently. "You really want some sleep now. Come on."

"You don't take this seriously," I realized as he was pulling me to my feet. "You think this is something fabricated."

I pulled my arm away from his grasp and staggered backward.

"What the hell?" he growled.

"Come on into my mother's room," I insisted, my voice a bit higher than I wanted it to be. "I'll show you the loose floorboards."

"Do you honestly expect me to believe that you just sauntered up here tonight and miraculously found evidence of your deeply troubled ruminations just like that?"

I turned quickly to go back into my mother's room, lost my balance, and collapsed onto the hallway floor.

"That's it for you, buckaroo," Andrews said, completely out of patience. "You're getting into bed now or I'm calling Lucinda."

I struggled to stand, couldn't quite figure out where I was or what I was holding in my hand, and then everything went black.

21.

When I came to, it was morning. It was early, the sun was barely up, and it had snowed quite a bit during the night. Like most early spring snowstorms, it wouldn't last. The sun would rise, the snow would melt, and crocus and jonquil bulbs would all be happier. But the first look out my window was cold and white.

I heard voices downstairs, and after considering that Andrews might, indeed, be talking to himself, I recognized that the other voice was Lucinda's. She sounded very angry. I thought, then, that staying in bed and pretending to sleep might be my best option. But after a minute more, I decided that I had to rise and take my medicine.

I sniffed, ran my hand through my hair, and sat up. I was still in my clothes from the day before, including boots. I got to my feet and was suddenly very eager to brush my teeth.

Alas, the second my boots hit the floor Andrews and Lucinda had stopped talking.

A moment of silence was followed by a bellowing voice.

"Fever Devilin, you get your be-hind down here! I need to kick it all the way to *Memphis*!" Lucinda's voice—though quite loud and genuinely angry—was still music to my ears.

I shifted my weight, tested my legs, and launched myself out of my room. All things considered, everything went smoothly.

I made it down the stairs and into the kitchen without a single hitch.

The kitchen was warm. The countertops took on the gold of the early morning sun, and a kind of haze hung in the air of the room, doubtless from the cooking oil Andrews had used to fry his eggs. He was seated in front of an empty plate, a generous gathering of paper towels tucked into the collar of his sweatshirt. Lucinda sat in front of a glass of orange juice, turning it distractedly. She was dressed for work, in her hospital whites.

"It snowed last night," I said, delighted, headed toward the espresso machine.

"Thank you, Captain Obvious." Andrews, clearly, was in no mood for my brighter side.

"I'm working on having you arrested." Lucinda was so mad at me that she wouldn't look up from her glass.

I rested against the kitchen counter and really took them in. Both were simmering, and I certainly understood why.

"Look," I began softly, "I know that you're both worried about me."

"Not me," Andrews interrupted. "I think you're an idiot."

"And I'm just mad," Lucinda chimed in.

"Yes," I conceded, "but what's at the root of all that discomfort? You're concerned about my health. And rightly so. But if I could just say this: I wouldn't be the person that I am if I just wanted to loll about the house not caring what happened to me. I mean, can either of you honestly say that I'm the sort of person who would do that? Would I ever just let Skidmore handle it; not want to get involved? No matter who had been shot in my house? And the fact that, well, *I* was the one who was shot in my house, can you possibly imagine that I would just say, 'All right, fine, let the sheriff handle this, I'll just knit and watch PBS?' Seriously? Have you met me?"

Andrews pinched his lips together. They were thin, and then

they disappeared altogether. "He does have a point," he admitted softly after a moment.

Lucinda finally looked up at me. "Is it too late for me to get out of this relationship?"

I smiled. "Yes."

"Okay, then." She stood. "I'm going to work."

She downed her juice and headed for the sink with her glass, but I managed to catch hold of her arm. "You understand that I really . . . appreciate your concern, right?"

"Damn it, Fever," she said softly.

I leaned close and kissed her on the cheek. "I'll take that as a yes. And?"

"What?" She looked down.

"I love you."

She sighed.

"This is a—I'm living in a brave new world, then," Andrews stammered. "Last night Dr. Devilin was rambling on about race in America. This morning he says those three little words that I, frankly, didn't think he knew how to say. Strange days indeed."

I was still staring at Lucinda. "I don't say it often enough. But you know it's always there."

"I know." She nodded.

A very difficult silence reigned in the kitchen for far too long before Andrews saved the day.

"So. What the hell was it that you think you found last night?" he wanted to know.

"You didn't look?" I couldn't believe it.

"At what?" Lucinda asked.

"He claims to have found something in his mother's room last night," Andrews explained. "But when he fell down, I lost interest in his fantasies."

"I can't believe you didn't look at what I found. Where's the tin?"

"The tin box?" Lucinda asked. "You found it?"

"It's another tin box," Andrews said, rolling his eyes, "that magically appeared in his mother's room, under the floorboards."

"Like 'The Tell-Tale Heart,'" I mumbled. "Did I say that last night?"

"It's probably still on the floor up there," Andrews sniffed. "I really didn't want to play any reindeer games last night. I was tired, I was irritated, and I didn't believe a word of what he said. And then he passed out."

I headed out of the kitchen and up the stairs. "Wait until you see this stuff."

"I have to go to work," Lucinda called after me.

"No," I insisted. "Just wait a minute. Just—you have to see this."

I took two or three steps at a time, landed at the top of the stairs, and saw the red-rimmed tin sitting there, as if it had been waiting patiently just for me. Then I had a sudden, prickly feeling that it had been waiting for me for a couple of decades. I drastically reduced my pace. I seemed to pick up the box in slow motion. There, sitting on the floor beside the tin, was my mother, dressed in her black dress, arms folded, frowning.

"I heard a preacher on the radio this morning," she told me. "He said that if God had wanted the races to live together, He would have made us all the same color."

Then she started laughing so much that I thought she might choke.

"You showed me this box after you told me about that," I whispered. "When I was eleven."

She nodded.

"You showed me where it was hidden." I stared, but it was getting harder to see her.

She nodded.

"Why didn't I remember until now?"

And she was gone.

I squeezed my eyes shut. The vaguest possible hint of Unforget-table perfume hung in the air.

"Fever?" Lucinda called. "Are you talking to us?"

I reached down and retrieved the tin. "What?"

"Are you talking to yourself up there?" Andrews yelled.

I stared for a moment at the place where I had seen my mother sitting.

"Yes," I answered him after a moment.

God bless her, Lucinda called into the hospital after she'd taken a quick look at the contents of the red tin. She only allowed that she'd be a half an hour late, but at least it gave me time to get a few things clear in my mind. I didn't always have to say things out loud before they became real, but I did then.

I splayed the three items on the kitchen table, facing Andrews and Lucinda.

"This first one," I began, haltingly, "the photograph of 'Birdie,' is jogging something uncomfortable from my childhood. I re-member my parents arguing about money left to us by my great-grandmother. My father didn't want anything to do with the inheritance, though he never told me why. The argument was their worst, the angriest words I ever heard between my parents. My father won. I remember my mother calling the woman *Birdie*. And I also recall—I think I recall—riding in this Hudson Terraplane. I think the woman in this photo is my great-grandmother."

They were silent, so I plunged ahead.

"This letter," I went on, tapping the hospital stationery, "is cer-tainly proof that a man named or called Chester Morton was born in New Orleans in 1902."

Andrews couldn't resist that one. "So he couldn't, really, have been the one who tried to kill you three months ago, or took pot-shots at you very recently busting out the window of your truck."

"What?" Lucinda almost stood up. "Someone shot at you?"

"Did I forget to mention that?" Andrews answered sheepishly.

"Could I make my point," I insisted.

"No!" She stood. "You cannot make any more points with me! I'm calling Skidmore."

She shot to the phone and dialed before I could even get to my feet.

"Nice work, Sherlock," I mumbled to Andrews.

"Yeah," he admitted, "I probably shouldn't have. . . ."

He trailed off as Lucinda began shouting into the phone.

"Somebody shot Fever again!"

"No they didn't," I called out. "I'm fine. They shot my truck."

"Yes he got out of the house!" she went on, ignoring me. "Because Dr. Winton Andrews is worthless."

"Hey," Andrews protested.

"You do something about this right now, Skidmore Needle, I know where you live!" She slammed the phone down.

Lucinda spun around and glared at us. If we'd been two shiny apples, we would have withered and turned black.

"I'm actually glad you called the sheriff," I said calmly. "I'd like to show him this new information. And discuss the implications thereof."

"I'd like to discuss *your* implications," she snapped.

"You have to sit down and let me connect these dots for you," I pleaded, "and all of this will make more sense."

"Look, old chum," Andrews interrupted. "I'm afraid I'm on Lucinda's side in this. And not just because she's a nurse and knows eighty-seven ways to kill a man."

"A *hundred* and eighty-seven," she corrected, squinting.

"But also because," he went merrily along, "you're not right. You're—I'm sorry, Fever—you're a little bit out of your mind. I don't think it's anything too dire, because you were always giving off hints of this sort of thing. But a coma is a *coma*—it's not some-thing to be trifled with. And you're trifling with it. Ask anyone."

Lucinda's expression softened. "Sweetheart, he's right. If you could see yourself from the outside, the way we see you, you'd be really worried too. You're having hallucinations, you're passing out, you're making things up as you go along and you think they make sense, and maybe they do to you, but they're just . . . they're very nonsensical."

"Very surreal," Andrews agreed.

I was momentarily at a loss for words. They'd knocked the wind out of me, certainly. But they'd also held up a mirror, and I could see myself a bit objectively. I did appear to be crazed. And I hadn't even mentioned talking with the ghost of my mother twice very recently.

On the other hand, there was the red tin and its contents. I turned to look at the items on the kitchen table.

"Then what do you make of these things?" I asked them.

Lucinda sighed. "All right, let's say that you did just find this tin in your mother's room, after all these years. These things are just her keepsakes, her mementos. You know what a strange per-son she was. Who can say why she kept these things?"

"I'm not making up the connection between the letter and the newspaper article." I tried to sound more convincing than I felt. "You can see that the article is about missing relatives of Jelly Roll Morton and that the letter is about a boy born in New Orleans, where Jelly Roll was from, whose last name was given as Morton."

"I can see that your mother thought there was some connec-tion, maybe," Andrews shrugged. "For some reason."

"All right, but you don't think it's strange that my mother had in her possession a letter addressed to someone in the Newcomb family?"

That silenced them both.

The Newcomb family had founded the town when our mountain was first settled. We had been called Newcomb Junction until the 1920s. The family had ties to great wealth in other parts of America, but this particular branch had helped to define the concept of Southern Gothic. One of their offspring, Tristan, was the famous, self-named Newcomb Dwarf, who had owned the traveling show that had employed my parents. And most people in town still refused to discuss Orvid Newcomb, another little person—and a professional hit man—who claimed to have been a relative of mine.

"And at the very least," I continued, a bit more sure of myself, "you have to admit that I'm not making up the name *T-Bone Morton*. There was such a person, and he was somehow connected to this Chester Morton who is somehow connected to me."

"No," Andrews insisted. "No such thing. You're making random items into a pattern. That's what your brain does, it finds meaning even where there isn't any."

"You can't be serious," I said, irritation growing. "I said the name Chester and less than a day later I found evidence of Chester. You think that's a coincidence?"

"Do you hear how crazy that sounds?" he shot back. "Do you understand that from my point of view you wanted to prove something so you went and found something you already knew was in your house that would make a connection—?"

"Why the hell would I do that? What would be my motive?" I was nearly shouting.

Thank God Lucinda was there. She stood up and stopped us both. "All right, look!"

Andrews had never heard that tone of voice from her, and I had only very rarely. It was the sound of absolute authority, and it silenced us both.

"I don't know what any of this means," she said to Andrews, "or if it means anything at all. But Fever has a history of being right when everybody thinks he's wrong. He's also just reminded me that he is who he is, and that's fine with me. I like who he is pretty good. You can't *make* the rain stop from falling just because you don't like to get wet. He's got to do what he does. I know that."

"Fish gotta swim," I said to Andrews. "Birds gotta fly."

"Shut up, Fever," she snapped. "I'm getting to you. I brought you back to this life for a reason, and I'll do it as many times as I have to, because I'm not going to hang around this old world without you. But you're taxing my patience. You have got to quit trying to deliberately kill yourself!"

"I promise," I answered instantly.

"And you have got to set a date with me. By the end of the week. Or else, and I mean it."

"A wedding date?" Andrews asked, hushed.

"Hush!" She was staring at me.

"Hm. What's today?" I asked, dazed.

"It's Thursday." She wore no aspect.

"So. By the end of the week means, what? Tomorrow? Saturday?"

She looked away. "I'm going to work now. You'll do what you'll do."

It sounded like a threat.

"Can I come over for dinner on Saturday?" I scrambled toward her. "We'll talk about it then?"

"Why don't I come here," she sighed. "That way it'll make you come home from wherever it is that you're going to go and at least I'll know that you're still alive."

"Seven o'clock?" I said, softer.

She turned to Andrews. "You watch out for him, hear?"

"Yes, ma'am."

"And you remember that he's usually right when most people think he's wrong."

Andrews smiled. "Well, I have to admit that's true."

She left. I tried to follow her out the door, but she waved me off, clearly still perturbed.

Andrews clapped his hands, rubbed them together, and cleared his throat. "That was fun. What's next?"

"We have to find this guy," I answered, heading upstairs.

"Chester?"

"No. The so-called Earl of Huntingdon. I'm taking a shower and changing clothes."

"Where do you think you can go to find *him*?" Andrews demanded to know.

"We'll start at the hospital. I think he might work there."

"Oh for God's sake," he mumbled.

But he followed me up the stairs.

22.

Andrews complained all the way to the hospital. His comments were generally punctuated by inventive profanity, some of which approached a kind of poetry—if that poetry had been written by William Burroughs or Charles Bukowski.

Otherwise, the morning was lovely. Snow was melting but still white, sun was warm and golden, cardinals shot though the barely budding maple limbs like red arrows. Andrews alone was impervious to the beauty of the almost-spring.

He posed his final question as the hospital came into view around a curve in the road. "Why didn't you just mention this to Lucinda before she left your kitchen?"

"Plenty of reasons," I answered him calmly. "The primary one is that I didn't think of it until after she left. But even if I had, I think I probably wouldn't have brought it up. She was pretty angry, don't you think?

"She was that," he reasoned.

We pulled into the visitor's parking lot.

"And I thought you might be eager to see young Nurse Chambers," I concluded, eyeing him sideways.

"Shut up."

He actually blushed, which took me completely by surprise.

"Wait," I managed to get out, "you actually like Stacey."

All he could do was nod.

I shook my head. "Love finds Andy Hardy."

"You watch too many old movies," he mumbled, climbing out of the truck.

Across the parking lot, in through the automatic doors, and straight to the first-floor information desk, Andrews avoided looking at me.

The person at the desk didn't recognize me, but smiled at Andrews. Her name tag said "Becky Mayfield."

"Dr. Andrews," she said, as if they had shared some secret.

"Hi." He blushed again. "You remember Dr. Devilin."

Her eyes grew wide. "You're Fever Devilin?"

"I am," I confirmed.

Her hand shot out. "I'm very pleased to make your acquaintance."

I took her hand. I couldn't figure out if she had heard wild stories about me and was fascinated to see the thing in the flesh, or if she was overdoing her manners because the head nurse of the hospital was my fiancée. But there was something more to her behavior than simple, polite curiosity.

Whatever her ideas, I charged ahead. "We're actually looking for someone who helped me when I was a patient here recently. He's an older African-American man with an obvious New Orleans kind of accent. Do you by any chance know who I'm talking about?"

"No." She frowned, thinking. "I don't think there's anyone like that working here, unless he's very new."

"Is there any way I could have a look at some kind of list of employees, like orderlies and nurses, that sort of thing?"

"Oh, I don't know," she answered, clearly conflicted. "I mean, I'd have to check with Lucinda Foxe, you know, to see if that would be all right."

"I understand completely," I told her. "I'll speak with her my-self."

"Okay, good," she sighed, very relieved. "I expect you'll have a better chance of getting her to say yes than anyone in this hos-pital."

"Is Nurse Chambers on duty?" I asked, with a sideways glance at Andrews.

"She sure is." Becky Mayfield was very obviously aware of the relationship between Andrews and Nurse Chambers. Her grin was so significant that it threatened to crack some of her teeth. "Shall I page her?"

"No," Andrews said quickly.

"Actually, we would like to say 'hey' to her," I added. "Do you have any idea where she might be?"

"Let me check." She couldn't stop grinning, and consulted a clipboard and then her computer screen. Finally she concluded: "Second floor, try the station first."

"Will do," I assured her, "and thanks."

As we hurried away toward the escalator, Andrews leaned close to me.

"Are you just trying to embarrass me?" he asked.

"No," I assured him, "I'm trying to find this Earl of Hunting-don character. And Stacey, despite her current choice in amorous companions, is generally very smart. She's also a great gossip. If this guy actually works here, either she'll know him or she'll know who would know him. Don't you think?"

"Well," he admitted, "you're probably right about that."

We stepped onto the escalator and we both leaned forward. I felt a little dizzy, and took hold of the moving black rail. It seemed to be moving at a slightly different speed than the silver stairs, and I was further disoriented. Mostly to focus on some-thing else, I tried to laugh.

"And don't you want to see Stacey anyway? She really likes you."

"I know," he answered sheepishly. "We became something of an item during your long winter's nap."

"She told me."

"I think it might be getting serious."

"Oh," I realized, "and that's making you uncomfortable."

"If by *uncomfortable* you mean *panicked,* then, yes."

We came to the top of the rise. I stepped off the stairs, took a few more strides, and tried to get back my equilibrium. Unfortunately, Andrews noticed.

"Are you all right?" he asked, taking my arm. "You're not going to pass out again, are you?"

I shook him off with a little less patience than I should have. "I'm fine."

He stopped walking.

"Sorry." I closed my eyes. "I really can't stand people treating me like an invalid."

"Okay," he said slowly, "then quit acting like one. If you stop falling asleep at odd moments, I'll stop grabbing you when it looks like you're about to. Deal?"

I sighed as heavily as I could to show my discomfort, and motored ahead toward the nurse's station. As luck would have it, Stacey was there, staring at something on the desk in front of her.

"Nurse Chambers," I began, still ten feet away from her, "I've brought you a surprise."

She looked up and her entire body lit up. "Winnie!"

I winced. "Didn't we have some sort of arrangement about your using that name?"

She ignored me completely, stood, and tried to get at Andrews over the counter of the station. Despite himself, he was grinning like an eleven-year-old and moving at an alarming rate of speed toward her open arms.

Their embrace was relatively brief, but it made up in quality what it lacked in duration.

Before they could speak, I felt I ought to interject, "We're here on business. We're looking for a hospital employee, someone that I think is connected to my situation."

Stacey glanced my way. "You think somebody that works here shot you?"

"No," I said quickly, "but there's a man who gave me tea in my room who knows something about the whole business."

"Stop saying *business*," Andrews snapped. "I'm humoring your weird hunches because Lucinda told me to and because, in this particular instance, I get to see Stacey. But this whole mess in your head is anything but businesslike."

I addressed Nurse Chambers. "I'm looking for an African-American man in his fifties who works here as an orderly or a nurse or a nurse's aide. He has a very distinguishable accent."

Stacey grinned. "Very funny."

I took a step closer to her. "Why would that be funny?"

"Well," she answered, a little uncomfortably, "we only hire female nurses, our aides are all student interns from the college down in Habersham County, and the cut-off age for orderlies is thirty."

"Really?" I marveled.

"We're run by a business group, Dr. Devilin," she said, her voice lowered. "They have rules and insurance issues and all kinds of other instructions for us and we have to follow them because we want to stay open. Because the people in this county need us. If I don't worry about all that too much, then I can just fill out the right forms, give the right answers to ten or twelve questions every month, and I get to do my job, which is making people better. Like you."

I had clearly hit a nerve. Nurse Cambers was obviously unhappy about the way the hospital was run. It seemed ill advised for me to pursue that particular line of questioning at that moment, though I felt compelled to take up the matter of political and economic considerations in the running of county hospitals with the head nurse—at another place and time.

"So the man I'm describing could not really be an employee here," I concluded.

"No." She exhaled, realizing that she'd gotten a little more upset than she should have.

"That tells me something." I nodded.

"It tells you that this is a dead end." Andrews took Stacey's hand and said, "Sorry to bother you."

"Anything unusual about any of the orderlies that you do have working here?" I asked on impulse.

She thought for a second and said, "There was one who came down here from up North, studying to be a radiology tech, I think he said, but he quit or got fired—we're not supposed to ask. He got here in January, I think, but I haven't seen him in a while."

"Mean anything?" Andrews asked.

"No," I admitted.

"Sorry the man you're looking for isn't here," Stacey said sweetly.

"Well, if he's been around these parts for any time at all," I said vaguely, "someone's got to have seen him. He's 'as inconspicuous as a tarantula on a slice of angel food 'cake."

"Nice," Andrews grinned. "You stole that from Raymond Chandler?"

I shrugged. "He stole it from Dickens—the spider on Miss Havisham's wedding cake."

"What are you talking about?" Stacey said.

"Metaphorical language," Andrews said. "The grammar of dreams."

I had decided that a trip into the actual town of Blue Mountain was in order. If our man had been anywhere around the area, people would have noticed and would have opinions and gossip about him. It was the nature of our town, maybe all small towns, that a stranger would be welcomed, treated with respect, and then talked about behind his back. Especially a flashy stranger with a funny accent.

I realized as we drove down Main Street that I hadn't been into town for more than a month before my attack, so it had been closer to five months since I'd seen the place. Nothing was different, of course, from the last time I'd seen it except for the snow. It was mostly melted, the air was clean, and no one was outside. Still, I looked at Main Street with new eyes—the eyes of a man returned from the dead.

I felt very sad to approach the empty storefront where Miss Etta's diner had been only the year before. A sense memory filled my head with the glorious smell of golden squash and onions, fried okra crisp as popcorn, cornbread like cake that a bride would eat at her own wedding. Etta had opened her dining establishment at the age of twenty and, without much further effort on her part, she had turned seventy-five before she'd passed on. I still imagined her, asleep as usual, in a very uncomfortable chair close to the kitchen door, her hair like white smoke, wreathed in a pale halo just above snowy eyebrows. Her face, ancient but barely wrinkled, had always been the very model of serenity.

But her diner was just a big empty room now.

Andrews refused to look at it as we drove up, but we were both thinking the same thing: who's going to feed us all, now that Miss Etta is gone?

"Pull over," I said suddenly. "In front of Miss Etta's."

"Really?" Andrews sighed, a little exasperated, but he pulled the truck into a spot right in front of the place. "I guess I miss her too, or, truth be told: her food. Hard to say that you knew the actual woman since she was asleep most of the time. But, man, was everyone in the state at her funeral, or what? I've never seen so many—"

"I saw something," I interrupted, staring in through the dirty storefront window.

"Saw something in there?" He clearly didn't believe me.

"Humor me," I said.

"My brother," he answered, "our entire relationship is based on my humoring you."

"So why stop now?" I asked him, getting out of the truck.

He turned off the engine and followed me to the door of Etta's place. It was locked.

We stared in. The place had been left exactly as it had always been. Mismatched Formica tables, a wild variety of chairs, even tablecloths and napkins were all still in attendance. Sometimes people would go in and sit there, eating a sack lunch of some terrible fast food, just to remember when they'd had it better. I was, in fact, a little surprised to find the door locked.

"Try around back," I mumbled. "She never locked the kitchen door."

"But," Andrews protested, "she's not here anymore."

"Didn't I just say 'humor me'?"

"God," Andrews whispered.

But he followed me.

To get to the back of the building was a simple matter. Only a wooden gate guarded a small alleyway between two buildings. It had been nailed shut but was nearly rotted at the ground and easy to squeeze by. Then it was only a matter of sidestepping bricks and trash and the occasional dead animal, and there you were, around the corner from the back door of Miss Etta's place. Andrews had never gone that way, but he was enjoying following me.

"This is disgusting back here," he muttered. "Is that a cat?"

"Well," I said, eyeing the bones and hank of hair, "it probably used to be."

Through the tall weeds and over a pile of bricks that had obviously fallen from near the top of the old building, we made it to the narrow confines of the back driveway, the primary home of perhaps the smelliest Dumpster in America.

"What the hell!" Andrews covered his nose and mouth with both arms.

"Yes," I agreed, "it's quite a remarkable stench."

"Call somebody," he said from behind his sleeves. "Have this Dumpster removed. To Cleveland. And even then we might still smell it."

"What have you got against Cleveland?" I took hold of the solid metal back door to Miss Etta's.

The door swung inward toward the old kitchen and I heard shuffling noises. I shot a look back to Andrews. He'd heard them too. I took another step inside, trying to be quiet, but the door scraped the floor, and the floorboards creaked. I froze, but it was too late, the noise I'd made was already in the air.

A figure appeared, backlit and difficult to see, but the voice was unmistakable.

"What took you so long, boy?" he asked me in his thick Creole accent. "I been waiting for you for a couple of hours. You got your faithful Indian sidekick, Tonto, with you?"

Andrews stepped up next to me. "I'm not Tonto," he complained. "I'm Watson. Sometimes I'm even Holmes."

The old man laughed at that. "Okay. I guess if I can be the Earl of Huntingdon, you can be anybody you want."

"Thanks," Andrews said in a very insulting tone.

"This is something of a—weird coincidence." I stammered. "We've been looking for you."

"You have?" he asked. "Come on in. Sit down."

We followed him into the dining area, past the giant old stove. It was colder, by at least three hundred degrees, than I'd ever known it to be—and that added to my sadness.

"Why in the world you want to go over to the hospital and ask about me?" he began before Andrews and I were even in the dining room. "Nobody there knows me."

"Wait, how would you know that we were at the hospital?" Andrews asked. "We didn't mention that."

"Not important," he snapped, ignoring the question, staring at me. "And this is not a *coincidence*, Sherlock. I told you to meet me here today. Apparently you just don't remember it."

Andrews stopped walking. "You told him to meet you *here*?"

"You think I don't know who he is?" the man asked, his obvious irritation growing. "You think I don't know he's got a sentimental feeling about this place? About this food? Food is a power. It's more than just fuel for your tank. He knows that. I know that. You're from England, so it's harder for you to understand, because you didn't ever have a good meal in your life until your old girlfriend took you to Tamarind on Queen Street for some of that hot Indian stuff. I believe her name was Hyacinth. That's a pretty name. Come on. Sit down."

Andrews stared. I did too.

"You knew I was coming here?" I asked, feeling very thickheaded.

"Damn, didn't I just say I *told* you to meet me here?" He shook his head. "You got to believe that I know what I'm doing. And that I'm here to help you."

"How the hell would you know about Hyacinth?" It was clear that Andrews couldn't decide whether to be in awe or to take a swing at the old man.

"You put some sort of—you made some kind of posthypnotic suggestion," I said slowly, "when you gave me tea, that obviously drugged tea, at my house."

"Something like that." He nodded slowly.

I examined the man for, really, the first time. His face wore the genuine serenity of the enlightened mind. There was nothing hidden, nothing guarded, nothing sinister about that face. He seemed otherworldly in exactly the same way as the Buddhist monk Thich Nhat Hahn had seemed when I'd seen that man speaking in Atlanta. In fact the resemblance was striking—except for the fact that this man, the self-proclaimed Earl of Huntingdon, was obviously insane.

He read my face and smiled. "When you don't know anything," he said softly, "the truth sounds like madness."

I was startled to have been so transparent to the man, but an overwhelming curiosity about him supplanted every other instinct or observation about him.

"What are you doing here?" I asked him. "Why are you doing this to me?"

He turned to Andrews. "Hyacinth Burke was a lovely girl. She runs a theatre now. My family comes from England, you understand, and we know a lot of people, and we keep in touch pretty good. I believe she is currently producing a very nice version of *The Birds*."

"How do you know about Hyacinth?" Andrews demanded, his voice rumbling.

The man sat down and folded his hands across his chest, beaming at us both. "You boys, you're just like everyone else in America. You're too quick to judge a book by its cover. I am the Earl of Huntingdon, a human repository of knowledge in a time when knowledge is dangerous. We are guardians of that knowledge, our whole family. I can name and date the lineage of a thousand families from our origins in England. Including the Wakefields. Including their vile poison. Now you listen and you listen good."

For some reason beyond reasoning, I felt compelled to be silent, ordained to listen. Andrews, apparently, felt the same compulsion.

"When you were shot," the man began in very soothing, storytelling tones, "I heard the noise. I heard it because we watch out for our own. I got to the hospital, took care of you, whispered in your ear so that, even in your coma state, you would dream. You would dream the story the way it happened, and it would be easier for you to hear it now. You would wake up troubled. And it is truly said, 'Let everyone who seeks continue seeking until they find. When they find, they will become troubled. When they become troubled, they will be astonished, and then they will rule over the All.'"

"What am I supposed to be seeking?" I asked slowly. "Because you're talking about something more than just my looking for the person who shot me, I can see that."

"That's right," he answered, his smile growing. "So let me tell you a part of the story, something you ought to be prepared for. It's about a woman named Lisa Simard."

"I know that name," I said, trying to figure out why it would be familiar to me.

"You know it because I told it to you in the hospital while you were asleep. She ran a nightclub in Paris in the 1920s. She fell in love with a man called T-Bone Morton. Saved his life. He was a saxophone player, and his natural father was Jelly Roll Morton, and you know who he is."

I nodded. "The man who invented jazz."

"Maybe," he said curtly, "but the point is, this T-Bone, he fell in love with Lisa right back, and they had a baby. Everything would have been just fine, but Lisa was a woman who spoke her mind. That's something to be proud of. Unfortunately she ran up against some of these men who didn't care for the way she talked, and they killed her. T-Bone almost killed himself then, and he might have, except for the fact that he had a little baby daughter to take care of. He didn't know what to do. He was laid down low with grief, and a little afraid for his own life, so he came back to America."

"He played with King Oliver," I said, feeling as if I might be in some sort of fugue state, "in Chicago."

"Yes," he said gently, "but now we have to go back in time to T-Bone's mother, a woman called Eulalie."

"Eulalie Echo," I whispered.

"She had T-Bone by Jelly Roll—and now that I say that out loud it's funny sounding, but that's the truth. She also had another boy by another man, and that other boy, T-Bone's half brother, was called Chester."

"Chester," I repeated.

"Now this boy Chester," the man went on, "he could be the poster child for a certain kind of American poison: he was raised to hate. He was taught to hate. He was fed on burning coals of bile. He slept in the broken glass of rage. Wait."

He leaned forward, took out a red mechanical pencil and a small spiral notepad from his coat pocket, clicked the pencil, and wrote.

"What'd I say? 'The broken glass of rage,'" he said to himself. "I got to remember that. That's good."

"What?" I glared at the pad.

"Oh," he answered absently, "I give this speech a lot and sometime I'll say a new phrase or sentence that's too good to use just once. Don't you like 'the broken glass of rage'?"

"It's a good image." I nodded. "And the fact that he slept in it, very powerful."

"What in *the* hell?" Andrews began.

"Sorry," the man said quickly, putting away his pad. "The point is, Chester was a white-hot Yankee racist of the first order because, you see, he was white, and his mother was white, and T-Bone wasn't because Jelly Roll wasn't."

"I'm confused," Andrews muttered.

"I don't understand a lot of this myself," the man admitted. "I'm just trying to get through the story."

"Why?" Andrews demanded. "What does *any* of this have to do with *anything*?"

"Because," the man answered in a stronger voice, "Chester tried to kill T-Bone, and Lisa killed Chester. Lisa saved T-Bone's life by killing Chester. That's a matter of record."

"Why did Chester want to kill his own half brother?" I asked.

"What does it matter?" Andrews roared, slapping the table with his hand. "Jesus!"

"Because T-Bone was evidence," the man said looking directly into my eyes, "that Chester's mother laid down with a black man. Chester had been taught that it polluted the purity of his whole family's white blood. T-Bone had to be extinguished from the family line, you see. He couldn't be allowed to go on, him nor his baby daughter. That's what Chester was taught by his mother. They couldn't have a whole branch of the family that sprung from Jelly Roll Morton, you understand."

"But Lisa Simard killed Chester instead," I said softly. "Stabbed him in her own club."

"That's right." The old man nodded.

"And shortly thereafter, T-Bone came back to America." I realized that I was grinding my teeth.

"But Chester's mother, Eulalie, she found out about that. Found out that T-Bone was back home in Chicago, and she sent men to finish the job that Chester had started, and to avenge her white son's death. She sent men to the Lincoln Gardens ballroom one night. T-Bone was playing there. But angels once again guarded T-Bone's life, and he escaped harm. A strange bargain was made after that."

"It was Bix's idea," I mumbled. "Bix Beiderbecke."

"Yes," he confirmed. "T-Bone gave his daughter to distant relatives, kin in New Orleans, thanks to Bix. Then T-Bone disappeared."

"That kin in New Orleans," I whispered, "was your family?"

"Eulalie vowed then to keep her hate alive," he went on, ignoring my question. "Her desire for revenge, it lived for generations, searching for the missing man and daughter. She was sure and certain that T-Bone and the girl would eventually be found. And when they were found they would be expunged. She wanted to wipe out any trace of nonwhite blood in her family, you see. She was absolutely insane—not entirely human. As sometimes happens with these demon-people, Chester's mother lived a long time and poisoned the minds of her children and grandchildren, and their generations."

"Wait." I was struggling with some deeply embedded, nearly lost information from the deepest caves of Mnemosyne.

But he wouldn't allow me to finish the process.

"You didn't get what you needed from those boys over at Fit's Mill," he said urgently, his eyes burning holes in my cornea. "Go back and get into the basement under the meeting hall. They keep records. Go now."

"Wait," I said again, feeling dizzy.

I was just about to come to some fuller understanding of something, like a realization of something that had always bothered me, or the removal of a bullet that had been stuck in my chest for a while, when we were all startled by a loud banging on the locked front door of Miss Etta's establishment.

Sheriff Skidmore Needle was standing there, scowling at the three of us with a fervor that threatened to break the front window.

"Uh-oh," the old man said, rising so quickly that he knocked over his chair. "Got to go."

He shot toward the back door of Miss Etta's faster than I would have imagined he could move.

"Wait!" I jumped up.

Skidmore began pounding on the glass and yelling for us to let him in.

"What's the rest of the story?" I called out after the old man, but he had vanished through the kitchen and out the back door.

Andrews shot to the front door and unlocked it for Skid.

"I've a great mind to draw my gun and shoot you both," he fumed. "I locked this place up for a reason!"

"The back door was open," Andrews began innocently.

"No it wasn't," Skid snapped. "Not at six thirty this morning when I checked it."

He raced past us after the so-called Earl of Huntingdon. I followed at only a slightly slower pace, suddenly afraid that Skid might inadvertently hurt the old man. My feet hit the ground of the back alleyway immediately after his did.

The Earl of Huntingdon was gone.

23.

Skid spent six or seven minutes yelling at us before I could get a word in edgewise.

"This man is trying to help me," I finally managed to insist.

"This man could very well be the person who shot you!" Skidmore countered. "He's been identified at the hospital. Even though he's never actually been employed there, several people recall seeing an older man with a funny accent in your room, dressed like an orderly. They assumed at the time he was a private nurse."

"But, see," I began, "that probably means he's *not* the man who tried to kill me since, you know, I was in a coma and he was alone with me in the room and all he would have needed to do was to take a pillow—"

"Shut up!" Skid growled.

"Okay," I agreed.

Always best to agree with an angry, armed officer of the law.

"Now I discover that you know him? That you're talking to him?" Skidmore asked, doing his best to seem calm, though his face resembled nothing so much as a Cherokee Purple tomato. "Who the hell is he?"

"He is the Earl of Huntingdon," I said, doing my best to sound serious.

Skidmore turned his ire on Andrews. "If you don't tell me what you know about this man," he snarled, "I will lock you up and I mean it."

We could see that he did, in fact, mean it.

"What, exactly, is the matter, Skid?" I asked calmly. "You're mad that he broke into Miss Etta's? Everybody does that. We eat lunch in here all the time. We bring our sad little sack lunches and bottles of pop. We miss her. And as to the old man, he's really not the person who tried to kill me. He's helping me find who did that."

"What?" Skid turned to me sharply. "So you do know him!"

"No."

"Then why would he be trying to help you?"

Skidmore wasn't calming down, and that was cause for concern.

"Seriously, Skid," I tried again, "what's going on? Why are you so riled up?"

"Could it be that I'm worried about my oldest friend?" he demanded, his voice getting higher. "Could it be that I can't find the man who almost killed him? And it's been more than three months and I still don't have the first clue?"

I looked at Andrews. He looked back at me. Then we both answered Skidmore's questions together.

"No."

Skidmore stood silently for long seconds, and then he exhaled so ferociously that it hurt my feelings.

"It's Melissa Mathews," Skid began softly. "She has cancer."

It's funny what happens to most people when they hear that kind of news, when they discover that someone they care about is in trouble. Suddenly I lost all interest in my own concerns, I completely forgot what I had been thinking about so intensely for days. All I could think about was Melissa, and Skidmore, who loved her in an altogether chaste and brotherly way.

"Okay." I took several steps closer to him and put my hand on his arm. "You just found out."

He wouldn't look at me. "Coincidentally, I found out kind of because of all this mess. You were just at the hospital talking to Becky Mayfield."

"Who?" I asked vaguely.

"The nurse at the information counter," Andrews said softly, standing in the doorway to the kitchen. "What's this about Melissa?"

"Becky called me right after you all left," Skid said. "She wanted to tell me that you had got her to thinking, and she said she did remember an older man in your room over these last couple of months. She said she hadn't thought about it much because she just assumed you'd hired some outside help so that Lucinda could get on with her work and not all the time be running into your room to see how you were."

"Okay," I said quickly, "but about Melissa."

"Right." He nodded his head several times, trying to think of the right words. "Anyway, Becky told me that she was sorry to hear about Melissa and I said, 'Sorry to hear about what?' And she said 'about her cancer.'"

He let go another heart-cracking sigh. "I tried to act like I knew what she was talking about, so I said, 'She seems to be doing all right.' Which is true. But Becky said, 'I don't know, she was just in for another one of her treatments.' So now I have to talk to Melissa and find out what's going on."

"Skid," I said, my hand still on his arm. "You know how tough she is."

"Yeah." He drew himself up. "Anyway, I was headed out the door to find her when I saw your truck parked here. And then when I came over to, you know, tell you about everything, there you were, sitting with the mystery man. And when he saw me, he took off so fast I thought—I don't know what I thought, really. I kind of lost it for a second. I mean, I just found out that you'd been asking about some stranger in your room, and from Becky's description, there he was, sitting at the table with you—in Miss Etta's diner. It was very . . . what's the word?"

"Surreal?" Andrews suggested.

Skidmore shrugged.

"Do you want someone with you when you talk to Melissa?" I asked.

"God, no." He scowled. "I think she doesn't want anybody to know what's going on with her. She would have told me."

"This Becky at the hospital," I said, "just assumed that she had already told you. Because, ordinarily, she would have. That's why you're so worried."

"Right." He closed his eyes. "I mean, I knew there was something wrong with her. She gets tired a lot now. She's taken more sick days in the past several months than she has the whole time I've known her. She's lost weight. I thought maybe she was worried about some boy or other. I never thought it was—this."

I could see his distress, and I felt it too. It didn't matter then that I'd been in a coma, or that dreams and reality were mixed in my perceptions, or that a very odd stranger was dogging my path. I could even ignore the foul stench from the nearby Dumpster. At that moment, I was only one of three men in a back alley of a small town in the mountains, worrying about a sweet young woman who was in trouble.

Images of Melissa filled my head. During her tenure as a deputy she'd risked her life a dozen times or more, broken into a murderer's hotel room, jumped into the Nantahala River to save two elementary school children, and fired her pistol often in the line of duty. But a half-hearted *hello* from a boy who was beginning to like her: that would send her into paralysis. It was truly said that she was the shyest woman on the planet.

There had been rumors about a possible affair between Skidmore and Melissa for years, partly because of their working relationship, mostly because small minds in small towns are open to a limited number of choices when it comes to relationships between men and women. Gossip is gossip the world around.

Part of the reason Skidmore was so upset, the psychologist in my head told me, was that he had conflicting feelings at that moment. He was genuinely terrified that something might happen to Melissa, a person about whom he cared deeply. But he was also afraid that if he showed his emotions too plainly, some people in town would nod wickedly, assuming that they knew what carnal bonds lay at the root of his concern. The conflict between those two tensions was the true cause of his anger at us, and his deepest distress.

"Talk to Girlinda about this," I said on impulse.

He looked up. At first, the anger rose to the surface again, but it only took a second for him to realize how much talking to his wife would help. She would absolve him of any conflicting feelings. She knew there was nothing to the rumors about Melissa and Skidmore—knew it in her marrow. She would comfort him, she would worry about Melissa, and she would begin to cook. Food was more to her than physical nourishment to her; it was a metaphorical sustenance, a spiritual communion.

"Okay," he said after a moment. "Good idea."

Then I realized, quite suddenly, that we were uncovering one of the reasons Skidmore hadn't had as much success in the matter of my assault as he usually had. He'd not only had to work with less help from Melissa, he'd also been worried about her; distracted. No wonder, I thought to myself, he was so overwrought.

"Look," I began, my voice assuming a tone that I felt was quite authoritative, "I've been going at my problem in a completely incorrect manner."

Skid and Andrews turned my way.

"I've been flailing around like a man who was shot and sank into a coma," I continued. "Like someone who's lost in the labyrinth of his own thoughts and experiences and dreams."

"Again the labyrinth?" Andrews sighed.

"But you *were* shot, and you were in a coma, and you're almost always lost in your own thoughts," Skidmore told me impatiently. "How the hell do you think you're supposed to be acting now?"

"I am supposed to be acting like myself," I answered him, "looking at someone else. I am supposed to be using the same techniques I would use on anyone else under these same circumstances. I've been letting events shape my perceptions rather than allowing my perceptions observe the events."

Andrews got it. "You've been letting the facts change your skills rather than using your skills to attack the facts."

"Exactly!"

Skidmore blinked. "I have no idea what you're talking about."

"I'm going to Fit's Mill," I said quietly, "to do field research, investigate a cultural history. Only this time, instead of looking for other people's stories, I'm researching my own personal folklore, the stories of my family. My history."

"I see." Skid got it. "Well, I'm going to have to play the role of sheriff now, and tell you not to do that. *Tell* you not to do that. I'm not asking. I'm not explaining. You are to go home now and quit interrupting my investigation. You are to leave off participating in these shady rendezvous situations with miscreants who might have tried to kill you. And I would prefer it if you'd just get in bed and stay there so that Lucinda won't take a chaw out of my hide. You hear me?"

I looked down. "I hear you."

"Fever," he warned.

"I understand," I told him fervently.

"If you get shot and killed again," he said, "don't come running to me."

"I'm on the job," Andrews said, stepping up. "I'll do the driving."

Skidmore shook his head. "Like that makes me feel better."

"I really will watch out for him," Andrews said very seriously.

"All right." Skid rubbed his forehead for several seconds, sighing. "Well. I've got to go find Melissa. And I've got some other business to take care of that might just get us further down the road in the solving of your attack. So go home, and I mean it."

Andrews and I nodded as if we were both in church. Skidmore locked the back door to Miss Etta's and disappeared down the alleyway.

We were halfway to Fit's Mill before I managed to say to Andrews, "Thanks for driving this way and not back to my house."

"I could have wasted a good deal of the morning arguing with you about this, but the fact that I'd eventually lose was clear to me. And I heard what the old man said."

"Plus, third time's a charm," I allowed. "Why is that, exactly?"

"Why is *what* exactly?"

"Why is the third time a charm?" I specified.

"Shakespeare," he answered instantly.

"No." I shook my head. "Shakespeare isn't the answer to everything."

"But in this case," he chided me, "we have but to refer to the witches in *Macbeth*. 'Thrice to thine and thrice to mine and thrice again, to make up nine. Peace! The charm's wound up.'"

"Well, I might give you its Scottish origin," I admitted, "because it *is* listed in Alexander Hislop's *The Proverbs of Scotland*. 'The third time's lucky.' But that's later—1800s. The expression's been around longer than that, surely."

"And you think?" he asked.

"I think we may have to go back to the Bible. The trinity seems pretty lucky to a lot of Christians."

"All right," he argued, "if you're going to do that, you might as well go back to Pythagoras. His entire mathematical gestalt was based on the number three, like it had magic. Why are we talking about this?"

"To distract you," I admitted. "To keep you from fully realizing that this little bit of sociological archaeology is liable to be fairly dangerous. We're going to try to get into the meeting hall of some crazy supremacist organization and break into their basement vault. They have guns. What have I got with me? A Shakespeare scholar."

"No," he corrected me instantly. "You have a kick-ass Rugby player with you. Haven't you seen the bumper stickers? We eat our dead."

"Yes I know all that," I answered. "I actually meant that your knowledge of Shakespeare would come in handy. If you try to beat them up, they'll just shoot you. But if you try to talk to them about Shakespeare the way you usually do to me, they'll be asleep in two minutes and we can just sneak past them. Like Cerberus after a sop."

"Ha-and-I-do-mean-ha." He gripped the steering wheel.

Once again we decided to go the slightly longer way around, avoiding the woods. The air sucked in through the open back window was very cold, and I didn't see the point in risking more broken glass.

The sun had ridden high into the late morning air, and there were no more snow clouds to be seen. The sky was a more springtime blue, even a robin's egg blue, like something about to crack open.

As we drove down the decaying roadway toward the nearly abandoned town, a sense of excitement took ahold of me. My chest thumped and my head was lighter.

"I'm having an intuition," I announced.

"Well, roll down the window," Andrew answered. "Don't throw up in the truck."

"I'm going to find something important in the records they have downstairs in this building."

"If those men don't kill us first," he reminded me.

"Right," I agreed.

Andrews nosed the truck forward toward the tumbledown building where we'd met with Travis and the Sons of Wingfield. About the size and shape of a small house, it looked different in the light of day. It actually looked more ominous than it had at night. The windows all had yellowed, stained newspaper in them to prevent anyone's looking in. The building was made of wood, not bricks as I had misremembered. Most of the paint was gone, the wood was well rotted, and the roof was corrugated tin that was entirely covered in reddish rust and nut-brown kudzu vines. In a month or so, the roof would have a nice green head of leaves, and the kudzu would begin creeping downward to cover the front of the building, the windows, and the doors. Unchecked, it would engulf the entire town within a few years. And it didn't appear that anyone in town had cared to stop it.

"Do you have anything remotely resembling a plan?" Andrews wanted to know.

"I don't think you could call it a plan." I opened the door to the truck before he'd come to a complete stop right in front of the building.

As I was getting out and Andrews was pulling up the emergency brake, I noticed a small crest above the door, like a family shield from English peerage.

"Hey," I called to Andrews, "have a look at this. What does it look like to you?"

"What does *what* look like?" He turned off the engine and climbed out of the cab.

I pointed. He looked.

"It's a coat of arms," he said, staring.

We were looking at a shield with three sets of wings in a diagonal design on a stripe of red, a helmet of armor above it, a bit of ornate background, all topped with the motto: *Fidélité est de Dieu*— Faith is in God. I had to shift a little to the left to get the light on it just right, but then I could clearly read the name *Wingfield* at the bottom of the crest.

"Well," Andrews said softly, "it looks like the genuine item. I've seen a million of these things."

I stared up at it. "I've never quite been able to understand some people's obsession with ancestry. Lineage is an accident, I think. I just haven't ever put any stock in it."

"That's because you've always secretly hoped that you were adopted," Andrews said, only half in jest. "You'd rather not believe in family history because your family is so very, very strange."

"Fair enough," I sighed.

We stood a moment more, looking up at the Wingfield crest. I was trying not to think too much about it. Andrews was trying to peek into the building through the old newspaper in the windows. Neither of us was having much success.

"Shall we?" I said finally.

I put my hand on the door, turned the handle, but, of course, it was locked. Just as I was about to suggest that we go around back, as we had at Miss Etta's with such success, we were startled nearly out of our wits by sudden, blasting music. Human voices created a wall of sound that rattled the windows of the little building, and shook the newspaper rags.

"And am I born to die?" the song began. "To lay this body down? And must my trembling spirit fly into a world unknown?"

"Do these people meet all the time?" Andrews whispered incredulously.

"Didn't Elder James tell us that this is a special season?" I asked just as softly. "I got the impression there's some outside impetus for so much activity."

The song continued to spill out into the air.

"I know this tune," Andrews whispered, astonished. "Why would I know this song? Is it that Sacred Harp crap?"

"A little reverence, please, for a genuine American folk art form," I said, speaking barely over the music.

"But I mean how would I know it?" he insisted.

"Well, it's possible that you know it because they used it in a movie called *Cold Mountain.*"

"Oh." He seemed a little less spooked. "I did see that movie. Creepy song, though."

"I think we can use this as our cover. We could slip into the basement while they're distracted with their singing."

"You're not serious." He stood his ground. "You can't possibly consider breaking into this place with those gun-toting crazies actually in it."

"I'm not leaving this town again empty-handed." I knew that I wasn't rational. I knew that I was being insane. I didn't care. I simply pointed to the side of the building where several windows lay in the cinder-block foundation. "They seem like they'd be easy to get into. You can stand guard if you want to."

He glanced at the windows. "I hate this plan."

"It's not so bad," I reasoned, completely irrationally. "They're occupied in there. We can hear everything they're doing. We can keep tabs on them. If they stop singing, we'll get out."

"You don't think they can hear us too?" he said, barely audibly. "The truck pulling up, the door slamming, our voices before they started singing? They heard us before."

"Maybe." I shrugged. "But they don't know it's us."

"They don't? They knew it last night!"

"It's part of the beauty of my current insanity. They'd *never* believe we'd be stupid enough to come back here today. I mean, would you believe it? Didn't they do their absolute best to scare us far, far away?"

"One should have thought," he opined in his finest Noel Coward. "And yet, here we stand."

"But not for long," I assured him, heading for the side of the building. "I'm going down into their basement. You can get back into the truck if you want to. You can be ready to take off in case there's trouble."

He actually thought about it for a second before he said, "Lucinda would kill me dead if I left you here. And *me* she wouldn't pack in snow and revive. I'd just be dead. Then she'd just leave my body on some lonesome mountainside to be eaten by crows and, I don't know, bobcats."

"Probably right," I agreed over my shoulder.

"You do realize that you've completely lost your mind and we'll probably be killed."

"Uh-huh," I agreed. "So why are you going along with me?"

He shrugged. "Because you said you had an intuition. And when you say that, you're almost always right. What did Lucinda tell me? That you have a habit of being right when most people think you're not, something like that? So, it's really her fault that I'm in this with you. Our murders will be on her conscience."

"Nice bit of pretzel logic," I said, smiling.

I knelt down beside the first window. These weren't covered and I could see in. Dimly lit tables and file cabinets filled the space. I put my face close to the glass. The place was unkempt but seemed to be organized—after a fashion. I put my hand on the lower part of the window and pushed. It didn't budge. The singing in the hall seemed to grow louder. I looked up at Andrews.

"I might have to break the glass," I said softly.

"Try the other windows first, Igmo."

"Igmo?" I glared up at him.

But I did slide over and try the other windows—with no luck. I absently took in a few more lyrics in the remarkably loud hymn: "And see the Judge with glory crowned, and see the flaming skies!"

"Now can I break a window?" I insisted, crouching down by the one farthest from the front of the building.

"Can you do it quietly?" he whispered.

I nodded and began to use my fingernails to chip away at the ancient molding around one of the panes of glass. I thought it might be possible for me to dislodge the pane without breaking it, just lift it away, and reach in to open the whole thing. It would take a bit longer, but it would certainly be quieter.

But Andrews would not be pleased. "What's taking so long?"

Irritated, I picked at the brittle putty faster, and in another minute—a span of time made longer by tension—the windowpane came free. I reached in and pushed the lock. The window creaked, but opened wide enough for me to crawl through, headfirst, eventually managing to put my hands on the cluttered table against the wall under the window. I did my best to be careful, but the posture was awkward, and several file folders or large envelopes slid off the table and patted onto the floor.

"Sh!" I could hear Andrews entreat me.

Alas, it was at that moment that the folly of my endeavor came clear: there I was, half in and half out of the basement records library of an organization of raving, rabid lunatics. I was forced to wonder if, perhaps, my mind might not be working properly after all, and that everyone else had been right. Maybe I should have been at home in bed.

That moment did not so much pass as dissolve into the next, and I found myself floundering ridiculously on the disordered tabletop before I managed to find relative stability standing on the dirt floor of the basement.

Having seen my little ballet, Andrews decided that a different approach would be better and so came in feetfirst. It was not, after all was said and done, any better an idea. His feet hit the table, but could find no purchase, and he slid out of control, genuinely injuring his back as it scraped on the windowsill.

But there we were, the lame and the halt, in the midst of the Backwoods Branch of the Official Library of Hell. A small smoke of dim light managed to filter in through the dirty windows. It gave the entire endeavor a rancid luster. The space was lined with tables, cabinets, old crates, cardboard boxes, and resembled nothing so much as a hoarder's attic. At one end where the back door would have been there was a rickety wooden staircase that obviously led to the meeting hall. The walls were unpainted cinder block; the floor was dry, packed dirt. We stood staring for longer, much longer than we should have, just looking around before we got to work, randomly, examining files and cabinets.

"You realize this is hopeless," Andrews whispered. "There's absolutely no system to any of this."

I nodded and kept looking.

After what seemed like days, I realized that there was, in fact, a system. It was not linear, and it was not alphabetical, but it was a system. The entire "library" was organized by states. It was laid out according to a map of America. It began with the northernmost states at the end near the stairs, and at the opposite end in the corner was the section on Florida. Further quick investigation of this phenomenon uncovered the fact that only the original thirteen colonies were represented. When I finally pointed out this system to Andrews, he confessed that he'd already given up.

"Okay," he shrugged, his voice hushed. "But look at this."

He showed me a hand-drawn map of Delaware. On the back there had been written the names of dozens of Dutch families. The page looked very old.

"No," I said quickly, "I mean, this section over here? It's Georgia."

I pointed.

He shrugged.

"Fine," I said, apparently to myself.

I stumbled over boxes in the dirt, and made it to the haphazard section concerning the mountainous regions of my state, and with very little effort after that, found a part of file cabinet concerning Blue Mountain.

A quick pawing through that enclave revealed a folder with the name *Devilin* on it. Even though I had been certain I would find something like that, I was still a little taken aback. I took a second deciding if I really wanted to see what was in it or not, but curiosity was a powerful demon. I opened.

As I leafed through the several dozen pages—cryptic notes, official government documents, letters, a few old photographs—I had the dizzying sensation that I was looking at the contents of the missing tin box, the one stolen from my home. I was certain that some of the things I saw there had even been in that box, or the one from my mother's secret hiding place. The name Newcomb appeared on many of the pages, but I told myself that it didn't really matter: our town had been founded by the Newcomb family, a Newcomb had owned the weird traveling show that had employed my parents for most of their lives; surely there was nothing more than that to link my family with theirs.

But something from the darker, watery depths of my subconscious was thrashing so violently that my dizziness increased and I was suddenly afraid that I might fall asleep again. I looked around desperately, trying to find something that might snap me out of my increasing stupor.

Thank God Andrews noticed.

"What is it?" he whispered, moving quickly to my side.

"I found it," I told him lamely, holding out the folder.

"Okay, well, then, Jesus," he stammered. "Let's get out of here."

He took the folder out of my hands and moved with surprising agility toward the open window. He held out the folder and motioned to me as if he were trying to coax a wild animal out of his house.

"Come on," he said gently.

I moved, wading through honey, not in complete control of my limbs. The sensation of impending sleep would not leave me. I shook my head furiously, eyes squeezed shut. I felt my knees weaken.

Andrews wore a panicked look. He was clearly not certain what he should do.

He was about to toss the folder and come to drag me out the window when a sudden noise froze us both. Someone was unlocking the door to the basement. A split second later there was a voice.

"I heard it too," Travis called to someone in the meeting hall. "I'll check the traps. We got two really big rats last week. You know how they love to eat paper. Why do they eat paper?"

Andrews was scrambling out the window in the next instant. I flew over the boxes in my way and clambered up on top of the table. My cohort's legs were in my way. I pushed on his feet. He grunted and moved faster. I shot a look out past his bulk to make certain that he had the all-important folder in his hand.

"Hey, gee, you'uns hear that?" Travis called out. "Sounds big. Come on. I'm not going down there myself."

His hesitation gave me the extra seconds I needed to scrape out the window after Andrews, ripping my pants, skinning my hands, and hurting my left foot, the one with the missing toe.

I dragged myself out onto the ground, the window slammed down, and Andrews took off running toward the truck.

I scrambled up just in time to hear as significant a stream of cursing as I had ever known in my life. No deity, parent, or sexual activity escaped its scope. I assumed Travis and others had discovered that someone had broken into their Fortress of Decrepitude.

I had barely made it to my feet when the first shots were fired.

Running despite aches and pains and the lax muscles of the recently un-comatose, I nearly caught up with Andrews before the next shots whizzed past my head.

"Christ!" I called out, ducking.

"Fever?" Travis's voice called out.

Someone else yelled, "That sumbitch!"

"Hold your fire, damn," Travis yelled back. "Stop it!"

I didn't look back. I shot forward as fast as my legs could make me. Andrews was already in the truck and starting the engine. I was wheezing like a steam engine, but I made it to the door. Before I even opened it, Andrews began backing the truck up.

"Wait," I coughed, like a drowning man.

"Come on, then!" he answered, not slowing the truck one whit.

I managed to open the door and jump in just as he shoved the gearshift into first. He slammed down the accelerator, and instantly shifted into second gear, spewing mud and slush and dead leaves everywhere behind us.

We were a mile down the road before I realized what had happened.

"Wait," I said, my heart still threatening to explode. "Travis told them to stop shooting at us. And they did."

There hadn't been a shot fired after Travis's directive.

I turned to look out the back of the truck where a perfectly nice rear window had once been.

"And no one's chasing us," I continued. "Something's weird."

"We just got shot at!" Andrews yelled. "Again!"

"I know, but—"

"Someone was trying to kill us!" He wouldn't calm down. His face was red and his eyes were bulging.

"But, see, when they saw that it was us, they stopped shooting."

He eased back on the pedal just a little. "They did?"

"And they're not behind us now. They're not coming after us."

He glanced in the rearview mirror. "That is weird."

"He called my name. Travis called my name." My breathing was still a little out of control.

"What's going on?" he asked, his face returning to its typical London pallor.

"I don't know."

I glanced down at the stolen folder that lay on the seat between us. Andrews saw that I was staring at it.

"Go on," he urged. "Have a look at the thing that almost got us killed. Again."

Against almost every fear I had to the contrary, I picked it up and began to examine its contents.

After a time—seconds or hours, I had no idea—I offered my halting summary. "T-Bone Morton was, according to some of this information, a long-lost son of the jazz genius Jelly Roll Morton. T-Bone Morton and Lisa Simard, a woman from a famous French wine family, had a daughter. That baby was given to a member of the Newcomb family, the branch that lived in New Orleans. But one of them, a man called Jeribald 'Tubby' Newcomb, brought the girl to this part of Georgia. He was, as I have told you, one of the original founders of Blue Mountain. The records reveal—I mean, I think this is what they say: that the girl, T-Bone and Lisa's daughter, a baby who had been smuggled out of Chicago on the run from men who wanted to kill her—that girl married a Devilin when she was seventeen."

"Wait," Andrews said, letting his foot off the accelerator. "What?"

"This is what the Earl of Huntingdon wanted me to find." My shoulders sank as I truly relaxed for the first time in days.

"I don't understand," Andrews said, turning to look at my profile.

"That girl, the daughter of T-Bone and Lisa," I said slowly, a smile coming to my lips, "was my maternal great-grandmother."

24.

I couldn't stop smiling for the rest of the drive back to my home. Andrews contributed to my mood significantly.

"You get to be related to Jelly Roll Morton!" he kept saying.

"It is a bit like finding out you were a descendent of George Washington," I admitted.

"Except George only founded a country," Andrews said. "Jelly Roll invented *Jazz*."

"I want to study the things in the folder a little more closely," I said. "I want to compare this stuff to the stuff in the box I found in my mother's room. Plus, I think some of these things were in the other box, the famous blue box that was stolen from my home when I was shot."

"Why are there two boxes?" It was a simple question.

"My parents were psychotically secretive. I believe that my mother hid information about a lot of things all over our house, buried in our yard, probably other places too. My father certainly buried money in different locations on our property. It's actually possible that the stolen box could be one of dozens. But some of the things in this file were in that blue box, I'm almost certain."

"Hang—hang on." Andrews stammered a bit soberly, "wouldn't that mean the man who shot you has been to the meeting hall in

Fit's Mill—wait, one of the men who just shot at us back there might be the—Travis! Travis is the guy who tried to kill you!"

He squirmed excitedly in his seat, having solved the crime.

"Before the past couple of days," I said, somewhat more skeptically, "I would have agreed with you. Completely. But now puzzling evidence to the contrary gives me pause."

"What *evidence*?"

"You started it," I told him. "Travis seemed to be trying to tell me who was trying to kill me. He has recently been much more cordial to me than he's ever been. And just now he stopped his cohorts from shooting us."

"He can't just gun you down on the main street of his home town," Andrews objected, "especially knowing that your oldest friend is the sheriff of the next town over. Of course he told them to stop."

"Well, that's a good point," I admitted.

"We have to tell Skidmore what's just happened." Andrews stepped on the accelerator again.

"We have to tell Skidmore that we broke into a private library, stole documents, and fled the scene under gunfire?"

"Well," he demurred, "that's not the way we'd say it."

"Exactly how would we say it?"

"We'd say," he told me emphatically, "that we think Travis is the one who tried to kill you. Skidmore would go arrest him and get the truth."

"But we don't think that Travis is the one who tried to kill me."

"We don't?" he asked.

I looked down at the folder then, and realized something about it.

"Hey," I said. "This folder is a different color and kind from every other folder that was in the drawer about Blue Mountain. Look."

I held it up.

"I can't look, I'm driving," he complained. "What is it?"

"It's not like any of the others in the drawer, I'm saying."

"So?"

I set it back down on my lap. "I don't know. But it means something. It might mean that the person who stole the things from my house, who tried to kill me, and who collected all of this information about this genealogy—that person might be from someplace else. Not from around here."

"Because it's in a different colored folder?" he asked.

"Well," I answered, looking down at it, "kind of."

"Has it concerned you at all," Andrews began slowly, "that you've taken us on a series of very strange adventures in the past couple of days?"

"Strange adventures?"

"Well, for one thing," he began, "I've been shot at more times in the past seventy-two hours than in the previous, say, six years."

"People often shoot at you when you're with me. It's not you, it's me."

"That's right," he agreed a little too enthusiastically. "You're the Kiss of Death, you are. But that's not my point. These little escapades have been some of the most, I don't know, *surreal* ever— and I think you'd agree: that's saying something."

"You're right about that too, but what's your point?"

"You've been sleeping for three months. Shortly before that, you were dead. I have to take everything you say with a whole shaker full of salt, and even then it doesn't seem seasoned enough to eat."

"What?" I asked.

"Maybe you're not entirely in command of your faculties," he explained softly. "Maybe your interpretation of events isn't the most stable."

I nodded. "I was just worrying about that," I admitted, "when I was halfway through the window back there."

I was surprised to look up and discover that the trip had flown by. We were clattering up the mountain toward my house. For some reason, I was *not* surprised to see a police car in my yard.

Skidmore was sitting on the front porch. Deputy Melissa Mathews was pacing back and forth. We hadn't even pulled up into my yard before Skidmore was down the steps and headed toward my truck, talking.

We couldn't understand what he was saying, exactly, but the gist of it was clear: he was upset that we hadn't done what he'd told us to do.

By the time I got my car door open, he was rounding the truck toward me with a look of righteous fire in his eyes. He actually had his handcuffs out.

"So I am officially arresting you," he was saying, "and confining you to your home under penalty of the law, the harshest penalty I can come up with!"

"What?" I managed to say before he took me by the arm.

He was shoving me in the direction of my front porch and Andrews was loping beside us trying to figure out what was happening.

"I've brought Deputy Mathews with me to enforce this injunction."

Melissa was trying very hard not to laugh.

Skidmore hustled me up the steps and into my living room. He deposited me onto my sofa and began lumbering around me.

"You leave the hospital before you're supposed to. You won't stay in bed and eat Girlinda's soup. You gallivant all over the county. You get shot at! I mean, have you *seen* the back window of your truck!"

"Well, of course," I began.

"Shut up!" he roared. "You are to stay in this house and keep away from any more investigation of anything beyond what to eat for lunch, you hear me? I have to drag Melissa off your own case and make her stay here to keep you from killing yourself because you won't do what anybody tells you to do for your own good! Have you just been to Fit's Mill?"

"When I tell you what we found—" I began again.

"Have you just been to Fit's Mill?" he interrupted, louder than before. "Against my explicit instructions to the contrary?"

"But the thing is—" Andrews started to say.

"You!" Skidmore turned his ire toward Andrews. "I've a good mind to have you deported."

"I have dual citizenship," he said quickly. "But the point is—"

"The point is," Skidmore ranted, "that I came over here to show you what I've been doing about your case, and you weren't here. You weren't here like I told you to be less than two hours ago!"

Only then did I notice that several laptop computers were set up on the kitchen table, along with what looked like an old stereo system.

Skidmore saw me looking at the setup and seemed to calm down a little.

"That's what I brought you," he said, sighing, exasperation filling every word.

"What is all that?" Andrews said, following our gaze.

"That, gentlemen," Melissa said proudly, edging into the kitchen, "is the most current and up-to-date voice recognition software in America. It's what the sheriff's been waiting for. He got it from the FBI."

Andrews looked at me, not Skid. "FBI? Really?"

"That's right," Skid said, a little of his anger subsiding in the face of the new gadgets he'd brought. "This software has taken a sample of your attacker's voice from his 911 call that I played you in the hospital. They say it can be as significant as a fingerprint."

"It's going through every database in the country," Melissa said, sitting down in front of one of the computers. "It's listening to every 911 call ever recorded, every phone call to every police station in the past ten years, every anonymous tip or threat or—I mean, I hate to think of what else it's listening to. But it's already found three potential matches and we've only had it set up for half an hour."

"We haven't listened to anything yet, you understand," Skid explained. "We have to let it finish what it's doing."

Melissa was staring at the screen in wide-eyed wonder. "Isn't this amazing?"

I found myself transfixed by her expression, and trying to think how old she was—twenty-four or so? I reminded myself that she was a person who'd been born into a world of computers. All I could think about was my grandparents sitting at that same table when they were her age, a time when the cabin had no electricity. I thought about a time, fewer than a hundred years before, when wood fire in the oven cooked the food, oil lamps lit the living room, and a lap dulcimer and cheap guitar made all the evening's entertainment. And there I was, waiting for a computer, something the size of the file folder I was clutching, to check every human voice ever recorded in America.

"I know you don't want to hear this," I said to Skidmore calmly, "but I did find something at Fit's Mill that bears scrutiny—yours and mine both."

It was clear from his posture, the tension in his neck, and the way that he turned to look at me that the last thing he wanted to do in the world was hear what I had to say. But to his credit, he forced himself to ask, "What did you find?"

"You're not going to believe it," Andrews joined in.

I held up the folder. "I think I found some of the things stolen from my house when I was attacked. And I think I might have found out a lot more than that."

"He's related to Jelly Roll Morton!" Andrews exploded.

"Who?" Skid said calmly.

"You can't be serious," Andrews said.

"Not the point," I insisted. "The point is that someone in Fit's

Mill, or someone from somewhere else who came to Fit's Mill, collected genealogical records about me and my maternal heritage."

Skidmore shifted his weight to one leg and let out his breath. "I have no idea what you're getting at."

"Right." I sat back. "This is going to require—I'm going to have to try to piece some of this together as I go along. Do you want me to just talk, or do you want me to put it all together and then make some sort of presentation?"

"Fever," Skidmore began, the irritation returning to his voice.

"I don't know what it means," I said quickly, "but my mother was hiding, for most of her life, something about her family heritage. And somebody else, maybe my father, maybe this strange character who keeps referring to himself as the Earl of Huntingdon—"

"The old guy you saw us with in Miss Etta's this morning," Andrews filled in.

"But somebody wanted me to find out what she was hiding," I continued. "Somebody left clues. They were in the tin box behind the clock on the mantel for most of my life here in this house. I ignored them, the way you ignore a lot of things about your parents and your family when you're a younger person. It didn't make any difference to me at the time. All I wanted was to get away. I couldn't wait to leave this place, and I couldn't have cared less about my family heritage."

"I don't see what this has to do with anything," Skidmore mumbled.

"It's the root of what's happened to me," I told him. "Could you sit down?"

"No."

"Look." I shifted my weight on the sofa, "if you just sit down and listen for a moment, I can tell you what I think is the motive for the attack that almost killed me. And I can offer up a couple of prime suspects."

"A motive." Skidmore looked away.

"It's the thing I haven't wanted to think about," I admitted. "I certainly haven't wanted to talk about it. Why would a total stranger walk into my house, shoot me, call 911 to brag about it, and have such intense anger in his voice when he did? I may not be anybody's favorite person, but I certainly can't remember doing anything that would provoke that kind of venom."

"I've thought about this every day," Skidmore admitted, finally taking a seat in one of the overstuffed chairs across from the sofa. "Lots of times I come to the conclusion that it's my fault. Somebody wants to kill you because you've helped me in my work. You've been involved in the criminal world around here because of me. You've made enemies."

"Huh," Andrews said absently, collapsing onto the sofa beside me. "I guess I'd kind of thought it might be somebody from the university. Academics? They really know how to hold a grudge."

Skid and I looked at Andrews.

"You have no idea how vicious that world is," he explained to Skidmore. "You make an enemy in academia, you'd better sleep with a pistol under your pillow."

I smiled. "This is a nice bit of Freudian follies. You're both interpreting the motivation according to your own fears and foibles."

"And that's a nice bit of alliteration, Dr. Devilin," Andrews responded, "but I do, upon immediate examination, agree with your assessment."

Skidmore seemed less certain, but didn't say anything.

"No," I continued, "I have to tell you the abbreviated version of a much longer story, a story that my mother may have told me, and also that might have been whispered to me when I was in a coma. It's about my great-grandmother."

"God Almighty." Skidmore shook his head, entirely exasperated.

"You have to wait for the voice recognition program to work its voodoo anyway," I told him. "Why not give this a chance, what I'm about to tell you?"

He folded his arms in front of him, a thinly veiled, traditional gesture of unwillingness to listen, to accept.

I plunged ahead anyway.

"Early in the twentieth century in New Orleans," I began at a healthy clip, "there was a man called Jelly Roll Morton. He is one of the people who might rightly be cited as the inventor of jazz. He was certainly the first published jazz composer. He played the piano."

"Damn it, Fever," Skidmore swore.

"If you interrupt me," I said politely, "this will take longer. I'll hurry."

He sighed deeply and closed his eyes.

"Jelly Roll had a son, may have had many children, but the particular son in whom we are interested for the purposes of our story was named T-Bone. His mother was a Storyville prostitute called Eulalie Echo. T-Bone was raised in the brothels, taken to Chicago as a youth, and became a saxophone player. He fought in World War I, stayed in Paris when the war was over, and fell in love with a French woman named Lisa Simard. Unfortunately, the mother, Eulalie Echo, had other children. She was addicted to cocaine, a little crazy, and had followed Jelly Roll when he'd left New Orleans to go to Chicago. Jelly Roll did not recognize or acknowledge her and it made Eulalie Echo crazier. She raised another son, a boy who—have I mentioned that Jelly Roll Morton was an African-American and Eulalie Echo was a Caucasian?"

"What?" Skidmore asked, more out of irritation than curiosity.

"That's an important part of this story," Andrews chided me. "You should have mentioned that at the top."

"I forgot." I shrugged.

"You forgot?" Andrews sat forward. "It's the most important element of the story!"

"Right," I agreed. "Right. Let me start over."

"Please don't start over," Skidmore said quickly. "I have a gun."

"This woman, the prostitute, was white," I went on immediately, "and so T-Bone was a bit mixed. But the woman had another son by a white man, an anonymous white man, and that son was named Chester Echo. He is, apparently, the crux of the biscuit."

"I hate that phrase," Andrews mumbled.

"Please shut up," Skidmore said in tones of mock-civility.

"Chester Echo," I went on, "was fed on the—fed on the burning coals of racial hatred, and he slept in the broken glass of rage."

Andrews sat up. "Now there you go," he said. "That's great."

"Not mine," I admitted. "The point is, Chester was raised on racism, taught to hate, and the primary object of his hatred was, as it turns out, his half brother, T-Bone Morton."

"Why?" Skidmore asked, in spite of himself.

"Because, as I have been told, the mother, Eulalie, was ashamed or enraged that she'd slept with a black man," I answered, "or lots of black men, as a prostitute. Her general shame and rage, exacerbated by what may have been a prodigious amount of cocaine, made her insane. Her insanity poisoned her son Chester. Her son Chester determined that the only way to rid his mother of her troubles was to go to Paris and kill T-Bone, then wipe out all knowledge of his existence and the evidence of his mother's degradation."

"It's all very Shakespearean," Andrews opined.

"Not now," I snapped at Andrews under my breath.

"Hold on," Skidmore said, unfolding his arms. "This has got something to do with that Klan-type operation over there in Fit's Mill."

"You know about them?" I asked.

"Sure. They're organized as a nonprofit church, so their business has to be on record with the county. They call themselves

the Sons of Wingfield, whatever that means, and they're connected with several white supremacist organizations all over the
country."

"How in the hell would you know about this?" Andrews had to
know.

Skidmore turned a withering gaze toward Andrews. "Being
sheriff is not my hobby, Dinkus. It's my job. And I'm really good
at it. You don't understand how I could get all this computer
stuff from the FBI whenever I want it? I work with them all the
time. Fever, here, doesn't participate in every case I have. There
are a hundred other police matters outside the confines of his
little escapades with me, and you. The FBI, along with local law
enforcement, has kept the Sons of Wingfield under fairly close
surveillance—especially since September of 2001."

"Wait." Andrews nodded slowly. "Because they're considered
a—what? A domestic terrorist organization. Good. They are."

Skidmore exhaled.

"Okay but what I'm trying to tell you," I broke in, "is that Chester Echo went to Paris to kill T-Bone Morton. Instead, this Lisa
Simard, the woman T-Bone loved, killed Chester. Then T-Bone
and Lisa had a child. Then Lisa was murdered. Not sure who did
that, but T-Bone brought his baby daughter back to America. He
landed in Chicago, which he knew to be the jazz capital of the
world at the end of the 1920s. Turns out that Eulalie Echo found
out that he was back and sent some of her friends, Chester's friends,
more Klansmen, to kill T-Bone in a dance hall. That didn't happen, but T-Bone, for the safety of his daughter, gave the child to
some people back in New Orleans who happened to be named
Newcomb. Some of that family had already come to these mountains, as you well know, and founded Newcomb Junction that has
now become Blue Mountain. They sent the baby daughter here,
the child of T-Bone Morton and Lisa Simard, who married a Devilin and became my great-grandmother."

That broke through all of Skidmore's walls. "What?" he said very loudly.

"That's what I said!" Andrews butted in. "He's related to the man who invented jazz. Fever! Can you imagine?"

"That's what your little story means?" Skidmore asked me incredulously. "You have African-American kin?"

"I'm not certain *that's* the most significant point of my story . . ."

"But you think it tells you why someone wanted to kill you?" he asked more slowly.

"It might even tell me *who* tried to kill me," I answered.

Andrews turned fully my way. Skidmore leaned forward. Even Melissa, from her place in the kitchen, turned in her chair to see my face.

"Who?" Skidmore asked.

"The ghost," I told them all, "of Chester Echo."

25.

Little explanation of my suspicions was needed. Skidmore thought he understood immediately.

"These boys, these Fit's Mill boys," he said, "they found out about your family, your great-grandmother, and they didn't like it."

"I'm trying to tell you that it's more complicated than that," I said, staring down at the folder in my hand.

"I think Travis did it," Andrews insisted. "That seems obvious to me. He shot at us. At least twice."

"Travis," Skidmore said, almost to himself.

"I don't get any of this," Melissa called from the kitchen, her attention turned back to the computer screen.

"You don't get any of what?" Andrews asked.

"I don't think Dr. Devilin is right about this thing," she said, not looking our way, eyes still glued to her work. "Sorry, Fever, but who cares about that stuff these days? I mean, who doesn't get it that we're all mixed-something-or-other. I saw it on television, the—what's the percentage of black people in America that's related to Thomas Jefferson? Like, did you ever see that show from the seventies that was actually called *The Jeffersons*? I guess they knew even way back then, right? We're all mixed."

I stared blankly at Melissa's profile. "I don't know where to begin. I mean, I don't know which one of my seven hundred re-sponses comes first."

Skid smiled. "She's young."

"I know," I railed, "but she doesn't ever watch the news? She doesn't see what's going on in America?"

"I see," she said matter-of-factly. "I just think that it's all older people who have these problems. Nobody my age worries about that kind of thing anymore. Nobody cares what *race* you are, gee."

I looked over at Andrews and said, "Wouldn't it be great if that were actually true?"

"Yeah," he answered, looking down, "but it's not."

"I know."

Skidmore cleared his throat. "Maybe I should actually take a look at what's in that folder you've got there."

I nodded and handed it to him.

He opened it, sorted through the pictures, read the documents; chewed on the inside of his lower lip.

In that silence, I finally had a moment to let a few things sink in. I had a chance to consider the new facts of my maternal heri-tage. I didn't completely understand it, but I felt a certain dawn-ing, odd pride. My body carried the genes of genius. On the other hand, the life experiences of Jelly Roll Morton could not have been further away from mine if we'd been born on different plan-ets. I had no more understanding of his life, or the life of any person of color in America, than Andrews did. So I was left to wonder what the new revelation truly meant.

I had always fallen down on a kind of Buddhist approach to family: biology is an accident of birth. You have to find, in this lifetime, your true family. It's comprised of people you know and trust and love, no matter what the biology is. It had never made any sense to me that some people put so much stock in genealogy. On a practical level, I had always celebrated the fact that I was nothing like my mother, and even less like my father. So if it was the case that someone had tried to kill me because of ancestors I never knew, never even knew existed, then reality was, at best, a tentative and transparent folly, a play, or maybe a tale told by an idiot, filled with sound and fury, signifying nothing.

I smiled at that, and leaned over to nudge Andrews. "Isn't it about now that you should be giving out with the appropriate quotations from the Bard?"

"I wondered what you were thinking about just now," Andrews responded. "You seemed so deeply sunk in."

"I was."

"And didn't you just tell me that not everything had to do with Shakespeare?" he asked.

"I did."

"But now you want my pronouncement."

"I do."

"Well, oddly," he began in his best scholastic tones, "Shakespeare does have a great deal to say on the subject of race."

I smiled.

"In *Othello,* Iago hates his commander because of his race. To get even, he tells Othello lies about his wife to enrage him. He says, 'I'll pour this pestilence into his ear,' which is exactly what Eulalie Echo did to her son Chester all his life. She poisoned her son with a unique brand of hatred until he was insane."

"Yes, *Othello* would have been the one I'd have started with."

"Or how about the Prince of Morocco in *The Merchant of Venice,*" he went on, as if I hadn't spoken, "who says, 'Misslike me not for my complexion.'"

"But—" I began.

"Or let's try 'Hate all, curse all, show charity to none.' That sounds a lot like Eulalie, her son, and the boys of Wingfield or whatever they call themselves, doesn't it?"

"It does," I confirmed. "What's that from?"

"*Timon of Athens,*" he told me.

"You've been collecting these in your mind for a while now, haven't you?" I asked.

He nodded.

"Just waiting to say them."

"I have at least a dozen more," he admitted.

"Well, amusing as that is," Skidmore said with absolutely no amusement in his voice, "I would like to interrupt with a little, well, useful thinking. I'm going to make Melissa stay here and babysit so that you don't leave this house while I go to Fit's Mill and see can I get some answers."

"You don't want to wait until the program gets done with everything?" Melissa asked.

"I don't have any idea how long it'll take for that to happen," he snapped, "and if these two morons just came from breaking into some secret vault they got over there, I need to get over there and mess with Travis before they clean it up."

"Well I guess you could also get a recording of Travis's voice," Melissa snapped right back, "so we can see does it match up with the one on the tape!"

Skidmore exhaled. "Yes. Good idea. I should use the—?"

"Use the shoulder radio-recorder that the State Patrol gave us," she sighed. "That way you just wear it, it looks official, you turn it on before you get out of the car, and it records the entire conversation."

"Okay." He shook his head.

"Did you talk?" I whispered, glancing into the kitchen at Melissa.

"Didn't get a chance to," he whispered back. "After I left you'uns, I saw her pull in at the station with all this computer mess."

I nodded.

"Melissa?" he called out.

"Sir?" she answered.

"If either one of these two children tries to set one foot out of this house while I'm gone," he told her in no uncertain terms, "you have full authority to shoot them both."

"Both?" Andrews asked reflexively. "If he tries to leave, I get shot?"

"Teach you both a lesson you won't soon forget," Skidmore told him.

"Shoot to kill?" Melissa asked cheerfully.

"You do what you have to do," he answered.

"All right," I said, hauling myself off the sofa and wincing at my sore leg, "then you can see yourself out. I'm going upstairs to check my wounds."

"Wounds?" Skid asked, genuinely concerned.

"I hurt hands and feet getting in through the window over there to get that folder," I told him, heading toward the stairs. "I want to anoint myself with Neosporin."

"I hurt my back," Andrews chimed in, following me.

"Good," Skidmore concluded. "Go upstairs. Stay there. I'll be back directly."

Melissa made a great show of taking her pistol out of its holster, checking it for bullets, and laying it on the table beside her laptop, all without looking our way.

"Sheriff," she said very casually, her eyes still on the computer screen, "before you leave over there to Fit's Mill, would you have a look at this? I think you're going to find it very interesting."

I started to say something about how that might be the moment for Skidmore to talk with Melissa, but Andrews read my mind and shook his head. So I began, instead, to hobble up the stairs.

Melissa called after us. "You'uns don't mess around with the sheriff today, hear? He's got something on his mind that's worrying him. I don't know what it is, but he's in a rare mood. Fair warning."

I heard Skidmore say, "You know I'm worried?"

But I didn't hear the rest. I realized at the top of the stairs that

I had successfully fought off a sleep attack, and was quite pleased with myself, but also entirely exhausted.

"I think I have to lie down," I mumbled to Andrews.

"I should think that would be the case," he agreed. "You haven't had a nap in—what?—three or four hours?"

"Very funny," I mumbled, lumbering toward my bed. "You didn't think I should mention Melissa's . . . situation just now?"

"I did not." He followed me into my room. "If she wanted to chat about it, she would. Clearly, it's a private matter."

I nodded my agreement and collapsed onto my quilt.

"Look," I announced as he took a seat at my desk, "I've been thinking."

"Oh, God," he said instantly. "Not that."

"What does it really mean if I'm related to Jelly Roll Morton?"

"It means enough to Travis and his ilk," Andrews answered, "that they want you dead."

"No." I tried to focus clearly, squeezing my eyes shut, willing myself to stay awake. "Travis might not like it and he might even make fun of it or use it as a kind of justification for all the weird anger he's felt toward me since the school days. But it wouldn't mean enough to him to want to kill me. All this time up here in these mountains, and you still don't understand that it's all right to torment the oddballs, but ultimately we're family. If you started saying the same kind of thing to me that Travis has said to me all my life, and he heard you? He'd kick you to the ground before you knew what was happening. We can make fun of each other, but if anyone else does? Hell to pay."

" 'He may be a fool, but he's our fool.' "

"What?"

"It's a Randy Newman song. Something about Lester Maddox, the cracker governor of your state back in the bad old days. 'He may be a fool, but he's our fool.' "

"Well, I don't know the song," I admitted, "but the sentiment is right on the money."

"You don't think Travis tried to kill you," he went on. "Despite evidentiary events to the contrary."

"I think it's a family problem."

"What?"

"Who was it, when they were describing the conflict between Judaism and Islam, said that family squabbles are the worst?"

"I don't know what you're trying to say." Andrews inched his chair closer to the bed. It was clear he thought I was falling asleep again

"I think that someone related to Chester and Eulalie Echo is trying to kill me," I said as plainly as I could, "and anyone else related to the mixed-race coupling of T-Bone Morton and Lisa Simard."

"Because?"

"Because that kind of hate is a cellular poison," I explained. "You teach it to your children from the day they're born, and they stay mad about it for all the rest of their lives."

"But—no, wait," Andrews said haltingly.

"I'm descended from Eulalie Echo too," I reminded him, "*if* I'm really related to Jelly Roll Morton. In this scenario, they would be my maternal great-greats or something like that. Maybe three greats."

"You're heir to madness and rhythm." He smiled. "I like that."

"If it's true." I yawned.

"Don't you want to believe it?"

I smiled. "Not if it's not true."

"Why?"

"Because I've spent a long time trying to become exactly who and what I am," I said, lying down on the bed. "That's been difficult enough so far. Throw into the mix that I have this kind of thing to deal with, and I could easily become distracted from the real job."

"What real job?" His voice seemed to be coming from a long way off.

"The job of becoming who I am," I murmured. "I just told you."

He said something else, but it seemed to be in a language I didn't know. And I could barely hear his voice over the cornet solo.

The tiny club was very loud. T-Bone Morton sat in a chair far away from the bandstand, but his left foot was still keeping time with the drummer. The tune was "Honeysuckle Rose" and the cornet solo was red hot, very high, and confection sweet.

T-Bone was not on stage because he was minding the baby. His infant daughter lay sleeping in his arms as if she were in a peaceful forest or a silent nursery. T-Bone couldn't stop smiling.

"That's my girl," he was thinking to himself, staring down at her as she snored. "Loud jazz is mother's milk."

Out of the crowd came a tall, thin man in a black suit. He was not smiling. He walked with stilted purpose through the obstacle course of human bodies and bar stools. Lisa saw him before T-Bone did. She swept around from behind the bar and planted herself between the man and her family.

"*Qui êtes-vous?*" she demanded.

"*Sturmabteilung*," he mumbled in German.

"*Allez-vous!*" she yelled.

The man looked directly at T-Bone and said very clearly, "*Schwarzes tier!*"

There was suddenly a pistol in his left hand. The only thing between the barrel of the gun and T-Bone's heart was the infant daughter, still sleeping.

Lisa smiled at T-Bone over her shoulder as she took one step to her left. It was like a dance, a graceful dip and sway, very beautiful. She did it just as the gun went off. The bullet went though her but T-Bone had already bent his body over their child. The bullet thudded into the wall behind the table where T-Bone had been sitting.

Lisa seemed to drift to the floor like a feather sifting through the air.

The man with the gun stood over her, staring down, watching her bleed. He raised his gun again, to aim it at T-Bone, but T-Bone was gone. Suddenly the man was shoving and grunting past the stunned members of the immediate crowd. The band hadn't stopped playing. No one knew, for another few seconds, what had happened. By the time they did, the man with the gun had made it to the door and vanished into the Paris midnight.

Lisa Simard was dead. In the alley behind the club, T-Bone Morton couldn't breathe; his baby opened her eyes and started to cry.

Suddenly I could hear Andrews over the baby's crying and the echo of the gunshot, like distant thunder.

"Get up!" he was yelling, headed out my bedroom door.

I opened my eyes, disoriented. I blinked. I could hear Andrews crashing down the stairs. There was a louder noise on the front porch, and something else I couldn't quite make out.

Just as I realized something bad had happened, I heard Andrews from below.

"Oh my God!" he howled. "Melissa!"

I realized that the gunshot I had heard had been downstairs in my kitchen, not just in my dream. I bolted out of the room and down the stairs. I could see, as I descended, that Andrews was frozen in the doorway. I was scrambling so fast to get to him that I nearly fell.

I hit the bottom of the stairs, and couldn't figure out why Andrews hadn't moved or spoken.

I lumbered toward him and knocked him forward, onto the front porch.

He stumbled sideways and shouted, "No!"

And I was presented with an almost exact image from my nightmare. A tall, thin man in a black suit stood over Melissa Mathews, watching her bleed. When he looked up, and our eyes met, I registered recognition. He was young. His crew cut made his ears bigger than they already were. He was a funny-looking, goofy kid. I struggled to place where I'd seen him before.

He seemed to be watching my confusion. It made him grin.

Andrews had tumbled to his side because of me and I instinctively went to help him up.

"Let him be," the kid said. He sported an unusually midwestern accent.

I only half-heard him, and disregarded him utterly. Which proved to be a permanently terrible mistake.

Without even looking directly at him, the kid casually pointed his pistol directly at Andrews and fired twice. Andrews never made a sound. His body thudded to the deck of the porch and was still as a stone.

"Upstairs," the kid said, the gun pointed squarely at me.

"What are you doing?" My head was swimming.

"Upstairs, I say," he told me, flailing the air with his gun.

I stumbled backward, grabbing the door frame. He flew toward me; jabbed the gun in my ribs.

"That's right, you son of a bitch," he said into my ear. "It's me."

I had no idea who he was.

He spun me around and shoved me forward. I fell toward the

banister and righted myself just as I felt the stab of the pistol in my lower back. I was genuinely terrified that I would pass out. There was no question of my being able to defend myself in such a disoriented frame of mind—and body. All I could do was stagger up the stairs and try to breathe.

We reached the landing and he kicked me toward my room.

"I want you in that bed," he growled, "so I can finish what I started, exactly the way I done before, only right this time, don't you know."

My head was pounding, and my brain felt as if it might be boiling in my own blood. I could barely hear him—or move, or breathe, or speak. I was absolutely certain he was about to shoot me very dead.

Something frenzied in me tried to catch hold of anything I might use as a weapon. The door? Could I slam the door on his gun hand? My lamp? Could I bash in his head with my lamp? The bed? Could I throw him onto the footboard and knock him unconscious?

I happened to glance, then, at the Currier and Ives picture of a sleigh being pulled by two horses, and everything suddenly seemed to go into slow motion. I felt light-headed, and barely moved. My breathing was shallow, and the images of ordinary reality faded.

I saw a face that was not a face and it said, very softly, "Do you recognize me?"

"No," I think I said. "Should I?"

"We only have a moment together." It hovered like a mist in the room beside my bed. "Do you have a story to tell me?"

I could not look away. "A story?"

Then the angel vanished.

In the next second, the kid was shoving me forward again, and I tumbled into my bed.

He stood over me and for the first time I saw him in the right light. He was the goofy orderly I had seen when I'd first awakened in the hospital.

"Are you Albert?" I asked. "Are you the orderly who was going to bring me soup?"

"So you know who I am," he sneered, the gun inches from my head. "I was afraid you might give me away at the hospital, but when I saw that you didn't recognize me, I still thought I had a chance. Until Earl showed up."

The gun in my face was like the nail I had used several days previous: it worked to keep me awake. But I felt the impending, familiar, sickening sensation of slipping into unconsciousness about to overtake me. I thought that if I could rouse myself, I could over-power the boy and call for emergency help. But my limbs were lead, and my head was filled with vapor.

"Who is Earl?" I sat up with my back against the headboard.

"You know very well who he is," he snapped. "Earl Hunt. Your guardian angel. Only he ain't around now. I seen to that."

"I don't know you," I said, trying to stall and let my head clear, "and I don't know anybody named Earl Hunt."

"I don't care what you say," he told me, and I believed him, "I'm going to kill you today for good."

"You were in the meeting hall at Fit's Mill, with Elder James," I realized. "I saw you but I didn't see you."

"So it's all coming clear to you, is it?" He grinned. It was not a happy expression.

"No," I said firmly, the clouds in my cortex dispersing only slightly, "none of this is clear to me. But I guess you're the one who shot out the back window of my truck."

"What?" he sneered. " I ain't shoot up your truck. All I want to shoot is you. And you know why."

At that moment I saw that he was holding my other tin box, the one I'd found in my mother's room. He had it tucked under his arm, near his armpit. For some reason, that made me angrier than anything else. Then, for some reason not entirely clear, the anger actualized something in my brain. I realized why I had seen an "angel" in my room. I knew that my own subconscious angels were directing me to do what my conscious mind had already conceived. I had to wake up to my true self. I had to use the tools that I had always used. I couldn't muster the strength needed to overcome this particular demon physically, but I also couldn't allow him to take my own personal folklore away. So I had to attack him on the battlefield of his own mind.

"I think you have something interesting to tell me," I said calmly. "Do you? Do you have a story to tell me?"

He cocked his head like a troubled dog. "A *story*?"

"I'm asking because I have to be myself," I told Albert, partly to confuse him, partly to say out loud what I was thinking, to convince myself.

"What?" He did, in fact, seem confused for the first time.

"I've been letting events shape my perceptions rather than allowing my perceptions to observe the events." I exhaled.

"Are you trying to mess me up?" He raised his gun. "It won't work."

I settled in my body and in my mind. I assumed the tone of voice and facial expression I had used all my life, hundreds of other times, to get people to tell me their stories.

"I know," I said soothingly. "But you do have something you want to tell me."

"About what?" he growled.

"You want to tell me why you're here," I said simply. "You want me to know what this is all about before you kill me. That's why you didn't just shoot me on the porch with the others. You wanted me to understand what I've done wrong, and why this retribution is righteous."

He nodded without realizing it. "You need to know, all right."

"Then tell me." I sat back and waited.

Silence, as I had so often learned and relearned, could be an interviewer's best instrument. If I sat comfortably in my own silence, ignoring the gun that was pointed at me, oblivious to anything but the boy's face and voice, he would fill the void.

"I wouldn't even know where to start," he sneered. But I could see that he had already begun to think about what he wanted to tell me. It was in his eyes as clearly as if he had already begun.

And that reminded me of another lesson often learned: most people operate under the illusion that they aren't transparent. Most people think they can hide what they're thinking and how they're feeling. But they can't. Not from me.

"Why don't you begin by telling me about Chester and Eulalie Echo," I said.

It was a gamble, but not much of one. If he didn't know who those people were, he'd continue in his confusion. If he did, he'd want to tell me about them. Or it would make him angrier and he'd just go ahead and shoot me. Either way, I'd have less to worry about.

"That's right." He grinned. "That's where it started, you bet."

I smiled before I realized it, because his accent was funny to me. Years of living in the mountains, though punctuated by European travel, had given me an ear for our dialect, but the hard biting, midwestern, quasi-Scandinavian syllables were amusing—even under such dire circumstance. He misunderstood my grin.

"You think you know," he sneered, "but you don't."

"You've heard of them," I suggested.

"Yes, God." He laughed as if I were the stupidest person he's ever met. "Proud to say. Chester started our chapter of the SW."

"The Sons of Wingfield." I nodded.

"Shut up."

Good, I thought, he wants to talk now.

"Chester was dedicated," Albert said proudly. "His whole life was devoted to our work."

"Tell me about that work."

"Our work is you!" he snarled. "People like you. You make me sick to my stomach. I mean, the blacks, they can't help it. If they could all just go on back where they came from, they'd be happy little monkeys in their boom-boom jungle and we'd be shed of them all for good. But people like you, you look like everybody else. Nobody can tell you got a sewer in your blood. Not by looking at you. That's what my people, and Chester and his mom, that's what they did to help. They started the library."

"The library?" I asked before I could think.

"Don't you play like that," he snapped. "You was in the library, the local branch they got around here, just today! We know that was you."

"It was," I acknowledged. "Would you like to sit down?"

He blinked.

"You could sit in my desk chair," I went on. "It's very comfortable."

"Okay." He kept the gun trained on me but maneuvered the chair close to the bed and sat.

"So Chester and Eulalie started some sort of library," I prompted.

"Did you know that Eulalie Echo was not her real name?" he asked me. "She never knew her real name. She was forced into prostitution by the blacks in New Orleans when she was a little girl. I can't hardly stand to think about that. But she was a strong woman, and she bided her time until she could escape New Orleans and get to Chicago where she'd be safe." He nodded for emphasis.

"That's where Chester was born?"

"Yes," he snapped, irritated. "That's where Chester was born. This was back in the ancient times, almost a hundred years ago. I know because we're taught all about it in our church school."

"Church school?"

"SW is a church, you ignorant Son of a B." He sighed, exasperated with my lack of common knowledge. "We got Sunday Bible school just like anybody else. We learn about God and Jesus and General George Gordon and Nathan B. Forrest and Chester Echo—all the men who made this country great."

"I see," I answered contritely. "So Chester Echo started some sort of library, you were saying."

"Yes, damn," he said, shaking his head. "They started the blood library."

"I see."

He blinked. "The problem with this country, see, is that the people who started it got off on the wrong foot."

"How did they do that?"

"They did not keep Captain Edward Wingfield as the first president."

"The first president of what?"

"Damn it," he sighed, "I thought you went to college. You don't know that Wingfield was the first president of America?"

"He was—he was British," I stammered, remembering the brief history recounted by Andrews.

"Yes, he was born in the area of Huntingdon over in the old country, in 1550, but he was the real founder of the original settlement in America. He was the first elected official in this country, voted president by the men of Jamestown colony. He just wanted hard work and purity. That's what was going to make this a great country."

"But something happened," I urged.

He nodded. "After only four months, he was let go. On September 10. They made him a scapegoat and he was sent back to London."

He was obviously remembering some kind of rote-learned lesson. His eyes rolled upward when he sought to recall dates and certain phrases.

"Why?" I asked.

"Weather," he snorted.

"Sorry?"

"That year in Virginia was the worst drought in nearly eight hundred years. Crops failed and they had no food. Lots of people died, either starved to death, got sick and died, or got killed by the naturals."

"The naturals?"

"These so-called *Native Americans*," he sneered. "They tried to kill us, wipe us out of our own land that the king had give us fair and square."

"I don't understand," I told him. "Captain Wingfield was sent back to England because the colony had bad luck?"

"They charged him with being an atheist," Albert said softly, "just because he didn't believe in the Catholic gods."

I struggled not to react physically to that. "The Catholic gods?"

"Wingfield wanted to keep the country pure American," Albert responded angrily. "No Catholics, no coloreds, no slack-offs!"

"Oh." I couldn't think what to say more than that.

"And then that bastard John Smith took over. And you see what he did: took up with that red girl."

"You mean Pocahontas?"

"Shut up!" He leveled his pistol at me again.

I shut up.

"Suddenly anybody could do anything," he mumbled, somewhat incoherently.

"But Chester Echo didn't want that. He and his mother were trying to fix that?"

"They started the blood library," he said again.

"I don't know what that is."

"The hell you don't. You were just in one." He held his pistol steady, pointed directly at my chest.

I tried to take a calming breath. It wasn't working. I tried to keep Andrews and Melissa out of my mind, but there they were. I realized that I was clenching my fists, willing Skidmore to come back to my house, to help them—and me.

I forced myself to keep talking, keep my mind on the immediate.

"The blood libraries," I began tentatively, "are records of people who have mixed heritage."

It was a guess, but seemed an obvious deduction.

"As we say, these people, these blacks, they can go on back where they came from and leave us be. And us whites, we're all fine, of course. But it's mongrels like you that's the problem. If we let you live, by and by there won't be any way to tell who's what."

"Everybody would be one color."

"Right," he said, misunderstanding my argument. "Everyone would be polluted."

I moved slowly to sit up, trying to ready myself for a sudden move when the time was right. I knew I had to begin my ploy because Albert's hand was beginning to shake.

"You do understand that this entire enterprise is built on Eulalie Echo's insanity. She was a cocaine addict and, very likely, suffered from syphilitic dementia. This is all about her strange revenge for imagined abuses."

That lit the candle. Albert's face flushed red the color of a stripe on a flag. He stood up so fast that the chair beneath him flew backward and crashed into my desk.

"I will be so happy to kill you dead," he raved, his hand now wildly twitching. "I took your little tin box before, the one you had on the mantel, so there'd be no physical evidence of Eulalie Echo's shame. I give the contents to the library. But I knew there was another one. You had another box hid. This one."

He wriggled his left arm until he had the other tin box in his hand, the red one I'd found in my mother's room. He held it up close to my face.

"I didn't have it hidden," I told him. "My mother did. How did you know about it?"

Suddenly, with a blinding flash of insight, I realized why one tin box had been kept in plain sight on the mantel, like the Purloined Letter, and another had been hidden in my mother's secret place. That had been done to protect the information against someone like Albert. He'd broken into the house, he'd found the tin—it was obvious. He'd thought he had all the information, and that would be that. But unbeknownst to him or anyone, there was another tin hidden. That is, until I unearthed it and left it lying around for anyone to find.

"Right." He lifted his pistol. "Well, now I'm going to shoot you a whole lot of times so it don't really matter at this point."

"Wait!" I shouted. "You have to tell me: how did you know there was another tin box? You just said you knew there was another one."

He smiled. "I'm happy to tell you that. Your mother. She used to eat over there at Travis's barbecue place and she would talk, especially once she'd had enough to drink. She used to brag about it. Travis egged her on, said he didn't believe her. She told him there was proof hidden in a secret place at her former home. She was actually proud of it, proud, she said, of her family history. But we got the truth, all right."

"What do you mean?"

"One of our brotherhood," he told me, smiling, "some man named Ramsey—he was sweet on your mother, and she liked him too, I guess. She told him all about your family, all about where to find proof. And then Ramsey, he was all tore up when she died, when your momma died. I say good riddance to trash."

Out of nowhere, a knot of grief like a cannonball pounded me into silence. It was a strange, baffling sensation: having sudden great sympathy, and great affection, for my mother. I'd never felt anything like it before, and I nearly lost myself in it.

"In fact your whole family's tainted all to hell," he rattled on. "Dwarves and carnies and hit men. We've had our eye on the whole lot for some time now."

"There must be a lot of you," I mumbled, not really thinking, "if you can keep up with everybody in the country who has mixed heritage."

"You're talking about question number nine."

"What? I am? I don't know what that is." I tried to focus.

"Question number nine on the census form, numb nuts," he sighed. "All they got is five races listed, and a box called 'other.' Only a little more than two percent of the people in this country say they're 'other'—but it's lots more than that. Our records show that nearly half this country's a mongrel, one way or another. I can't hardly stand to walk through the streets of Chicago know-ing what a cesspool it is. Anybody you brush up against could be one, you can't tell just by looking anymore. Take you, for example. Just to look at your face, you'd think you were all right."

"But I'm not?"

He laughed.

I kept straining my ears for the sound of Skidmore's car, trying to will him to come back and see what was going on. I had another completely unfamiliar sensation then: I had an impulse to pray. I found that I only wanted Andrews and Melissa to be saved, and didn't much care what the man with the gun did to me. It would be lovely to report that such a feeling was altruistic, but there was more agony than agape in my thinking.

I couldn't stand the idea that something terrible might happen to Andrews, or to Melissa. I didn't care so much about myself because it had already happened to me. I'd been shot, I'd been in a coma, and I knew I wasn't the same. I had an overwhelming sensation of being on borrowed time—that I'd been revived only to tell one more story, only to say a proper good-bye to the people

I loved. And the evidence of that apprehension was standing two feet away from me holding a gun.

Rousing myself in an attempt to stall Albert long enough to be caught, I stabbed at the only thing that I could.

"Who is Earl Hunt?"

"What?" he snapped.

"You mentioned—"

"You damn well know who Earl Hunt is!" He jabbed the barrel of the pistol into my right cheek. "He's that bastard from New Orleans who got me fired from the hospital. I would have got you then, but he was always around. I even called you in your room, but he was there, watching over you. Always sneaking up behind me. And then when you'd turn around, he'd be gone. He's got some kind of strangeness about him."

I managed to concentrate—the gun touching my skin was significantly bracing. I could tell that he was afraid, in a very primal way, of the strangeness he perceived in this other man.

"I don't know what that sentence means," I said calmly, "the part about his strangeness."

"He's from New Orleans," Albert said, as if it were a complete explanation.

"The Earl of Huntingdon," I said, smiling, feeling very stupid for not comprehending that obvious fact before that moment.

"So-called," Albert sniffed.

"He's the reason I'm still alive."

"One of them, yes," Albert admitted. "We'll get him eventually. We'll also get that nurse you're sweet on. She's the one."

I deliberately focused on the facts instead of the emotions of the moment, although the wall I had constructed between the two was thin and tenuous.

"You want to get Lucinda because she's my fiancée?"

"No."

"Because she saved my life," I concluded.

"No. She's a nurse. That's her job."

"Then," I began haltingly, "why?"

"You know." He looked down at me the way certain young boys look down at a cat they're about to torture.

"I honestly don't," I fully admitted.

"She's got so much Cherokee blood in her," he snorted, "she couldn't have gotten a drink of liquor anywhere in this state a hundred years ago."

The full impetus of Albert's thinking, and the work of the Sons of Wingfield, finally penetrated my brain. They were pursuing a phantasm: the illusion of racial purity. No mixing of any sort was permitted in their pinheaded folly. Their fantasy of pure blood was driving them mad—because the more they did any genuine investigation of any family tree, the more they realized that very few people on the planet could claim the sort of pure blood they were seeking.

For reasons I could not even begin to fathom, I decided to taunt Albert with the facts.

"You have to realize that a subconscious impulse to mix bloodlines is a biological imperative," I began. "The survival of the human race depends on acquiring the full panoply of genetic attributes, the best that every allegedly separate race has to offer. As we do, we become stronger. Eventually, and it may not even be that far in the future, there will only be one race on the planet."

"Shut up!" he warned.

"I mean," I went on, ignoring him, "I'll admit that something's lost in completely forgetting ethnicity. Cultures, traditions, folktales, folkways, cuisine, music, art, dance, language—I could go on and on—are all beautiful in their diversity. Astonishing, in fact. But when everything is said and done, I always discover more similarities than differences, and find the similarities more engaging. Take, for example, the fact that almost every culture on the planet has its own variation of what is basically the same creation mythology."

"I said for you to shut," Albert insisted, smiling, cocking the pistol.

He moved slowly around the bed, close enough to me that I could smell him: a weird combination of liquor, formaldehyde, and Old Spice. He stood with his back to the door, blocking any hope of a sudden escape, his eyes locked on mine.

I looked into those eyes for the first time, really. He was clearly a stupendously ignorant soul, and one who could be manipulated. I stared deeply, and I brought all the overwhelming energy of my fear and grief and passion to bear in that gaze.

"I don't care if you kill me," I told him, and I meant it. "But I do care that you've hurt my friends. If anyone else dies, you won't know a moment's peace ever again. I'll see to that from the other side. I'll crawl up out of my grave. I'll marshal a force of every other spirit ever sent to the grave by you and your kind, and we'll be in your mind, in your heart, in your cells, in your blood, in your *sweat* every second of every day until you run screaming down the corridor of your own death. And that will just be the beginning. You look into my eyes right now. You'll see it's true. *Albert*."

Say the demon's name; it helps to undo its power if you can name it.

His forehead began to glisten. He blinked several times in rapid succession. He tried once or twice to speak before he managed to say, "You got that from Earl, that devil way of talking."

"Yes," I said, even though I had no idea what he was talking about.

"You got his powers." Albert was having a difficult time breathing.

Realizing then what he meant, I launched into the first thing I could remember from my research on gris-gris hexes.

"Ogun Akirun, Ogun Alagbede, Ogun Alara, Ogun Elemona,

Ogun Ikole, Ogun Meji, Ogun Oloola, Ogun Onigbajamo, Ogun Onire, Ogun-un."

My ploy was working; I could see that it was. His eyes glazed, his hands began to quiver, and his mouth went slack. Unfortunately, I could also see that he was about to shoot his gun. I moved ever so slightly to the right, but that seemed to rouse him.

He grinned. "You sure ain't about to get away this time," he whispered.

I saw his finger squeeze the trigger. My right hand flew up and batted the gun to one side. It went off like thunder and the bullet cracked into the headboard of my bed. Albert seemed more confused than ever.

Then, out of nowhere, a shadowy form appeared behind Albert. Someone had come into the room from the hall. There was a flash of something shiny, and Albert was stabbed by something in his arm, and then in his throat. He dropped to the floor like a broken elevator. I thought I might have fallen asleep again, and maybe what was happening was part of a dream, because I was watching an exact duplicate of the scene in a nightclub in Paris, long ago, when Lisa Simard moved across the dance floor to stab Chester Echo and keep him from killing the man she loved.

Albert lay on the floor, his throat gurgling.

In the next instant, Lucinda was by my side, out of breath. "Did he hurt you? What happened? What did he do to you?"

"Nothing," I assured her. "I think—I think I'm okay."

"Thank God," she said, collapsing onto the bed beside me.

"God," I heard myself say.

Lucinda stared down at him. "Who is he? Did you figure that out?"

"You know him," I told her, "His name is Albert something. He was an orderly at your hospital."

"What?" She turned and tried to see his face in the weird light of the room.

I bolted up, struggling to stand. "Andrews. And Melissa!"

She looked at me strangely. "They're fine. Melissa's already on her way to the hospital," she said, her hand on my chest.

"Oh. Jesus." I was having a lot of trouble staying with her. "How did—how did that happen?"

"Well . . ." she began.

But I didn't hear the rest of what she was trying to tell me because Jelly Roll Morton and his Red Hot Peppers had taken up residence in the corner of my bedroom. They were playing a very spirited rendition of "Doctor Jazz" by King Oliver. I couldn't be certain, but the man on tenor sax could have been T-Bone Morton. I know he was looking at me, even as he was playing, and there was overwhelming love in his eyes.

26.

I woke up with a start in a cold, dark hospital room because the night nurse, standing at the end of my bed, had dropped my chart and the noise had roused me.

I blinked. She gasped.

"Oh my God," she whispered.

I slowly recognized Stacey Chambers.

"Nurse Chambers," I managed to say, struggling to sit up.

My voice was grating and garbled.

"Don't try to sit up, sugar," Stacey said excitedly. "We got you all hooked up."

A quick survey of my physical situation confirmed that I had an intravenous needle in each arm and several electrical wires depending from my abdomen. Everything was attached to machines. My bed was the only one in the room. The blinds were drawn. Only one chair sat in the corner. It was a beige hospital chair, all metal and vinyl. It didn't look particularly used.

"You try to stay awake, now," Nurse Chambers said, fussing with one of the machines to which I was connected. "I'm calling Lucinda right this minute."

She reached out and snatched up the receiver. "Hey, Reba," she said breathlessly into the phone, "it's Stacey. Get Lucinda right away. He's awake!"

A wave of déjà vu washed over me and I asked, quite uneasy about the possible answers, "Have I been in a coma again?"

She spun around, smiling. "God, no. You just got here a couple of hours ago."

I let go a sigh that could have cracked the walls, and sat back. "You have no idea how relieved I am to hear that."

"You had a severely elevated heart rate," she went on, all business, "combined with what appears to be fatigue and dehydration. You really shouldn't drink liquor right after you come out of a coma, you realize."

"I didn't drink any liquor," I protested.

"Winnie told me all about your little barbecue luncheon," she sniffed.

"Andrews!" I snapped forward again, and one of the machines to which I was connected began to bleat.

"He's fine, he's fine," she assured me, her hand on my shoulder, giving me what I thought was a very strange look. "It's Melissa we're worried about. She's gut shot, and it's a mess."

"How did they—who came to get them? How did Lucinda know?" I couldn't focus.

Nurse Chambers stopped moving. "Oh. Well. Let's just get Lucinda to tell you all that."

I rubbed my face. "I have to tell you," I mumbled, "that I'm having the weirdest sense of déjà vu ever."

"That's where you feel like you've already done something that you never really did, right?" She busied herself with something on the machine that had made a noise.

"Right," I confirmed.

"Well, isn't that *supposed* to feel weird?"

I had to agree. "I guess it is. Where is Lucinda, then?"

"She'll be right in."

"Thank God." I slumped back into bed. "Andrews is in some other room around here?"

"What?" she asked me, as if I had lost my mind.

"I have to see him," I told her.

"All right," she said sweetly. "We'll get to that in just a little while."

"And Melissa?"

"She's still in surgery," Stacey said, her voice a little more still. It was obvious that she wasn't going to say anything more at that point.

"Um," I began, hesitantly, "what about the man who—the one in my room that Lucinda—is he dead?"

"Dead?" Stacey stared at me. "You think Lucinda would kill someone?"

"No," I answered quickly, "but I saw a knife."

"No you didn't." She shook her head, sporting a half grin. "You saw a syringe, baby. She jabbed that man full of so much Desflurane, he may not wake up until next week."

"What is that?" I asked her. "Desflurane."

"Anesthetic," she answered simply. "Why don't you just wait and ask Lucinda all this stuff, so you can get the whole picture first-hand? You seem to be a little—I don't know—confused."

"Okay," I agreed. "I probably am."

I turned toward the window.

"Is it night or day?" I asked softly.

"It's morning," she answered. "You want the blinds open?"

"I do."

She came around the bed to the window and pulled the thin cord to raise the blinds all the way up. The morning sky was glorious, filled with golden sunlight and burnished clouds. As I gazed at them through the window, it appeared to me that they were a film, a documentary about clouds, or even a Walt Disney, *Fantasia*-style movie of gentle living things in the air and sky. Then I saw three minotaurs moving in the clouds. I was beginning to think that I might be hallucinating again, but before I could fully grasp what the clouds were doing, those mythological creatures, I was roused by Lucinda's brisk entrance.

"Out," she commanded Stacey.

Stacey vanished without a sound.

Lucinda leveled a devil's glee in my unprotected direction. "If I save your life one more time, do I get a free set of steak knives?"

"I know," I moaned. "We're going to *have* to get married now. People are starting to talk."

"People will say we're in love," she corrected.

"One of those. Look. I'm all turned around." I lowered my voice. "I'm feeling like this is the same thing as the last time I woke up in this room—you know, after my coma."

"Not the same room." She glanced around. "Look. You have TV."

I looked up at the set, and then glanced again at the dancing clouds. "So I do. But the odd feeling lingers. And I have a lot of questions about your heroic rescue of our protagonist."

"Oh," she mocked, "*you're* the protagonist?"

"You have to give me that," I told her. "I'm allowed to be the protagonist of my own story."

"Right," she agreed. "But this story isn't about you. It's about a beautiful nurse who rescues an erstwhile layabout—twice!"

"I have become something of a layabout lately," I concurred, "and I do see your point. But could we get beyond all the meta-fictional aspects of this exchange and on to the more pressing question?"

"And just what would that be?" she asked, her eyes burning into mine.

"What the hell happened in my house last night?"

She shrugged. "What did you want to know?"

"Most importantly, are Andrews and Melissa going to be all right?"

"Yes." She avoided looking at me. "Melissa's still in surgery. But, if you want the truth, it doesn't look good."

"And Andrews?"

"What?" She cocked her head. "He's fine."

"It wasn't serious?" I sat up a little. "It looked serious."

"What looked serious?"

"His gunshot wound," I said slowly.

"Gunshot wound." She sat on the bed. "Honey, Andrews didn't get shot, Melissa did."

"But—" I began, but I decided not to finish a sentence in which I told Lucinda that I had seen Andrews shot on my front porch. I was beginning to feel that some of the images in my brain might be slipping between various realities.

"What is it?" she wanted to know.

"Can you tell me what happened?" I settled back. "Skidmore left to go to Fit's Mill, Melissa was doing some computer work in my kitchen, and Andrews and I went up to my room."

"No, not exactly," she said, eyeing me suspiciously. "Let's see. You fell asleep in the middle of a fairly serious conversation with Andrews—which we'll have to talk about in a minute because who knew you'd be related to jazz musicians, but anyway—so Andrews came downstairs. Skidmore was still there, and Andrews apparently talked the sheriff into letting him go along over to Fit's Mill, since Melissa was there to protect you."

"I see," I said, trying to ignore what I thought had happened. "But then Albert came into the house at some point."

"He did," she affirmed. "Don't know how long after Skid and Andrews left, but that boy, Albert, he busted into your house real good, running. Melissa saw him but didn't get to her pistol quick enough, I guess. She managed to fire, but he'd already shot her two or three times in the abdomen. Albert—which we'll have to talk about him in a minute too—he went on upstairs to your room and Melissa managed to get off an emergency call before she passed out."

So. Waking up in my room to the gunshots, running down the stairs, seeing Andrews and Melissa shot, being shoved back upstairs and into my bed by Albert: all a phantasm. Or a dream. I decided that I would have to tell Lucinda about my delusions one day, but it was not to be that day. She was worried enough about me as it was. No need to add to her apprehensions. And, in truth, I was very happy to just put that particular set of images out of my mind for as long as I could, though discomfort lingered at having so vivid a series of hallucinations,

"Skidmore got the call from her," I said softly, trying to sound as coherent as possible. "And he called you?"

"Melissa called Skidmore, yes, but she was already patched into emergency services, calling for an ambulance. So when they saw the address, the ambulance drivers, they called me."

"You were here?"

"Yes, and I rode in the ambulance with them." She closed her eyes for a second. "Like before."

"Wait." I tried to add it up in my head. "You heard Melissa's distress call and you and the ambulance managed to get here before Albert shot at me? Did I talk to him that long?"

Her face lost a little of its color and it was obvious to me that she was trying her best to figure out how to say something. She settled on: "We got to your house in under eleven minutes."

I shook my head. "No you didn't. You can't get from here to my house in eleven minutes."

She looked away. "You can," she said softly, "if I'm in the ambulance and you're at the house with a gun to your chest."

I let the full import of what she'd said, and what she'd meant, sink in.

She thought something more than mere force of will had been at work. Urging the driver to go faster had only been the beginning. She meant that something metaphysical had happened. I chose not to argue the point—largely because I did not entirely disagree.

"So." I was momentarily at a loss for words.

"Anyway," she said after a moment, "we got there. Melissa was unconscious, the EMT got to her before I could. He told me to get upstairs, check on you. For some reason, I didn't run. I guess I must have heard your voice, and I wasn't quite sure what was happening. So I tiptoed up the stairs, and heard the other man's voice. It didn't take much to hear the hate in his words. I knew he was the one, the man who shot Melissa, probably the man who shot you last year."

She stopped, uncertain how to go on.

"So you—what? You had your kit."

"I had my kit." She nodded, mustering a bit more energy. "I wasn't thinking, I guess, I just—it was an impulse. I got a syringe filled up with Desflurane. I'm not even certain why I had it in the bag. Maybe I thought I'd need it for you in case you were all shot up again. But what I came up with was to sneak in your room and dose the man."

"You do realize," I said, trying to lighten her mood just a little, "that it was a crazy plan."

"Oh, God, yes," she agreed. "I look back at it now and I wonder what the hell made me think—anyway."

"You heard me talking to him."

"Uh-huh," she went on, "and I could tell he was distracted. And then you started up with that . . . what was that weird crazy talk you were doing? It was really scary."

"That's when you popped in and got him."

"Yes."

"So you heard my voodoo gris-gris."

"I don't know what I heard," she said.

"I'll tell you about it later," I promised.

"Well, all I know is that in one second I was in your room, there was a man with a gun, I jabbed him with my juice, and he went down like a broken elevator."

My breath momentarily caught in my throat. "What did you say?"

"Hm?" She was staring out the window. I realized that she might have been a little in shock, herself, or maybe just profoundly disturbed by the events of her morning—small wonder. But that particular phrase was eerily familiar.

"Why did you use the words 'he went down like a broken elevator'?"

"What?" She turned my way. "Is that what I said? I don't know. He did drop real good, real fast."

I sat back. "That he did."

"I'm kind of—I don't know—I'm kind of in a daze or something."

"Believe me," I assured her, "I know the feeling."

"I believe there must have been an angel in your room," she confided in a much softer voice.

"An angel?" I managed to ask.

"Oh, I know I don't talk about it much," she said, trying to make light of it, "but you can't work in a hospital for very long without considering the possibility that angels are around. I don't mean like pretty girls with swan wings in choir robes, nothing like that. I mean the kind of angels that live in sunlight, or comforting words, or the inspired actions of others—in the better blood of our biological yearnings."

"What?" I blinked. "Jesus, Lucinda, you've turned into a poet—a *religious* poet."

"I just never talked to you about this kind of thing." She smiled at me indulgently. "Because I don't want you to tell me it's foolish."

"No, but I mean," I took in a good breath, "I think you'd better tell me where you got a phrase like 'the better blood of our bio-logical yearnings.'"

"I got it from you," she said softly. "It was something you said once."

She was about to say something that I thought might be very important, when Nurse Chambers barged in, her face ashen. There were tears in her eyes.

"Melissa Mathews—they say she isn't going to make it. She's out of surgery, but they don't expect her to live."

27.

Andrews appeared behind Nurse Chambers in the doorway. She turned into his embrace, and they stood silently.

Lucinda reached for my hand.

I wasn't even certain I'd heard the news correctly. How could Melissa Mathews die? She was just in my kitchen.

Somehow Skidmore made his way past Andrews and Stacey and stood at the foot of my bed. He tried several times to speak, but couldn't seem to make any sound. His eyes were hollow, seemed carved out. I'd been with him, years before, standing in a field, when we'd discovered dozens of dead, decayed bodies. That was the only other time in our lifelong friendship that I'd seen the face he wore at that moment. It was barely human. It was Greek mask. All the muscles there contorted to conform to his grief.

All I could think about for a moment was the way Melissa's hair exactly matched the autumn leaves on a certain tree in our town square. In my mind's eye I could see those leaves fly upward in a sudden cold wind—upward and away. I could hear their sound, like a sudden rush of wings, and then the sky was clear: the leaves were gone.

"Your assailant," Skidmore croaked, "is awake and screaming for his lawyer."

284 | PHILLIP DePOY

"What?" I squinted in Skidmore's direction. "Albert wants a lawyer?"

"Oh, he's already got one. His organization has a very high-powered attorney on retainer. Or, lots of them, I think. This one's from Atlanta. On his way up now. Should be here in a couple of hours."

"The man broke into my house, shot a police officer, and almost succeeded in killing me. There are witnesses. What does he think a lawyer's going to do?"

"You don't know much about the way the law works, do you?" Skidmore shook his head slowly. "You have no idea what we're dealing with. This kid, Albert? He could very well get off completely. He's done it before."

"Done what?" Andrews growled.

"He and some of his cohorts," Skid said very softly, "they've gotten off scot free after they've done lots worse than this."

"What could be worse than this?" Stacey sobbed.

"No." Andrews held her tighter. "I'd rather not know what else these men have been up to just now, thanks."

I agreed with Andrews. I wanted to change the subject. The idea that Albert and his clan might get away with their crimes was too much to consider just then.

"So, you all were—you hadn't made it to Fit's Mill," I said haltingly to Skid, "when you heard Melissa's call, I guess."

"Right."

"We got there just in time to see the ambulance men run into your house," Andrews confirmed. "I have no idea how they beat us there."

"I've contacted our friends at the FBI, " Skid said, his voice a little stronger. "They're going to round up every one of those boys over at Fit's Mill and I'm personally going to interrogate them—all."

His sentence sounded more like a threat than anything I'd ever heard him say.

"For what it's worth," I ventured, "Travis appears to have been trying to help me—in his own, weird way. Andrews and I think he was hoping to make me realize that Albert was from Chicago, and that he was the one who tried to kill me. I think Travis may even have shot the rear window out of my truck in an attempt to scare me away. Although he denied it when we asked him. He really might not be such a—"

"Sympathy for the devil," Skidmore interrupted, shaking his head. "I don't care for it."

"Well," Lucinda said, but that was as far as she got. She couldn't seem to find the words she wanted.

"Also, I come to find out," Skid went on after a second, "there's been an undercover FBI man somewhere around here for a couple of months, ever since you got shot in December. They'd been following the activities of these so-called Sons of Wingfield—"

"Is that really an organization," Andrews asked, "or is it just some ad hoc gathering of criminal lunatics?"

Skidmore turned to look at Andrews. "Like a lot of these hate groups, they think they're more official than they actually are. They're a real nonprofit, but apparently they also tried to charter the name 'Sons of Wingfield'—you know, like you'd charter a lodge: the Rotary or, I don't know, an Optimist Club. But their petition was denied. And then the actual Wingfield family, those people over there in England? They got wind of what was going on with their name and issued some kind of legal proceeding against the group."

"I'd imagine that the family," Andrews offered, "were extremely unhappy about the use of that name for such a—I mean there have been Wingfields in Parliament since the fifteenth century, for God's sake."

"At any rate," Skidmore went on, "the FBI has had a man down here for several months now—"

"Wait," I interrupted. "Do you know who that is? Do you know the agent?"

He nodded. "I do now."

"Who is it?" Andrews demanded. "Have we met him?"

"I really can't talk about that. Why are you so interested?"

"Everyone is going to have to stop talking in a minute," Lucinda insisted. "This is a real live hospital room. There's a patient and everything. You have to hush."

I started to explain to Lucinda what was really going on. We were all trying to think of anything to say—anything to avoid thinking about Melissa. No one dared mention the place in the room, the very real place, where our sorrow was standing, a sorrow that was just as palpable as any person. It had a size and a shape and a shadow. We just agreed not to acknowledge it.

Instead of saying that to Lucinda, I tried to change the subject.

"Do I really have to stay in this bed?" I asked. "Hooked up to these bottles?"

"You're dehydrated, exhausted, in shock, still recovering from an older gunshot wound *and* a previous coma," Lucinda fired back a little more vociferously than was necessary, I thought. "So the answer is: *yes,* you really do have to stay in bed."

Stacey looked up from Andrews's shoulder and said to Lucinda, "I'm going to—could I take a little moment, here? I need to—I can't . . ."

"Let's go sit down," Andrews said instantly.

And they were gone.

Skidmore stood a little like a scarecrow in the late November rain. There was almost no life in him.

"Skid," I said very softly.

"Yeah, I know," he answered. "I just—I shouldn't have left her there."

And there it was, another specter haunting my oldest friend: undeserved guilt. There would be no telling him that what happened to Melissa wasn't his fault. He would blame himself no matter what. I'd seen him do it before, and I knew there was nothing I could do about it. I had a sort of helpless, drowning feeling, watching him tie his grief in black knots over something that could never be undone.

"You know, there's a certain variation of the Atlas Complex," I began, looking very deliberately at Lucinda, "which convinces a person that not only is the entire weight of the world on his shoulders, but that everything bad is his fault. And it's often a very strange connection between action and consequence. Sometimes the person will say, 'if only I hadn't picked up my spoon, that airliner wouldn't have crashed and all those people would still be alive.'"

"Shut up, Fever, all right?" Skid whispered. "Not everything can be made better by a little speech from you."

I glanced in his direction. "Okay," I told him softly.

He just stood there; so did Lucinda. I couldn't say whether minutes or hours passed, because all three of us were lost, for a certain span of indefinable time, in our own avalanche of images and regrets.

Finally Skidmore tapped his hand on the footboard of my bed. "All right." He looked around for a second as if he might find something important in the room, then he just left.

"He'll eat himself up about this," Lucinda said softly, sitting down beside me on the bed.

"How much would I have to pay one of these young orderlies," I said, "to put a pillow over Albert's face; rid us once and for all of that pestilence?"

"Fever," she answered sweetly, her hand on mine.

"All right," I responded, attempting to rally. "You do realize why I was asking about getting up out of this bed, right? I mean the real reason."

"What are you talking about?" she asked.

"I have to be in my home on Saturday night," I told her, taking her hand, "because I think I'm going to propose to my sweetheart then."

She shook her head and looked away, but there was a faint upturn at the corners of her mouth.

"Why don't you just tell me about your relation to Jelly Roll Morton?" she asked.

I knew she was only deflecting the conversation, maybe even hoping to distract me from darker thoughts, or to keep herself from thinking about recent events.

"Jelly Roll Morton," I obliged her, "apparently fathered a child in New Orleans, around 1900 or so, who was called T-Bone, by a Caucasian prostitute called Eulalie Echo. When Jelly Roll moved to Chicago, this Eulalie followed him. When he refused to acknowledge her or her son, she became embittered—though actually I think the word *embittered* doesn't even begin to describe what she became. She turned into a certain kind of personified hatred, partially fueled by drugstore cocaine. She then schooled her other children in that hatred."

"She had other children?"

"By other fathers." I nodded. "She had an entirely Caucasian son named Chester who seems to be reincarnated as young Albert who lies in a room close by, if you believe in that sort of thing."

"Oh." She cast an uncomfortable look toward the door.

"It's uncertain what happened to young T-Bone in his formative years," I continued, "but a good bet is that Eulalie abandoned him to be raised by others because she was ashamed of mixed-race progeny. Ordinarily a sad thing, I believe this particular case of abandonment might actually have been a blessing. T-Bone grew up with his father's talent and without his mother's insanity. He fought in World War I and ended up in Paris. He played jazz there, fell in love with a woman who saved his life, and they had a child, a daughter. That child—all evidence points to the conclusion that the child was my maternal great-great-grandmother, I think."

"No," she slapped my hand, grinning. "Get out."

"Well," I began, "I believe that my mother avoided telling me about it, tried to keep me from finding out, for some reason, but also possessed and kept, in our house, evidence that confirmed it—some of which was in the missing tin box from my mantel, remember that?"

"Your mother." She shook her head, grinning even bigger. "She is what you would have to call 'a caution.'"

I nodded. "I've only recently begun to reassess some of my perceptions about my mother. In her favor."

"Good." She stood up. "You can't stay mad at her for the rest of your life. She was a wild woman. People who're like that, they make better stories than they do parents, but look what an interesting person you turned out to be."

"Uh-huh," I mumbled. "If I were any more 'interesting' I don't think I could stand myself."

"Oh, don't I know it." She checked something about one of my IV bottles and then sighed. "Right. I'm going to see—I'm just going to find out a little bit more about Melissa."

"You don't want to hear about my gris-gris curses?" I asked. "That's what actually saved me this time, you know, not you. I really didn't need your help."

She gave me a look. It was her only answer. She left without another word.

The room, so suddenly empty, immediately took on the cold, depressed aspect of all hospital rooms: nondescript, vagrant; anxious. The random exhalations and flying molecules of a thousand other patients and their visitors layered the walls, pressed into the floor, clung to the curtains. Worry colored the air. Fear and pain and loss all crowded the invisible tension between light and shadow.

I began to wonder how any human being ever got well in a hospital.

I also began what I thought might be a common exercise for me in the ensuing months. I tried to go over certain events since I'd come out of my coma. Clearly, I had encountered a bit of difficulty discerning reality from hallucination, or even waking experiences from dreaming visions. How much of what I had thought was memory would turn out to be, upon examination, merely a dream, I wondered.

Unbidden, a quote from Poe, entirely unwanted and inappropriate in the spring of the year, invaded my thinking. "My days have been a dream . . . all that we see or seem is but a dream within a dream."

I considered that it might be comforting to some people, the idea that everything was an illusion. To me, a strong contrast between solid things and the ethereal world was essential. If we can only know light by having the darkness against which to judge it, then how much more would we need the tangible world to be clearly distinct from the realms of fantasy? A ghost is only a ghost if it had once been a living person.

Unfortunately, that line of thinking troubled me unmercifully as I tried to discern fact from phantasm in my days since coming out of the deep, dark sleep.

Did I dream my angel? Wasn't there some hidden letter that my mother had given me? Where was that? And what about my parents' strange, momentary escape attempt in the early 1960s, their bid to get out of Blue Mountain? Had that actually happened, or had I only imagined it as an explanation for my own flight from home. And if it happened, what if that had worked? What if my parents had never come back to Blue Mountain? What if they had stayed in the city, taken up politics, gotten real jobs? I would have been a completely different man.

Oddly, that thought settled me a bit, because, clearly, I was *not* a completely different man. I was the man I was. I could not be other than that. It seemed so simple an understanding of life: rail if you like, but your life is exactly your life—only what it is. There really was no other thing that I could have been.

In accepting that, I found some strange, physical release from the grip of a dark hand that had held me for most of my life, though I was at a loss to explain the feeling exactly.

Everyone, I concluded, has something like a phantom life at one time or another. We all mourn for the life we were supposed to have had, but didn't. We envy the life we should be living but can't. We long for the life we're going to have one day—when everything works out.

But none of these lives, not one, is real. We make them up.

"I cannot be other than I am," I said out loud.

Saying it out loud felt good. It made several of the shadows vanish; actually seemed to make the room brighter.

Then it didn't matter so much what was illusion and what was reality because both had conspired to create that moment, there in that bed, hooked up to machines, still alive despite every effort to the contrary.

I was so delighted and distracted by those thoughts that I barely noticed the man slipping into my room.

"You seem to be all right," he said.

I jumped straight up in my bed—like a startled cat.

"Whoa, sorry," he told me, smiling.

He was dressed in a crisp black suit, an antique narrow tie, and a pale pink shirt the color of a sunrise: the Earl of Huntingdon. He had one hand behind his back, something big tucked into his outside coat pocket, and he was carrying a thick, battered brief-case.

I exhaled. "You did startle me."

"Didn't mean to." He moved closer to the bed. "Came to say good-bye."

"You're leaving."

"Going home."

I realized that a good portion of his heavy Creole accent was gone.

"Your work here is done," I said.

"Almost." He brought his arm around from his back and set a small envelope on the bed close to my hand.

"What's this?" I stared at it.

"Look and see," he told me.

I hesitated, but couldn't resist looking. The envelope looked familiar. When I picked it up I could see that it said, *For Fever* on the front.

"Is this what I think it is?" I asked him.

He shrugged. "What do you think it is?"

I opened it. It was the letter:

> *Dear Fever,*
>
> *If your mother has given you this letter, you must already suspect something. You're looking at some of the photographic evidence. Maybe you've had an angelic visitation. Don't be alarmed. Everybody has those. If you decide to pursue this matter, you're in for quite a ride. If you find out who the woman is in that photograph, your life will change. Doesn't matter. Everything you think you know in this life? None of it is real.*

"But this letter is real." I could hear the relief in my voice. "I was just wondering about it. It is real."

"Real as me," he said.

"Right. You wrote this."

"Got this too." From his coat pocket he produced a tin box. It was the one rimmed in red, the one that had been hidden in my mother's room. "Used to have peppermint candies in it a long time ago, I think. It's from England."

I opened it: old letters, newspaper clippings, some photos, a few poems, and several legal documents.

"That's the evidence," he said. "Most of it."

"Evidence." I looked into his eyes. "Of what, exactly?"

"You know what I mean." He smiled.

"You got this—how?"

"Rather not say," he demurred. "Albert had it. I got it back." He stopped talking but I could tell there was more that he wanted to say.

"There's more of this stuff around, you know," I said. "I think I got most of it from the so-called library over in Fit's Mill."

"I know." He folded his arms. "But it's all about to be confiscated by the FBI. I slipped in, got everything that might be yours. Didn't want you to lose your precious keepsakes. It's all in there now."

"They're not my precious keepsakes," I protested.

"They were precious to your mother."

"How would you know that?"

"I knew your mother." He smiled.

"Yes, well," I told him, shifting around in bed a little, "I'm not surprised. A lot of men knew my mother."

He shook his head. "Not like I did. But I'll save all that for another time. Your mother wanted you to have these things."

"My mother pretended that she didn't want me to have them, or ever find out what they meant."

He grinned. "You know why she did that. She understood that the surest way to make you do something was to tell you to do the opposite."

"And she always let me think these things pertained to my father."

"But they don't."

"I know that now. She let me think it because she was under the impression that I liked my father better than I liked her, that I would consider these things more important if they'd come from him."

"Wonder why she thought that," he asked, but it was really more of a rhetorical question.

"Fine," I groused, "I get it: you knew my mother, she told you that we never got along."

"Yes."

"But would it interest you to know that I've recently had a— had a change of heart about her. A bit."

"Isn't *that* interesting?"

"When you almost die," I explained, settling back in my bed, "you naturally start thinking about death as an eventual destination instead of an intellectual abstract. When that happens, you want to know more about your history, or I did, anyway. Because if I can't be sure where I'm going when life is over, I can at least find out where I came from before life started. In short, I think, you become interested in genealogy."

"I suppose," he allowed. "Of course some people use a near-death experience to reflect on the events of their own lives, not the lives of their relatives."

"Yes," I agreed, "you also begin to examine your life and make new assessments of old facts. For example—just one example— I'm currently trying to discern the difference between how I felt about something at the time it happened and how I feel about that same event now, in the present."

"I guess for a person like you," he laughed, "self-examination is a daily chore."

"It is, it is." I nodded a bit too enthusiastically. "But now I'm looking at—now I'm interested in the larger picture."

"I see."

"All right." I folded my arms to match his. "If you're not interested in that, I have a more specific question for you."

"And what is that?" His smile grew.

"Are you going to tell me who you really are, or not?"

"Probably not," he answered casually.

"So all this nonsense about being the Earl of Huntingdon," I began.

"Oh, no," he interrupted, "that's all true. I am a more-or-less direct descendant of Guichard d'Angle, the Earl of Huntingdon in the fourteenth century."

"You're the actual—are you the only one?"

"God, no. These new ones, they're all from the Hastings family. Is this what you really want to know?"

"I'm not sure what I want to know," I confessed. "And worse than that: I'm not even sure what I *do* know. I'm having a little trouble distinguishing between fact and fiction at the moment."

"Well," he drawled, "part of that is your coma. You were asleep for three months. It's going to take a while before those dreams and images and memories are sorted out. And I will admit that part of your problem there is my fault. I told you a lot of things when you were in your coma."

"You're a very confusing person."

"That's deliberate," he admitted.

"You're a trickster figure," I told him point-blank. "That's who you are, with your—deliberate confusion."

He shook his head. "I don't know what that means."

"Trickster figures, they appear in all mythology and folklore," I snapped. "They're gods or people or anthropomorphic animals who play tricks, break the rules, deliberately behave in an odd manner."

"Reynard the Fox," he said, happy with his realization. "I know that one. My grandmother used to tell me stories—"

"Exactly," I snapped. "Classic example. And a French example, which is, you say, your heritage."

"I don't say it's my heritage," he corrected, "history says it."

"I don't know that. You're tricking me about everything else."

"Not everything's a trick."

"Fine, but the trickster is also a Jungian archetype."

"What's your point?" He was still smiling. "You seem to be getting all riled up."

"What you're doing goes beyond mere odd personal behavior," I answered him. "You're trying to mess up my mind."

"No I'm not."

"But we agree that you act this way on purpose," I said to him. "You tell me you're the Earl of Huntingdon so that when I recount that to anyone, I sound crazy. I know because I tried to use exactly the same technique, taking a page from your book, on young Albert just recently—when he had a gun in my face."

"Must have worked," he drawled.

"And your true identity," I went on, ignoring his comment, "I mean, God knows who or what you really are. It's hidden. I look demented while you vanish. That's right, isn't it? That's what's going to happen."

He shrugged, but the smile was still there.

"It's also a technique that some secret societies and government agencies employ," I ranted on. "You tell me all about your family history and your reasons for helping me, and when I relate that information to my friend the sheriff, he thinks I've lost my mind—or I'm still suffering from the aftereffects of the coma. You tell me these things to hide your tracks. Or to hide in general. Am I right?"

"I can see that my visit has upset you," he said soothingly. "That was not my intention. I really just wanted to give you back your box and say good-bye."

I lowered my voice and tried to sound absolutely sane. It wasn't easy. "Am I really related to Jelly Roll Morton, or is that another trick?"

"You'll have to come to your own conclusions," he said steadily. "But that is your box, that tin there. And the pictures in it? Your mother thought they were important enough to keep for you. They tell you a story. You remember all that."

"My problem now," I said, "is that I'm worried even those memories might be fantasies, not recollections of actual events."

"You want me to make you some more tea before I go?" he asked. "I don't like to see you this way. I worry about your health."

"And that's another thing!" I snapped. "At a couple of very key moments in this whole business, you've given me some kind of *tea*. I think you drugged me. That's what I think now. You've been drugging me and telling me things and I've come to believe them and you're doing it for some kind of weird or sinister purpose."

"That's strong talk." His voice was very calming.

"That's not going to work either, that hypnotizing voice. All your *soothing* talk, and on top of the doctored tea: it's actually a wonder I haven't lost my mind."

He started to protest, then thought better of it, though I didn't know why. "I see your point. I did put a lot of powerful herbs in all that tea. And I did use a little—language persuasion."

"Hypnosis."

"All right."

"Damn it."

"Well, you wanted to know," he told me. "Listen. I came here in December when I found out you were in a coma. There are a lot of reasons for that, but I don't see how they matter now since it all turned out about as well as anyone could have wanted: you're alive, Albert's caught, the Sons of Wingfield—those poor, stupid bastards—are all going to jail. That's pretty nice work, wouldn't you say?"

"Travis is going to jail?"

He nodded. "They're all in violation of the new Hate Crimes legislation."

I thought that sounded odd, a little stilted, and then I remembered several old news stories.

"No," I said, "I think the Georgia Supreme Court struck down the Hate Crimes statutes for this state—a while ago."

"I don't care about that," he said sharply. "This is a federal matter. The attorney general requires data collection on any crime that's committed because of the victim's race—or religion, disability, sexual orientation. Since 1992, the Department of Justice and the FBI have published a report every year on those statistics. That report is public knowledge: anyone can read it; anyone can do something about it. And then a couple of years ago the president signed the Matthew Shepard Act. You know what that is, don't you?"

"I do," I answered uncertainly, "but I'm not sure what it has to do with all this."

"Well among other things," he explained, a little irritated, "it dropped the requirement that the victim of this kind of crime had to be engaging in a federally protected activity before the law would apply."

"This is more—I don't know, more tricks. This boring government official routine, it's just another persona you're wearing at this moment to exacerbate your strangeness."

"Why in this world would I want to trick you?" He sighed. "I've been trying to help you."

"So you say, but that makes you what, exactly? Some kind of a vigilante? Some kind of—I don't know, you want me to believe that you came to my rescue when these men tried to kill me? Because of my bloodlines? Because we're related—are we related?"

He shook his head and the smile finally vanished from his face. "Look, Fever. I know you think this is a story about a man who gets shot and goes into a coma for three months. But, as is always the case, there is a larger story at work. You just got in the way of that larger story, one about a network of idiots and lizards who think that their work is to purify the American gene pool. That story started long before you were born, and, I am very sad to say, will probably go on long after you die. But the good news is: your part in that story is done. Go on back to sitting on your front porch, writing your little folklore articles; get married to that nice nurse. Have a life. Everybody in this town can try to get back to whatever it is that passes for normal around here."

For no reason I could think of, I blurted out, "Except for Melissa Mathews. You didn't do such a great job of helping her. And the man who shot her, may have killed her—he's going to get off!"

And just like that: the smile returned. "Oh, I don't know. You never can tell how these things might turn out."

"What?" Once again he had thrown me completely off balance.

"I'll leave you with this thought," he answered quietly. "Your mother taught you to believe in lies, your father wanted you to believe in magic, and yet your whole adult life has been about the truth and the facts. You study about things in the past, about folkways and stories and songs. Why is that? What are you looking for? And if you extend that curiosity to the study of your own past, your own stories—well, what are you looking for?"

"Stop it," I said, shaking my head to clear it. "You're trying to distract me, to break my concentration."

"I'm not trying to do a thing in this world but—wait, almost forgot. I brought your clock."

"You're doing it again!" I almost came out of the bed. "You're misdirecting the conversation!"

His answer was to toss his briefcase onto my bed and snap it open. "Glad I remembered this. Did you ever look at the underside of this thing? I left it in your bedroom for you to see, but I guess you didn't get a chance to examine it properly."

He produced my clock, the one that had been on the downstairs mantel for years, and had suddenly appeared in my room just recently.

"What—what underside of what?" I stammered.

"I was afraid of that." He rolled his head around, popping several vertebrae in his neck. "That's why you're still asking me if you're related to Jelly Roll."

"What's in the clock?" I demanded.

"Take it." He thrust it toward me.

I grabbed it out of his hands.

"Look," he insisted, motioning for me to turn it over.

I did. In small, engraved letters, nearly rubbed away by the years, I could barely make out the name "Simard."

"It's a family heirloom, you understand," he said softly. "Open that little panel."

I stared. "What panel?"

He pointed to a small hinge that anyone would have assumed was a door to the inner workings of the clock itself.

I unlatched it. A single piece of folded paper fell onto my lap.

"It's a birth certificate," I gasped.

"No." He shook his head.

"What, then?"

"Damn," he sighed, "just look at it."

I set the clock on my lap and picked up the paper. It had been folded four times. With each turn and unfolding, I felt an overwhelming rush of anticipation. When the page finally revealed itself, I was baffled.

"What is this?" I asked, staring at it.

"What does it look like?"

I stared. The paper was a piece of handwritten sheet music. The title, printed large, was "Birdie," and below the title it said, "arr. TBM for L."

"I don't understand what this is." But I couldn't take my eyes off it.

"All right." He winked. It seemed an odd facial tic more than an actual muscular gesture. "Do you know the song 'Angel Eyes'?

"Angel Eyes"? I leaned forward, uncertain what he'd said. "You're asking me about the Sinatra song?"

"I prefer to think of it as a Nat 'King' Cole song."

"My mother used to listen to it. That's what this is? A hand-written version of that song?"

"No, that's not what it is." He laughed. "I just wanted you to remember the last line of that song: 'Excuse me while I . . . disappear.'"

And he was instantly gone out the door. That odd exit was the final confirmation of my suspicions that his behavior was deliber-ately odd so as to foil any attempt to describe or explain him in any coherent way.

Suddenly alone once more, I had the sensation that there were pieces of a puzzle in my lap, but that I didn't understand them, like the sheet music in my hand. I felt there was something important I was missing, or forgetting, like a half-remembered dream. I was certain that if I could just collect my thoughts, I would be able to explain everything. In short, I was looking, as Einstein had for all his life, for that greatest of all impossible phantasms: my own per-sonal unified field theory, the explanation that would explain everything.

Maybe it was something about Albert that was bothering me. In cold examination under florescent hospital lights, it barely seemed possible that he had come from Chicago to kill me based on a nearly hundred-year-old grudge. Or maybe *grudge* wasn't the word for a blood feud, but it didn't seem so very likely that I would be singled out after so long a time. It seemed such a strange, dark path for a boy that young, especially in the twenty-first century.

I put down the sheet music and turned my attention to the tin box. It was packed. True to his word, the old man had stuffed it with everything I had ever seen on the subject of my mother's lineage. I sorted through it for a moment; stopped at the picture of a beautiful young woman, dressed for church, standing in front of a 1930-something maroon Hudson Terraplane. It was the edition of that car with the waterfall front grill, an expensive automobile for our part of the world in those days. As I was turning it over, I realized that it would say, on the back, in my mother's handwriting, "Birdie, 1943."

With a weird excitement, I realized that Birdie must be the daughter of T-Bone Morton and Lisa Simard, my grandmother, or possibly my great-grandmother. Even a cursory examination of her face, despite the age of the photo, revealed obvious signs of our kinship, and subtle signs of her mixed ethnicity. Then, as I stared back at the sheet music, I caught hold of a half-remembered coma-dream. It involved a melody that T-Bone had constructed out of birds sitting on wires outside his window in Paris. They'd looked like notes on a sheet music staff. After he'd whistled or sung the melody, the birds had flown away. It was his or Lisa's proof of the existence of God, because only God could remember that melody. But they had apparently named their child after God's messengers—if not angels, at least creatures with wings who had brought them the song. And just as obviously, T-Bone had done his best to remember the tune, his own half-remembered dream, and give it to his wife and daughter.

I had no idea why that thought made me want to cry, but it did. Maybe it was because Birdie herself had flown away now, as had Lisa, and T-Bone, and both of my parents—as well as Chester and Eulalie. All were gone.

Or maybe it was because I knew that their lives had been destroyed by secrets and events that had seemed monumental in their day but were barely noticeable in mine. A few generations previous to mine, a life could have been permanently altered by a discovery of mixed heritage. In my lifetime, that same discovery was little more than a colorful curiosity to most people. And if Melissa Mathews had been correct in her assessment of her generation, those secrets and adventures would mean nothing in the very near future. All the misery caused by those ancient hatreds: a woman gunned down in Paris, a man forced to give his daughter to strangers, an attempt on my life—the murder of my mother—all would be rendered into dust, barely worth noting.

Thank God I was not left to those melancholy devices for long. Lucinda came in, smiled oddly, and went right to one the machines to which I was connected.

"Where'd you get all that mess?" she asked, nodding toward the things in my lap.

"This guy brought them to me," I said in a deliberate attempt to be vague. "Did you find out anything about Melissa?"

"No," she answered. "They were all in consultation, her team, for some reason—and in a locked office. Very odd."

"So you came back to be with me?"

"Sort of." She had an air of studied calm. "Are you okay?"

She didn't fool me. "Why do you ask?"

"Oh," she drawled casually, "your EKG monitor got a little fussy. It set off a beep in the nurses' station. Something upset you?"

"I had a visit from someone, as I was saying," I began. "He gave me these things. They're very important. They're the reason Albert tried to kill me."

I lifted up the clock a bit for her to see.

"Uh-huh, that clock? And those old papers?" She sat on the bed. "Really?"

"Yes."

"You know, sweetheart, that you haven't been in your right mind since you came out of your coma, don't you?"

"Yes," I sighed, "but—"

"For example," she said patiently, "just for an example, I heard you mumbling all that—what was that you were doing to that boy in your room when I came in? All that mumbling and chanting?"

"Oh, *now* you want to hear about it? Well, that was a calculated ploy—a kind of psychic weapon."

"Go on," she said with the patient demeanor of a professional therapist.

I smiled. "I was trying to frighten him."

"How?"

"He was—it's a long story, but I was trying to remember any voodoo chants or speeches that I could from a very old study, something I'd done in undergraduate school. It was fascinating, actually, about the—"

"Could we just get to the point?" she asked wearily.

"Well, as I say, it's a bit complicated, and involves a strange older man from New Orleans, but I was trying to make Albert believe that I could put some kind of gris-gris spell on him, make him sick or make him drop dead or something. It was all I could think of to keep him from shooting me."

"What were you saying, those words, what were they?"

"Nothing really," I admitted. "I was just trying to remember, out loud, the various names and aspects of the voodoo god Ogun, a mythology associated with Hephaestus in the Greek or Bisva-karma in the Hindu pantheon. Ogun has power over fire and iron and politics and war and—"

"Fever," she stopped me.

"You asked," I told her innocently.

"Because," she said, her voice lowered, "it just sounded so . . . so crazy."

"I understand that," I said, "but you have to know that it was working until you burst on the scene with your hypodermic needle and your Superman Complex."

"Fine," she sighed. "The next time you die? No help from me."

Before further fussy repartee could ensue, Nurse Chambers bustled in, beaming, with Andrews close behind.

"Wait 'til you'uns hear!" she exploded. "You are *not* going to believe it!"

Lucinda spun around. "It's Melissa."

"Yes!" Stacey shouted. "She's fine!"

"What?" Lucinda and I said at the same time.

"She's more than fine, in fact," Andrews said, not looking at us. He was tugging in his left earlobe, his perennial gesture of preoccupation. "Not only are the bullets out and the damage more or less repaired—"

"Her cancer's going away!" Stacey interrupted, louder than ever.

"Wait." Lucinda stared. "No."

"It appears at the moment," Andrews said, "that her cancer might be going into remission."

"How is that—that's not possible, is it?" I asked.

"That's what I said," Andrews answered. "And the doctor told me some story about a guy in Colorado, a basketball coach, who had some sort of leukemia called 'sleeping tiger' and he was held up and shot at close range. When they took the bullet out, they discovered that his antibodies and white blood cells and whatever had not only rushed in to heal the wound, but they had begun to eat up the cancer while they were at it. That's what they think is happening to Melissa."

"Which doctor told you that?" Lucinda asked suspiciously.

"Franklin," Stacey said brightly.

"Excuse me." Lucinda bolted out of the room, clearly befuddled.

"It's good news," I managed to say.

"It's a miracle," Stacey said sweetly.

"You look better," Andrews observed.

"What's all that in your lap?" Stacey asked, coming over to the bed.

"They're—what would you call them?" I began. "They're precious keepsakes."

"Oh," she responded knowingly.

"Is that the famous tin box?" Andrews asked.

He ambled over to sit in the only chair in the room.

"It's the box I found in my mother's room," I told him, "but the contents include everything—the stuff from this box and the other one, the blue one that used to be on my mantel."

"How'd you get all that?" he asked slumping down in the chair.

"Our friend the Earl of Huntingdon," I answered slowly.

Out of nowhere, Skidmore appeared in the doorway. "Well, look who's better." He was very delighted.

"You're heard the news about Melissa," I assumed.

"Yes indeed," he shot back. "Don't know what to make of it. Don't care, really, as long as everything just stays the way it is right now."

I started to warn him that the chances of her actually being cancer free were spectacularly unlikely. But it seemed such a mean-spirited bit of factual invasion in the face of his current joy that I thought better of it. Let hope spring eternal, I thought. You never can tell how these things might turn out.

"I see you got your box back," he said happily.

"It's not the one—all right, yes, I got my box back." Details seemed unnecessary at that moment. "I was just telling Andrews that I got it back from the Earl of Huntingdon."

"Oh." Skid offered me his best Cheshire grin. "Him."

"What?" I sat forward. "You know something about him, the old man."

"Yes I do." But he wasn't going to say what it was.

"Come on." I set the box aside. "You have to tell me who he really is."

"Well, I'm not supposed to," Skid said coyly, "but since he's all done here, I guess it would be all right. They told me all about him, and his strange ways. You're not supposed to know."

"Who told you all about him?" I asked.

He lowered his voice. "He's with the team that's been investigating that group of idiots over in Fit's Mill. He's FBI, the agent that's been here for a while, like I was telling you about."

"The—the Earl of Huntingdon is—*he's* the FBI guy?" Andrews stammered incredulously. "That weird old man from New Orleans?"

"Sh!" Skid demanded.

"Wait," Stacey said, turning toward Skid. "You're talking about Earl Hunt? From New Orleans?"

We all looked at her.

"That's what Albert called him," I remembered slowly. "You said you didn't know him."

"What?" she asked, confused.

"When Andrews and I asked you about orderlies," I said, "you told us that none of them—"

"You asked me about orderlies," she said. "I didn't really think about Earl. He's the night janitor on this floor. He started last December, about the same time you came in, Fever. I mean, I never actually talked to him, but he's in the FBI about as much as I'm—I don't know: in the CIA."

"That man you caught us with in Miss Etta's," Andrews asked Skidmore, "is in the FBI?"

"That—that was him?" Skid's face contorted a bit. "I—well that's a surprise. I never actually met the man. I thought that guy you were with was—"

"Wait," I snapped, looking back and forth between Skid and Stacey. "Both of you just heard about him, but you never talked with him? Either of you?"

Suddenly Andrews sat up so forcefully that I thought he might launch himself across the room.

"Oh my God!" He shook his head. "I just remembered. I thought it sounded familiar. I—I'm an absolute—I can't believe he did this to us. You know who the Earl of Huntingdon was, right?"

"What are you talking about?" I asked him.

"Locksley is supposed to have been the Earl of Huntingdon," he groaned, rubbing his temples.

"Who?" Stacey asked.

"That's somebody in England?" Skid mumbled.

"Robin of Locksley is the Earl of Huntingdon in most of the stories," Andrews told them both, as if they were severely under-educated. "He was Robin Hood."

"Oh for Christ's sake," I fell back into the headboard of the bed. "He's made idiots of us all."

"That old man was messing with us from the very beginning." Andrews agreed, laughing. "He must have thought I was the stupidest man alive not to get the joke right away."

"What with your actually being British, and all," I agreed.

"Damn." Andrews shook his head again, still laughing.

"What are you talking about?" Stacey glared at Andrews.

"You mean he's not—he might not be in the FBI?" Skid had a very foolish look on his face. "But they said . . ."

"He might not even be the night janitor," I told him.

Before we could explore the stranger's wanton peregrinations any further, Lucinda burst back in, her face completely devoid of color.

"Sheriff, could you come see about something right away?" she asked, her voice hollow.

"What is it?" He looked instantly worried again. "Is it Melissa?"

"No, it's—it's that boy Albert," she stammered. "He's talking out of his head. He says he saw something. It scared him bad. I expect it's just a dream from the Desflurane I dosed him with, but he says he's got to tell you—he wants to confess. You've got to come now. He's a big old mess."

Skidmore and Lucinda both bolted out of my room, Stacey close behind.

Andrews and I looked at each other.

"What could possibly explain that?" I muttered.

Andrews smiled. "He saw the Earl of Huntingdon."

The awkward absence of talk that followed his sentence went on long enough to make us both uncomfortable, until I realized how some people explained such a silence.

"An angel must be passing by," I said very softly.

Andrews grimaced and slumped down in his chair. He closed his eyes and seemed to lose himself in thought. Or maybe he was just exhausted and wanted to rest. Who could have blamed him?

"You and Stacey seem to be getting along very well," I said at last.

"Yes," he answered absently, "we do seem to be."

"Good. That's good."

"You turned out to be something of an unwitting matchmaker in your comatose state." He smiled to himself.

"All a part of the service," I told him. "I'm going to set a date with Lucinda this weekend, you know."

"Uh-huh," he mumbled.

"I said that I would," I went on, "and so I'm going to."

"Why are you talking about this now?" he asked, suddenly a bit louder.

"Asking Lucinda to marry me?"

"No, I mean what exactly is the meaning of this line of conversation? Adventures in the banal?"

"No. I'm—I'm trying to get back to what passes for normal around here," I stammered.

"Oh." He slumped down further in his chair. "Well, good luck with that, then."

"Don't you want to talk about something—I don't know—more mundane at the moment? Don't you think we can be ordinary, just for a while?"

"No." He didn't look up. "I don't."

He closed his eyes again, and I stopped trying to talk.

I settled back into the pillows and turned to look out the window, staring at clouds. After a while it was nice to have the silence. As my own thoughts unwound, everything sinking in slowly, I finally came to an unusual, comforting conclusion about the clouds. They were clearly the first representatives of spring, not a last white gathering of winter. And after a few more minutes, they were even better than that: they were only clouds—ordinary, fluffy cumulus. They did not form themselves into imaginary, complicated, mythological visions as they had in December—before I was killed. Lying there in bed, a cloud was a cloud was a cloud. That was all.

At least the minotaurs of winters past were gone.